Contest of Wills

'Madam, you have ensnared me with your pale, scented body. I am obsessed with the need to have sex with you,' said Simmonds.

He pulled Melanie against him then transferred the grasp of her wrists to one large hand and began to pull at the bodice of her gown.

His near primitive behaviour thrilled and aroused her. The expression on the gardener's face told her that his pleasure was equal to hers.

Contest of Wills

LOUISA FRANCIS

BLACK
lace

Black Lace novels are sexual fantasies.
In real life, make sure you practise safe sex.

First published in 1997 by
Black Lace
332 Ladbroke Grove
London W10 5AH

Typeset by SetSystems Ltd, Saffron Walden, Essex
Printed and bound by Mackays of Chatham PLC

ISBN 0 352 33223 9

Prologue

'You have an interest in botany, Mrs Wilberforce?'

The proximity of the speaker, the smooth mellow voice and the slightly accented English sent delicious little goosebumps jumping along Melanie's spine. She turned her head slightly to cast a provocative upward glance from the corners of her eyes before returning her attention to the magnificent floral arrangement.

'I like flowers. We have many unusual native flowers in Australia but these –'

'Proteas.'

'– proteas, are quite spectacular.'

'My uncle is an ardent collector of native flora. Perhaps you would like to take a stroll through the gardens?'

Melanie turned to face her companion directly, her eyes searching his face for any secret message. An improper gleam in the clear blue eyes belied the socially polite mask of his features. Quelling her growing excitement, Melanie cast an uncertain glance towards the opposite end of the room. Her shipboard companions and their hosts were settling themselves at a card table.

'They will be too absorbed in their bridge game to worry about us. Unless, Mrs Wilberforce, you feel you should be chaperoned?'

1

'Not at all. And do call me Melanie, please.'

'Shall we go then, Melanie?'

When he took her elbow to guide her out through the French windows Melanie's goosebumps came back to life. She hoped she had not misread his intent, such was her anticipation of having his hand touch other, more intimate, places on her body.

While they strolled along the paths, her companion pointing out shrubs and trees of interest, Melanie mentally compared him to the lover who had made pleasurable the weeks prior to her marriage. Charming and cultured though Pieter van Heuren was, Melanie felt certain he would be as expert as the dangerous, unpredictable Matt Warrender in satisfying a woman's needs. And Melanie's were very much in need of being satisfied.

Dear Mr Wilberforce had managed to summon sufficient strength from his aging body to consummate their marriage with one brief and totally unarousing coupling. Since that night he had derived all his pleasure from the admiration Melanie drew from other men, his ego gratified by their envy. He received a vicarious thrill from knowing that men thirty and forty years his junior wanted to be in his shoes. Or rather, his bed. He also trusted his wife not to succumb to temptation. Nor had his trust been misplaced, though this was more from lack of opportunity than moral conscience on Melanie's part. On board ship sailing from Australia to England there were few opportunities for stolen sexual delights. After they reached England and during their tour of the continent she planned to make up for all she had missed.

'Why did your husband not come ashore with you?' The question intruded on Melanie's thoughts.

'He was feeling a trifle unwell. As he has been in Cape Town on several other occasions he decided to remain aboard.'

'So he entrusted you to the care of the Bartons who are now rather more interested in their bridge game than your safety.'

2

'Safety, Mr van Heuren? Surely I am in no danger?'

'Perhaps, perhaps not. That undoubtedly depends on your perception of what constitutes danger. There might be many things to cause a lady alarm.'

'I cannot perceive of any which might when I have so gallant a companion by my side.'

'I wonder if you would think me either gallant or a protector if you knew what thoughts are uppermost in my mind?'

Melanie paused, her head tilted for her to gaze into his face. Her eyes were as bright as the emerald which graced her marriage finger. 'What thoughts would those be, Mr van Heuren?'

'I believe you know quite well.' His gaze was bold, roving the length of her body in blatant appreciation of what he beheld.

Tendrils of deliciously wicked anticipation curled from Melanie's stomach to spread down between her thighs. She responded to the appraisal with an assumed coy expression. 'How can I know if you do not explain?'

His head was inclined in agreement. 'A valid point. There is a small cottage farther along this path. Perhaps we should go there so that we may discuss this matter in comfort.'

Melanie's eyes sparkled. She had been expecting a summer house or a secluded place in the shrubbery and prepared to put up with the inconvenience of either for the sake of satisfying her sexual cravings. Did Pieter van Heuren frequently lead ladies down the garden path? How glad she now was that she had accompanied the Bartons on this visit to their friends. She very nearly had not. A natural concern combined with her capricious conscience had dictated she remain with her husband. He had insisted she go ashore.

From the moment of being introduced to her intending seducer she had been pleased she had acceded to her husband's wishes. Pieter van Heuren, with his thick blond hair, blue eyes and tall muscled physique was like

3

a personification of some Ancient Greek deity. Melanie
had lusted for him immediately. Devious though she
could be when it suited her purpose, she had not been
able to conceive of any plan which might afford them
time alone together. The knowledge that the lust she had
expected would remain unappeased would soon be
sated enhanced her appreciation of the gardens. Proteas
would forever remain a favourite flower. They grew in a
grand profusion of pinks, cream and claret red along
either side of the path.

The small cottage sat in the middle of the proteas,
sunlight dancing off the panes in the mullioned windows. Pieter pushed open the door then stood back to
invite her, with a sweeping gesture of his arm, to enter
the cottage. Melanie found herself in a simply furnished
room. Two easy chairs stood on a worn rug near the
empty fireplace, with a small range, kitchen dresser,
table and chairs completing the furnishings. Faded curtains hung at the windows. If the spartan room lacked a
lived-in ambience it equally lacked any air of neglect.
Melanie cast a questioning glance at her companion.

'I come here from time to time when I wish to be on
my own. You have not met my cousins but I can assure
you they are a rambunctious lot.'

The smile which accompanied the statement suggested he was exceedingly fond of his cousins. Melanie
said as much.

Pieter laughed. 'As fond as one can be of two hoyden-
ish girls and three exasperatingly juvenile boys.'

'Surely they are not that bad.'

'They are.'

The heartfelt affirmation drew a delighted laugh from
Melanie. She was beginning to like Pieter van Heuren
more and more.

'Of course,' he continued, 'there are other reasons why
I like to use the cottage.'

'And what, I wonder, might they be?'

His lips quirked in appreciation of her quip. 'You like

to tease, Mrs Wilberforce. Do you want me to seduce you slowly or should I pounce on you and ravish you?'

Melanie's eyes glittered. 'I should be so lucky.'

To her surprise he threw back his head and laughed out loud. Then abruptly he stepped forward and caught her in his arms, his mouth hot and demanding upon hers.

Liquid fire ran through Melanie's veins. Lord, how long was it since she had been kissed so? Stretching up on tiptoe she wound her arms around his neck to return the kiss with unbridled lust.

'Ravish me,' she whispered when her lips were momentarily free, 'I can't wait any longer.'

Her bonnet was discarded in a moment and she was almost dragged into the bedroom. There she discovered her lover-to-be was no stranger to the intricacies of a woman's toilette. Melanie favoured the tie-back fashion, the straight tight skirt and fitted cuirasse bodice chosen for the manner in which they emphasised her feminine curves. Buttons and tapes presented no problem for Pieter and in no time at all the fashionable draperies were removed. When Pieter reached to loosen her stays, Melanie raised a restraining hand. 'I want to be ravished. Do you need me naked before you can do so?'

For answer he pushed her chemise from her shoulders to expose her breasts. His hands curved over them, his thumbs rubbing the already taut nipples to aching hardness. With her eyes half closed to better savour the arousing effects of the caress, Melanie gave a soft moan of approval.

In an instant he had pushed her back on the bed, following her down to press his hands against the insides of her knees and force them wide apart. Melanie did not resist. He parted the soft silk of her drawers to enable his fingers to make contact with the softer flesh beneath. So light a touch, yet so vibrant the reaction which coursed through Melanie's body. It had been too long. Far too long.

'Oh yes,' she whispered, her voice husky with need. 'Touch me.'

He played with her, teasing, tantalising, until she was gasping with frustration and attempting to push herself on to the elusive fingers. Opening her eyes, mouthing a plea, she saw the amusement in his and realised he was enjoying her torment.

'Bastard.' She swore lightly at him.

With a chuckle of satisfaction he made one swift movement to drag her hips upward, bringing her yearning vulva to meet his descending mouth. His tongue made contact, the blissful searing touch causing her to cry out aloud. Closing her eyes again she savoured the wondrous sensations which swamped her body. How delicately, expertly, his tongue aroused. The erotic tip found a way along each fold then circled the extremity of her vulva before darting at the moist opening. A hard point of flesh licked slowly up and down to stir her nerve endings to nigh unendurable awareness. Then, oh then, locating her clitoris to work so rapidly on that tender peak: Melanie could no longer contain herself. Any moment now heaven would be hers.

When he pulled away she almost sobbed her frustration. 'No! Please. Don't stop now.'

His eyes gleamed. Watching her. Enjoying the expression of near agony on her face. Waiting. Melanie begged. So close, so close. Lifted as she was, opened out to him, the removal of the stimulus had brought no lessening of the heat from her internal fire. Only when he saw that her torment had become nigh unbearable did he dip his head. Melanie's body gave one gigantic convulsion as the floodgates of her desire burst open.

Lord! Had anything ever felt so good? That firm male mouth sucking against her soft, swollen sex lips. The hard-tipped tongue working against her clitoris to ensure the peak of stimulus was maintained. Melanie was lost, drowning in the intensity of her orgasm, conscious thought subjugated to carnal sublimity. At length she

6

felt the plundering mouth leave her body, felt her hips being lowered to the bed. When the miasma of sexual gratification began to clear from her brain she opened her eyes to discover her lover was rapidly shedding his clothing.

Melanie blatantly admired his physique. Naked, his resemblance to a Greek god was even greater. He was golden all over, dark golden skin, light gold hair. Only his eyes gleamed sapphire blue in the sculptured perfection of his face. For several moments he remained motionless as if purposely giving her time to admire what she beheld.

Admire, Melanie did. How could any man be so perfect in both face and body? Was it possible for a mere mortal to possess such a magnificent penis? In contrast to his golden skin its purpled hue emphasised the fiercely proud manner in which it jutted from its nest of golden curls. Swollen with desire, the tip glistening with a diamond of lust, it reached up past his navel. The wondrous size of it filled Melanie with awe. Without really thinking about her actions she reached both hands down to press her fingers into her still tingling moistness, inviting him with her eyes to displace them with his organ.

When he did return to the bed it was to lift her as easily as a doll and turn her over to position her on her hands and knees. She felt him kneel behind her and opened herself to receive him, only to gasp at the sound of ripping material as he pulled the fine silk of her drawers to fully expose her buttocks. Hard fingers kneaded the twin mounds and an even harder shaft of muscle pressed against the sex-salved folds of silken flesh.

Suddenly he pushed within and Melanie gasped again in shock. He was so big. Too big. She did not think she would be able to take all of him. Easing back slightly he pushed deeper, then again and again, until the whole great length of him was encased in her hot tight sheath.

Stretched and aching, it seemed to Melanie that the head of that godlike organ was imbedded right up to her heart. When he began his rhythmic stroking she came near to swooning. Never had she known a lover like this one. How could her body endure being so stretched and filled? How could she bear for it not to be?

He began to move more rapidly, his thrusts progressively deeper and harder so that each one jerked her forward to propel a gasp from between her parted lips. Strong hands gripping her buttocks pulled her back to meet each thrust. Faster and faster he worked until she no longer had control of her body, her head and breasts rocking back and forth with each forceful pounding, her breath a continuous series of gasps.

Internally Melanie ached, throbbed and burnt with pleasure, all at the same time. So overwhelming was his possession that, even at the onset of her climax, she could produce no more reaction, only to close her eyes and surrender to the burning ecstasy – an ecstasy which seemed to have no end.

Nearing his own climax, he bent forward to encircle her with his arms, one hand pinching at her nipples, the forefinger of the other rubbing against her clitoris. A dagger-sharp stab of fiery pain shot through Melanie. Tears welled in her eyes to spill over, her fading orgasm being renewed with greater intensity. Sobbing, ecstatic, aching, gratified, Melanie did not know if she was nearer to heaven or hell.

Despite being extremely experienced in illicit sexual pleasures and capable of carrying off her activities with a superb aplomb, Melanie was amazed that no one appeared to notice any cause for comment when Pieter guided her back to the house some time later. True, her dress had been rearranged in its fashionable draping and her bouncing red curls smoothed to order beneath her bonnet, but Melanie was very aware of the nakedness of her lower body and limbs beneath her skirt.

Her entire being remained bemused by the magnitude of the sexual sensations she had experienced. She found it impossible to believe it did not show, that others were not as aware as she of the lingering sex scent. Apparently they were not. The older people asked if she had enjoyed the gardens, pleased when she answered in the affirmative. All the while she was acutely aware of every movement Pieter van Heuren made.

When the time came for Melanie and the Bartons to take their leave, he raised her hands to his lips in a gesture of gallantry. 'Meeting you has given me the greatest pleasure, Mrs Wilberforce.'

'Likewise, Mr van Heuren.'

'If you are ever in Cape Town again, please pay us a visit. You will always be welcome.'

'Thank you,' said Melanie, wondering if her husband would agree to a stop-over in Cape Town on their return journey. 'I will remember.'

'I won't forget,' murmured Pieter in a husky tone which challenged Melanie's composure. He had claimed her torn silk drawers as a keepsake, hence her naked limbs.

That nakedness only served to keep alive the memory of how his godlike organ had felt when deeply imbedded in her dainty body. From being subjected to such stimulation her body continued to crave the thrust of a man's. Encountering the Third Officer on her ascent of the gangplank she bestowed a smile full of promise. The officer had already shown himself willing. Melanie decided they must simply be inventive in devising ways of being together. After sex with Pieter van Heuren there was no way she was going to be able to remain celibate for the duration of the voyage.

She did not realise that when she greeted him with such provocative invitation in her sparkling green eyes he was forced to quell a surge of combined lust and jealousy. The Third Officer knew enough about women to recognise the unique radiance brought on by sexual satiation. He heaped silent curses on the head of the lucky man before bringing his mind back to the reason he had been awaiting her return.

'The Captain wishes to speak with you, Mrs Wilberforce. Would you come this way please.'

The official tone startled Melanie out of her sexual bemusement. She noted the grave expression in the Officer's eyes, her own growing wide and anxious as she glanced from his face to her companions then back again.

'Perhaps you should come with us, Mrs Barton,' the man said.

'What has happened?' cried Melanie.

Her frantic query went unanswered. 'If you please, Mrs Wilberforce.' And taking her arm, the Third Officer guided her to the Captain's cabin.

Mrs Barton hurried in their wake.

The Captain, who was recording the ship's log, glanced up at their entry and quickly laid his pen aside. Rising to his feet he greeted her with a gentle civility which only increased her agitation.

'What has happened?' asked Melanie again. A prescient fear made her knees sag and she clutched at her companion for support. 'My husband . . .?'

'My dear Mrs Wilberforce, I am so sorry to have to give you such news. Mr Wilberforce died of a heart attack while you were ashore.'

Chapter One

Alaric Wilberforce-Liddell reclined in his chair, long legs stretched in front of him, crossed casually at the ankles. With a glass of port, recently filled from the nearby decanter, in one hand, his indolent attitude suggested he was considerably less agitated than his half-sister.

He watched her pace restlessly back and forth, waiting for the explosion of temper he knew would soon erupt. She paused suddenly to face him, the hands she had been twisting together lifted in a gesture of angry exasperation. Her dark eyes, so like his own, blazed with indignation.

'How can you just sit there?' she demanded. 'Aren't you going to do anything?'

When he declined to answer, she continued in an even more vehement tone. 'You are your grandfather's only heir. Or should be. Now this – this – hussy, has got her avaricious little hands on everything.'

'The old man was perfectly entitled to change his mind.'

The apparently unperturbed manner in which that observation was made evoked an elongated gasp of anger accompanied by a fierce clenching of fists. 'Don't you care?'

'I care very much.'

'Then do something.'

'My dear Adeline –'

'Don't call me that. You know I hate the name.'

Ric's lips twisted in a malicious smile. Delie always rose to the bait. 'My dear Adeline,' he repeated with a grin for her venomous glare, 'pacing up and down will achieve nothing. Other than wearing more bare patches in the carpet. The solicitor informs me the will is quite legal. I can of course contest it since he was married but a few weeks.'

A snort of the kind which should never have issued from a lady graphically illustrated Delie's opinion. 'No doubt that was the little hussy's intention. Work him hard in bed until he had a heart attack.'

'Perhaps, perhaps not. We should not pass judgement until we know the truth about the marriage. This girl might have been genuinely fond of the old boy.'

'You don't believe that. Heavens above, he must have been fifty years older than her.'

Straight firm lips were compressed in a thin line, dark eyes made even darker by the anger Ric held suppressed. 'You are quite right. I don't.'

'So?'

'So what? I will definitely contest the validity of the will.'

Delie expended some of her pent up anger with a sigh. 'I am glad to hear it. I was afraid you were going to leave things be.'

A humourless laugh acknowledged her vehement admission. 'I do believe you are every bit as avaricious as our young widow.'

He was rewarded by a sulky glare. 'We need the money.'

'And the money we will have. No matter what it takes.' Ric swallowed the remainder of the port in the glass and rose. 'I am going out. No doubt you will find some way to amuse yourself for the remainder of the evening.'

The sardonic manner in which the supposition was made provoked Delie to a rage. If anything suitable had been at hand, a missile would have followed her half-brother's departure through the door. Instead she reached for the decanter to pour herself a generous measure of port. Defiance and anger dictated her actions.

Perched on the edge of the chair Ric had recently vacated, Delie sipped steadily at the wine while brooding on the injustices of the world. Liddell Hall meant more to her than anything, or anyone, in the world, even her infuriating half-brother with whom she shared a volatile love-hate relationship. Constantly antagonistic about so many issues, each could be fiercely partisan if the other was perceived to be suffering any injustice. Hence her fury on discovering Jeremiah Wilberforce had cut Ric from his will.

Most agonising of all was her uncertainty, even supposing Ric's contest of the will was successful, whether he would be prepared to spend any of the money on maintaining Liddell Hall.

Fresh anger surged through Delie. She looked around the room she loved, her gaze lingering on the beautiful old furniture and the valuable paintings. In the soft glow of firelight and lamplight the colours of the furnishings and carpets were rich and warm. Only in the honest light of day did one see how worn and faded they had become.

So much anger and agitation had created a restlessness which could be appeased in only one way. The mellow port warmed the blood in her veins and started a fire deep in her belly. Pouring herself a second helping of the heady wine, Delie carried it with her up to her bedroom. Once there she rang for her maid, pulling the pins from her hair while she waited for the summons to be answered.

The girl came running, knowing better than to keep

her haughty mistress waiting. She carefully assisted in the removal of Delie's elaborate evening dress. The predatory gleam in the dark eyes, which seemed to take no note of her, induced an almost sickening flutter in her abdomen. When she helped remove the fine undergarments she tried not to allow her gaze to linger too long on her mistress's voluptuous body.

'Will there be anything else?' she asked, hopefully, when Delie's nakedness had been covered with a robe.

'Open the curtains and place the lamp near the window.'

The girl's lips trembled from both jealousy and disappointment as she hastened to obey.

'Thank you, Annie,' said Delie when the signal had been set. 'You may go now.' She allowed the girl to move part way through the door before she added, 'I will ring if I need you again.'

Standing behind the lamp, Delie stared across at the darkened stables. A faint light glowed in the living quarters above. Patrick's room. He would be with her soon. He, too, knew better than to disobey her summons.

Delie smiled to herself, tipped the glass of wine to her lips and slid her other hand down to press over her pubic mound. The sexual power she wielded over her groom and her maid was as heady as any aphrodisiac. Tonight she craved sex with the urgency with which a condemmed man might hope for reprieve. She would ride Patrick, harder than he rode the horses. And he would allow her to do anything she willed. His lust for her was never fully satiated. She would not allow it to be.

Any moment now he would be coming through her door, an eager slave to her sexual whims. While he was of a build and strength to overpower her and take her any time he chose, he knew his place. Delie dictated when he could, or could not, have enjoyment of her body.

A superior little smile played around Delie's mouth.

14

Poor Annie. The maid knew she was second best. Patrick only bedded the girl when he could not have Delie. And Delie only took Annie when she wanted a change from a man's hard loving.

The sound of the door opening brought her around from the window. Clad only in shirt and trousers, his feet bare, the groom paused just inside the room. With his hand still on the door knob he watched her, his Celtic blue eyes hot with both lust and resentment.

'Shut the door,' Delie commanded in a quiet voice. Her hands were untying her robe so that it fell open at the front. With her gaze fixed firmly on her lover's face she slid one hand between her thighs while caressing her breasts with the other. Her eyes taunted him, her faint smile of contempt daring him to move. She rubbed her fingers down along her slit, back and forth, never taking her taunting gaze from the groom's face. The dark angry flush which stained his cheeks thrilled her as much as the degree to which his trouser front had become misshapen. Her intimate knowledge of the shape and size of the muscle which caused that distention precipitated a more avid flow of her love juices.

Motionless as a statue, fists clenched at his sides, Patrick stood watching her. The dark colour which suffused his face was heightened by anger that he should be so humiliated. One day, he thought, one day she would taunt him once too often. Then he would take her as he wanted, fuck her until she begged for mercy and not care if he lost his job.

'Undress,' Delie commanded, knowing exactly the manner of his thoughts and heady with her power. She liked the Irish groom more than any other lover. What he lacked in handsomeness of features was compensated for by muscular strength and endurance. Delie had decided he must provide her pleasure on the very first day of his employment. How willing he had been. How quick to learn the rules. Delie controlled the game. Patrick would not touch her until she bade him to. So long as he never forgot he was her servant he would always have a position at Liddell Hall.

With his shirt and trousers discarded he resumed his former position, hands clenched at his sides, every muscle in his body rigid. Especially the one which projected purple and defiant in front of his torso.

Shrugging off her robe, Delie turned to the bed. Seated on the edge she reclined a little, opening her thighs wide to afford him an unrestricted view of the moist pink opening of her sex. Her fingers toyed with her labial folds then rubbed lightly against her clitoris. The degree of her arousal was increasing by the second, her breathing becoming faster. Her gaze never left the groom's face.

'I am going to make myself come,' she informed him. 'I want you to watch, see my juices spilling out.'

The sight of her masturbating, a mocking smile on her face for his physical torment, broke his rigid self-control. In a rush he reached the bed, lifted her and flung her on to her face. He knelt over her and grabbed her hips, hauling them upward to meet the descending thrust of his throbbing organ. Delie shut her eyes in an ecstasy of triumph. Patrick was acting exactly as she intended.

His savage pounding exhilarated her with its mastery, pleasured her with the forcefully created friction between his hard rippled muscle and her soft internal flesh. Taking all her weight on her left arm, Delie reached with her right arm between her legs to grasp Patrick's balls. With her hand full of the heavy sac she held him deeply imbedded in her sheath. Her supple fingers rolled his delicate balls a manner which made his organ twitch within its silken nest.

Unable to move, held captive by Delie's grasp, Patrick reached around her body to locate the tight nub of her clitoris. Using his middle finger he deliberately rubbed too hard, laughing at her gasp of pain. 'Two can play at this game, mistress.'

For answer, Delie squeezed his balls harder. Patrick

rubbed her clitoris more vigorously. Fiery threads of delight coursed through Delie's body. They ran from his fingers along his embedded shaft to the core of her being before radiating up to her nipples and out to her fingers and toes.

'Yes, yes, oh yes,' she cried as the fiery threads became hotter, burning, enveloping her in an ecstatic conflagration. The release was almost painful, her hot juices seeping down the length of his shaft to moisten both his fingers and hers. Her gasps and cries filled the room.

Before they even began to quieten, Patrick withdrew both the stimulation of his fingers and the satisfaction of his shaft. He knew that his mistress, left hot, aching and only partly satisfied, would be like a wild thing, crazed for sex and all he could give.

He knew her well. Delie was so aroused, so hot, she doubted she could ever be satisfied. Demanding Patrick lie on the bed, she straddled his torso. With her weight supported on her hands she rubbed her burning quim against the equally heated head of his organ, teasing herself to a near demented state. Only then did she encompass him, pushing right down to grind herself against his pubic bone.

With her hands resting on her thighs she rotated her sheath around his rocklike organ, her sensitive peak sublimely stimulated by the dark wiry curls which ringed the base of his shaft. Delie's climax was rebuilding and she knew from the contortion of Patrick's facial muscles that his own was imminent.

'By all the saints!' He gasped and grabbed her hips, belting his shaft upward with such mighty thrusts they jerked her body.

Still Delie rotated her sheath around the pumping muscle until the air was filled with the cries and gasps of their orgasmic delirium.

Separated at last, sweat-glistened bodies continuing to throb with latent pleasure, Delie commanded Patrick to ring the bell.

Annie arrived so quickly Delie realised she had been listening at the door, the fevered expression in her eyes confirmation of her voyeurism. There was also a question in those eyes, an uncertainty of what was expected. 'You wanted something, ma'am?'

'Mm. I have decided to reward you for being a faithful servant.' Delie waited while Annie gathered her startled wits.

'Er, thank you, ma'am.'

'Then be a good girl and take off your clothes.'

The girl hurried to obey, her fingers fumbling in her nervousness. Just what her mistress had in mind she could not begin to imagine. She was reluctant to look at Patrick whom she loved, even though she knew he was enslaved by Delie. Nor had she told him of the times she had lain in Delie's bed, when tongues and hands were used to impart the pleasures normally taken with a man.

Patrick was equally confused, his confusion compounded by his physical reaction to the gradual exposure, layer by layer, of Annie's slim body.

Reclining on the bed, her hand again caressing between her thighs, Delie watched them both in amusement. The maid's figure was waiflike, her breasts tiny buds of femininity, her mound dusted with a sparse covering of hair as pale as that on her head. Her body was in every aspect the opposite of Delie's. Delie wondered if her groom also appreciated the erotic contrast between Annie's petite fairness and her own dark voluptuousness.

'Our poor Patrick is a trifle worn out,' Delie said when Annie was quite naked. 'I want you to bring him back to life.'

Patrick gaped at Delie. Annie's eyes widened.

'Do you mean me to suck him?'

'What else? Kneel in front of him and take his shaft in your mouth. You will taste me there but that will only heighten your pleasure.'

Before Annie was in position Patrick's organ was

18

already returned to close on full strength. His fingers twisted in her hair, guiding her head until her mouth closed over his sticky shaft. Neither registered the gurgle of amusement that came from the bed.

'That's right, Annie, lick him clean. Run your tongue all around his shaft and don't forget his balls.'

Annie would not have dared to disobey even if she had not been enjoying herself so much. In fact neither man nor girl was giving very much thought to Delie until the peremptory command rang out.

'Enough.' Delie sat up on the bed. 'Come here, Annie.'

When the maid reached the side of the bed, Delie slipped a hand between the girl's thighs. 'Oh yes,' she declared, 'you did enjoy that didn't you.' She stroked her fingers back and forth until the girl was trembling. 'Do you want to be sucked, Annie?'

'Oh, yes please.'

Delie cast a mocking smile at Patrick who had followed Annie to the bed. 'My desire is exactly the same as Annie's. Which of us will you please?'

Patrick's mouth opened then shut. Whatever response he gave would almost certainly be countermanded by their tauting, licentious mistress.

Delie laughed. Lifting one foot on to the bed she reached up to pull Patrick down. 'I see that I must make up your mind for you. You will pleasure me while I do what I can to satisfy our little maid.'

This she did. The deeper Patrick's tongue probed Delie's canal, the more deeply did her fingers press into Annie's tight opening. When both groom and maid were absorbed in the pleasures being imparted to and from their mistress's person, Delie lay back on the bed. Her fingers, pressed firmly inside Annie's quim, urged the girl to move with her.

'Suck my breasts and nibble my nipples. Pleasure your mistress, girl. I want to be stimulated all over.'

From long hours of training, Annie knew exactly how to impart all the stimulation Delie craved. She nibbled and sucked as she had so many times before, while Delie jerked her fingers in her maid's love hole and worked her own against the erotic action of the groom's tongue.

When Annie began to whimper, Delie pulled her hand away and shifted herself beyond reach of Patrick's oral caress. 'She is ready,' she said to him. 'Take her the way she is. I want to see how you fit that bulky shaft of yours in her tiny hole.'

Patrick needed no second urging. He straightened to a standing position and lifted Annie backwards on to his shaft. With his senses lust-dazed by the orgiastic situation, the gentleness he always used when first entering her was forgotten. His sudden swift embedment caused her to scream loudly, just once, before she began sobbing from the overwhelming onset of an incredible orgasm.

Carried away with her own libidinous excitement, Delie slipped from the bed to kneel behind Patrick. She twisted her head to enable her tongue to flick alternately at Annie's clitoris then along the glistening piston of Patrick's rod. She felt the shock then the immediate quiver of delight which surged through both their bodies. The action of her tongue was sending them both soaring to climaxes of hitherto unknown intensity. Delie did not mind. Let them have their pleasure. For the remainder of the night all their energies would be devoted to satisfying her in any manner she desired.

When Ric strode out of the drawing-room of Liddell Hall he had every intention of going to the stables for his horse. Out in the courtyard he had paused to absorb the crisp clarity of the night. The air was pleasantly cool. Brisk enough to be invigorating without chilling the bones. A three-quarter moon softened the edges of black shadows, giving light enough to see one's way. Ric decided he would walk the three miles to the village.

In the mood he was in he would not be able to sit on a horse's back without wanting to urge the animal to a reckless gallop. With more respect for his horse's well-being than to use it so, the exertion of a brisk walk was undoubtedly a far better method of releasing some of his pent-up emotions.

Despite the sardonic calm he had maintained within his half-sister's presence, he was almost murderously furious over the matter of his grandfather's will. His teeth gritted in anger when he thought back two years to the last time his paternal grandfather had visited England.

The old boy had been almost sickeningly sentimental over Ric's likeness to his long-dead father. Ric held no memories of the man he had known for only the first three years of his life. Quite unexpectedly he began to wonder what his life would have been like if Richard Wilberforce had not managed to drown himself in a flooded river.

Almost without him being aware of it, Ric's brisk pace eased to a casual stroll. If his father had lived he would have been raised in Australia. Delie would never have been born, though he might have had any number of other siblings. He tried to imagine life in the antipodes and failed miserably. Perhaps he had never really listened properly to his grandfather's stories.

'You have got to come to Australia, my boy,' Jeremiah had declared. 'It's your birthplace, your true homeland. Everything I own would have gone to your father if he had stayed alive. Since he did not, all my wealth will one day be yours, even if your mother did whisk you away to the other side of the world and rob me of thirty years of your life.'

'She was very young, Grandfather.' Ric defended the mother whose untimely death had brought him near despair. 'She had no family in Australia.'

'No need to get your dander up. I understand how she must have felt at the time. Fact of the matter is she very quickly found a replacement for the husband she had lost. You were all I had left of my son.'

A little of the hardness in Ric's heart softened at the old man's words. By the time the visit was at an end he had developed a certain fondness for the grandfather he had seen only a few brief times in his life.

'Why don't you come back to Australia with me?' Jeremiah had asked. 'You can keep me company on the voyage.' Ric had not known his relative well enough to understand the affable request was paramount to a royal command.

'I would if Mother was not so unwell.'

'She's got a daughter, and a husband, to look after her, hasn't she?'

'Delie and Mother rarely see eye to eye. My stepfather, as you may have noticed, is rather more interested in his own pursuits.'

'Bit of a gambler, isn't he?'

'You could say so.' Ric agreed to the grossest under-statement of the year.

'Tried a few times to wheedle a loan out of me.'

'I take it he was not successful,' Ric said with a faint smile. For all his innocent appearance and gentle manner, Jeremiah Wilberforce was nobody's fool.

'That wastrel will get nothing out of me. And when mine is yours, my boy, I trust you will have sufficient sense not to give him any either.'

'On that matter you may rest fully assured. I have no time for my stepfather.'

'Well, then, when are you going to come to Australia?'

Having no desire to remove himself from England's fair shores for the ruggedness of ones charted little more than a century ago, Ric prevaricated. 'As soon as my mother is recovered I will make arrangements to visit.'

His mother never had recovered and six months after her death her husband, by the simple expedient of falling down the stairs of a gambling den when inebriated, had joined her in the afterlife. Still in grieving for his mother, Ric had been relieved to be rid of his stepfather. Delie had not been overly concerned by the demise of either parent. She was far more shattered on discovering the

22

extremely impoverished situation in which brother and sister had been left.

Aghast at the idea of having to sell Liddell Hall, Delie had been gratified to discover Ric was no more keen than she to dispose of the family home. The sale of a number of valuable paintings and ornaments had given them a reprieve. While Ric had hoped that would be sufficient to see them through until Jeremiah conveniently passed on and left Ric his fortune, he had been obliged to write to the old man seeking a loan.

The refusal arrived with the advice that there was no way Jeremiah was going to allow his hard-earned fortune to be squandered on a crumbling English mansion. The terse missive ended with the statement that he thought it past time Ric made the effort to visit. He advised his recalcitrant grandson to rectify that matter forthwith.

Only a fool would have failed to recognise the implied threat. Before Ric had been half-way through making the arrangements necessary to voyage to the country of his birth a second letter had arrived telling him not to bother. Jeremiah would soon be setting sail for England.

Nothing more had been heard until the arrival this afternoon of the solicitor's letter. Whatever Ric had expected it had most certainly not been the information that his grandfather had died in Cape Town. Nor that the old man's entire fortune had been left to his young bride.

Conniving little bitch. The foul curses used to relieve Ric's fury were of a manner to have made the widow drop dead, albeit she was on the other side of the world. By fair means or foul Ric was determined to claim what was rightfully his. Ric strode on, fuelling his anger by planning ways in which to make the unknown Mrs Wilberforce regret her mercenary opportunism.

As was his half-sister, Ric was partial to the carnal indulgences of the flesh. Like her he needed sex to work

23

off so much anger and frustration. Unlike Delie he was perfectly satisfied to take one lover at a time. The majority of his mistresses remained in his favour for a year or more. Some had lasted rather longer. The extremely talented and inventive Cecelia, who was most definitely past her youthful years, had been able to retain his interest for close on three years.

Ric was well aware Cecelia's favours were not reserved for him alone. He never objected. After all he did not confine his physical releases exclusively to her body. She was always available when he wanted her and unfailingly enthusiastic in her endeavours to make sex both interesting and enjoyable.

She opened the door on his knock, drew him inside and reached up to brush a kiss across his lips. 'I was hoping to see you tonight.'

'Missed me already?' asked Ric, easing himself out of his coat. 'I was here last night.'

'For the first time in three weeks. I have a lot to catch up on.'

Ric scoffed. 'As if you would have gone without while I was away.'

'Does that bother you?' Head tilted to one side, Cecelia awaited his answer. For all her experience she could not keep from her eyes the hope she meant more to him than a compatible sexual partner. The mocking curve of his lips gave her her answer. He might just as well have told her he did not give a damn.

Cecelia shrugged. A bright smile intended to indicate she did not care either. She was willing to accept him on any condition he dictated. The subtly cruel streak in his nature attracted her as much as his physical appearance. Any good-looking man was pleasurable to Cecelia. Tall, dark men of satanic attractiveness with unfathomable eyes and thin, cruel mouths were irresistible. Ric Wilberforce was such a man.

'Have you any brandy?' he asked her now. 'I feel in

need of somethimg strong. Very strong,' he assured her on noting her stare of disbelief.

'Are you feeling unwell?' she asked. 'Never before have I ever heard such a statement from your lips. You are surely not developing a penchant for strong liquor?'

'Hardly. Having had a drunkard for a stepfather is assurance of that.'

Cecelia, knowing him well, placed a hand on his shoulder, her eyes raised to search his face. 'What troubles you, Ric?'

'Nothing which concerns you. I have received unwelcome news, that is all.'

'Ah, I see,' said Cecelia.

Ric glanced at her sharply, wondering if she guessed. He would not be surprised.

She took his hand to lead him to a chair. 'Come and sit down and I will massage your shoulders. You are very tense.'

Five minutes later Ric was beginning to feel considerably more relaxed, the brandy in only a small degree responsible. The matter of his grandfather's will receded from its place of importance in his mind. Trust Cecelia to work that wonder. Her clever hands were one of the things about her which he truly appreciated. They were equally adept at massaging the tension out of his body or the rigidity into his manhood. He suggested she turn her attention to the latter task.

Nothing loath, Cecelia knelt on the floor beside the chair. She rapidly freed his rod, which was already about as rigid as it could become, from the confines of his clothing. Her fingers ran in adoring caresses up and down its length. They moved lightly over the purpled ridges of the veins and across the velvety smoothness of the glans. When the first glistening pearl droplet seeped from the tiny crack, she tipped her head forward to flick it away with her tongue. With a passivity which falsely suggested he was unmoved, Ric waited for her to continue.

In delicate circles, Cecelia's tongue traced the rippled ring of foreskin before sliding down the line of the life channel to the base. She licked up one side of his swelling organ and down the other before returning to the head. At that point she removed her tongue to place her lips gently around the helmet instead. For several moments she held them motionless, gazing up under her lashes at Ric.

The corners of his mouth twitched slightly as he gazed back down at her. An appreciative gleam lit his eyes. 'Get on with it woman,' was all he said.

Cecelia was as expert at using her mouth as she was at using her hands. Her lips followed the path her tongue had taken, drawing him into her mouth until he was half encompassed. She released him slowly, softly teasing the highly sensitive head before repeating the action. Several times she pleasured him in this manner before relaxing her throat to enable him to push fully into her eager orifice. His ragged breathing indicated just how imminent was his climax. Relaxed and receptive, she used her hand to control his thrust until he was driven beyond the edge of control.

Using her tongue, she cleaned his shaft thoroughly. With that task finished she sat back on her heels to smile at him, her tongue cleaning her own lips. 'Was that good?' she asked.

'You know damned well it was.'

'Are you going to reward me?'

'I fear I am not able at the moment.' Ric cast a rueful glance at his limp, sated manhood.

Cecelia laughed. 'I will be happy to have your tongue as a substitute.'

'I doubt you have left me the strength to move.'

'Then do not. I am certain I can improvise.'

Rising to her feet she shed the loose gown which covered her nakedness. 'I think this will work,' she said, straddling Ric's lap with her back to him, then bending forward to tilt her buttocks upward.

Accustomed though he was to the range of Cecelia's inventiveness, the new position caused Ric considerable surprise plus a great deal of erotic stimulation. Eager though he was to taste the part of her anatomy thus presented, he discovered there was discomfort in bending his head so far forward.

'There needs to be a slight adjustment.' He lifted Cecelia's legs to place them up past his shoulders so that the inviting pink lips of her sex were raised closer to his mouth.

That her unusual position heightened Cecelia's erogenous sensitivity became apparent to Ric the instant his tongue brushed against her skin. Her lusty reaction inspired him to greater lasciviousness and pulsed new life into his flaccid shaft. Within moments she was panting and convulsing in total pleasure, twisting her head to take Ric's organ back into her mouth.

They were neither of them interested afterwards in using the bed for the continuation of their pleasures. For a time they rested, indolently caressing each other's bodies. A time during which Cecelia gradually stripped Ric of all his clothing. By then they were both impatient for total sexual union.

The table was a convenient height over which Cecelia prostrated her upper body in order to make available her rear for Ric's choice of opening. Ric pressed his thumb into her anus, his shaft sliding swiftly and easily into her moist canal. He knew she liked to be taken hard and wasted no time with teasing games. Indeed, he needed the physical power of driving her into a panting mass of sexual sensation.

Quite suddenly he stooped to curve his hands around her thighs and lift her legs to stretch them to either side of his body. Cecelia clutched frantically at the edges of the table, sending the centrepiece crashing in the process. Neither took any notice. With Cecelia spreadeagled half on the table, half off, Ric resumed his vigorous pumping. Though he held her legs, the force of each thrust jerked

27

her along the table. The tiny cries of pain she gave as her nipples were scraped along the table drove him to greater strength.

'Please, no more,' she cried. 'My nipples are burning.'

He turned her on to her back and once again lifted her legs over his shoulders. Guiding with his hand he teased the head of his rampant organ against her swollen vulva and over her burning nub. Only when her body began to convulse uncontrollably did he drive into her again. This time there was no stopping until they were both expended of all energy.

The day was nearing the luncheon hour before Delie made her appearance. Two hours earlier she had woken and rung for her maid. Annie had brought her cup of tea then dutifully arranged for the bath to be filled. When it was ready, Delie had risen naked from the bed and stepped into the water. Settling herself down, she commanded that Annie wash her, all over. Most particularly she had wanted the girl to cleanse between her sexual folds. When Annie did, Delie discovered the act of being caressed under water was highly arousing.

Though she had fallen asleep fully sated, the licentious activities of the night had left Delie's vulva tender, swollen and responsive to the most delicate stimulus. Annie's fingers were rapidly rekindling her sexual hunger. She lifted her legs to drape them over the sides of the bath with the demand that the maid pleasure her completely. An orgasm under water was a novel and exhilarating experience. Delie decided she must try it one day with a man.

Dressed, eventually, she made her way downstairs to locate Ric in the library. 'Have you decided what you are going to do?' she demanded of her unpredictable half-brother the instant greetings were exchanged.

'It is already done. I dispatched a letter to the solicitor this morning informing him I wish to contest the will.'

'I am pleased to hear it.'

'That is only part of my intention.'

'What is the other?'

'I am going to Australia.'

The calm statement stunned Delie. 'Whatever for? Surely the solicitor can do all that needs to be done?'

'No doubt. But it could become a very lengthy and expensive affair. My going to Australia will, I hope, expedite matters. I am also curious to meet the merry widow.' He laughed at Delie's startled expression. 'With all that money I am certain she is very merry indeed.'

Chapter Two

Wealth, luxury and the accompanying good things in life were not unknown to Melanie. Her parent's large house on the shores of Sydney Harbour was spacious without being ostentatious, furnished comfortably while remaining fashionable, and set in attractively landscaped grounds. In comparison with the mansion bequeathed to her by her late husband it assumed the dimensions of a worker's cottage.

For the first few months while she had striven to come to terms with her grief and even greater guilt Melanie had resided with her parents. Their love and the familiarity of her surroundings provided much needed solace. Despite the half-joking assertion made to her cousin that she was marrying dear Mr Wilberforce for his money she had, on her return to Australia, wanted nothing to do with the estate.

A trusted business manager, in conjunction with Jeremiah's long-time friend and lawyer, looked after the numerous properties and investments. Melanie was perfectly content to allow things to continue in that manner. Nor did she know, when she walked into any hotel or store, if it was one of the businesses or buildings of which she was now owner. And thus things might have remained if she had not received a disturbing visit from Jeremiah's solicitor.

His news had left Melanie momentarily dumbfounded. She had not been aware her late husband had any direct descendants. 'How do you know this man is not an imposter?' she asked.

'There is no doubt a grandson was taken to England at an early age.' Mr Bartlett was reluctant to mention the altered will.

'Does that prove anything? This man may simply be some adventurer, some opportunist, who thinks he has found an easy way to become rich.' The troubled expression in the large green eyes made the young widow appear so vulnerable that the solicitor found himself hoping this was indeed the case, even though he had argued long and vehemently with Jeremiah over his decision to change his will.

'If he is, his claim will soon be discredited. In the meantime I would advise you to take up residency in Arlecdon.'

Melanie now stood in the opulent hall of the mansion Jeremiah had named for his native Cumbrian village. The servants, aligned in order of seniority, waited to be introduced. Each was presented by the butler, Carstairs. While not relinquishing one shred of his haughty formality, he had still made Melanie feel welcome. The reactions of the other servants were varied. Some smiled, others masked their thoughts with expressionless greetings. Most, Melanie knew, would be wondering what kind of mistress she would make. Mrs Godwin, who had been housekeeper at Arlecdon for nigh on forty years and was of an age when she might rightly fear to be retired in favour of someone younger, compressed her lips and barely managed to be civil.

So, mused Melanie, the woman has decided to dislike her new mistress. She probably disapproved of both her youth and appearance. Melanie was well aware the black of her mourning rendered more vibrant the red of her lips, more sparkling the green of her eyes and enhanced her pale flawless complexion. Even with the maturity brought on by her unexpected widowhood she knew she appeared but a young girl instead of a matron of almost twenty years of age.

Melanie noted the awe of admiration in the eyes of some of the younger maids. She also recognised the uncontrollable gleam in the eyes of every male servant. So much silent flattery made her realise it was past time she allowed herself to renew her interest in life. Only in recent weeks had she finally been able to accept she was in no way to be blamed for her husband's death. Dear Jeremiah's heart would have ceased to function even if she had been at his side and not indulging her carnal appetite with Pieter van Heuren. And it had been with Jeremiah's persuasion she had gone ashore.

On reaching the end of the line of servants, Melanie turned slightly to cast her gaze back at the second gardener. He was muscular, thick of thigh and brawny of arm. Even with his person tidied and clad in his cleanest garments for the presentation, there was something so earthy, elemental, about him her senses were stirred. Melanie decided she would, before too long, make it her business to inspect the gardens.

This she did the very next day, locating the man in the shrubbery. For some minutes she provoked him by walking near him without speaking a word. Every now and then she stopped to admire the manner in which he trimmed the shrub, her attention being noticeably more on the ripple of his muscles than the foliage.

'Your name is Simmonds, is it not?'

'Yes, ma'am.' The man glanced briefly in her direction before returning his attention to his clipping.

'Have you been at Arlecdon for long?'

'Nigh on four years, ma'am.'

'Then I must presume you to be well acquainted with every corner of the estate. I want you to guide me on a tour of the grounds.'

'Now, ma'am? There are over twenty acres. To see it all would take some time.'

Melanie tilted her head in a manner suggesting she had not previously considered this fact. 'I believe you are right, Simmonds. Perhaps it will be better if you will show me a different section each day until I am – satisfied.'

There was no apparent reaction to the suggestive pause and altered intonation of the last word. He clipped a final errant sprout from the shrub then turned to face her fully. 'As you wish, ma'am. Where would you like to start?'

'I believe there is a maze. I have never been in a maze before.'

'You need only continue through the shrubbery to reach the entrance, ma'am. You will not need my assistance for that.'

'But what if I am unable to find my way out again?'

'You will not appreciate the maze unless you spend some time attempting to solve its secret. If you do not return in the time it should take I will come to your rescue.'

Melanie pursed her lips in consideration. His manner was far more cool than she had anticipated given the barely concealed sexual interest she had seen in his eyes the previous day. He seemed, from the monotone in which he answered her questions, intent on emphasising their respective positions within the household. As if Melanie would ever allow such a trivial consideration to interfere with her pleasure. Nor did she intend to relinquish the plans she had made to take that pleasure. Before venturing into the garden she had discarded her elaborate day dress for a simple skirt and blouse, her undergarments kept to the barest minimum.

Her contemplative gaze travelled from his face down the length of his body. For a few brief moments it rested on the crotch of his trousers. Was that muscle as well developed as the others? Melanie very much wanted to find out. While she gazed and wondered, she saw the fabric covering stir. A tiny smile of satisfaction played at the corners of her mouth. She raised her eyes, quickly enough to see the blatant lust before the mask of subservience was resumed.

'I believe you are right, Simmonds. I will explore the maze by myself. You will find me before I become hopelessly confused?'

'I give you my promise, ma'am.'

When Melanie had entered the maze she made no attempt to find the way out. She strolled slowly between the high hedges waiting for the gardener to find her and hoping he was not going to take too long. Anticipation had released a host of butterflies in her stomach. Though she had frequently attended to her own sexual relief in the past months, no man had driven his shaft to the hilt of pleasure since that fateful afternoon in Cape Town.

Unable to resist when she felt her nipples hardening, Melanie released several buttons to enable her to slide her hand inside her blouse. Her gentle caress made her even more eager for the rougher one which would soon follow.

The gardener came around a corner so suddenly Melanie was given no chance to withdraw her hand from her blouse. They both stopped to stare at each other, Melanie's lips parted with desire, his body tense, hands clutched at his sides. There was a degree of anger, and resentment, in his stance.

'I have a wife, ma'am,' he said at last.

'But I have no husband,' Melanie replied. 'A man such as yourself must surely be able to satisfy both a wife and a needful widow.' She removed her hand from her breast to rest it lightly against the now taut material of his trousers. 'Your body gives no thought to a wife.'

His eyes blazed for an instant before his self-control broke. He took one step forward to drag Melanie to him. Hard lips ground against hers while steel-like fingers

34

gripped her buttocks to pull her against the part of his body her fingers had so lightly touched. Melanie's insides melted.

He raised his head a fraction, his eyes burning down at her in a manner which made him master. 'If I would have you, ma'am, then I would have you naked.'

Exhilarated by the primitive savagery of his expression, Melanie undressed rapidly. At the same time he shrugged off his shirt and stripped off his trousers. Melanie's mouth went dry. The vibrant muscularity of the man made her knees feel weak. And if her mouth was dry, that other place, between her legs, most certainly was not.

His harsh libidinous gaze seemed to touch the fullness of her breasts, the narrow span of her waist then the gentle curve of her hips. 'Yes,' he declared. 'You were built for sex.'

In an instant she was on her back, legs parted with his body positioned between. He touched her only briefly, merely to confirm her readiness, before he drove his organ deep. Its swift passage home pushed pleasure to every portion of her body. Hands flung above her head, eyes closed, Melanie gave herself up to the unique delight imparted by manly muscle stroking her sex canal. How right the owner of that pleasuring organ was in his assessment. She was built for sex, thrived on it. From now on she intended to make up for all the months of penitent self-denial.

When her lover suddenly withdrew, Melanie opened her eyes with a silent question. A question answered when he lifted her legs to tip her knees back against her shoulders. Her pelvis was tilted, raising her to alter his angle of penetration. With the first re-entry Melanie discovered his stroke went deeper, stimulated different, more sensitive nerves. Unable to move, pressed down by her own legs and the weight of his body, she could only moan while the stimulus rapidly became too great, cry out when there was no holding back, with no control of the onrush of ecstasy which seared her body.

She was gasping out loud, her little cries sounding like pleas for mercy. Over and over his pounding continued, the grunts which accompanied it increasing in volume until, with a loud roar, he rammed as deeply as was possible. There he held himself for a few rigid moments before pulling back to resume his thrusts with undiminished virility.

Their fornication did not go unnoticed. Several windows of the mansion overlooked the maze. Mrs Godwin, while she tut-tutted in disgust and told herself she was right in her opinion of the hussy, watched with avid interest. Just to confirm the young mistress was no better than a harlot.

The butler happened to walk into a different room to discover one of the maids staring out of the window making strange little noises. Assuming something was ailing the girl, he walked up behind her to enquire of the problem. His very correct facade shattered when he saw the scene at which she gawked.

Immediately understanding what did ail the girl, and uncomfortably aware of his own uncontrollable physical reaction, he reached his arms around her to cup her breasts. Her enthusiastic response was to lift her hands to persuade his to knead vigorously at the mounds he held. This he did very briefly. He soon pushed the maid forward to lean on the window sill. His trouser fastening was released, her skirts pushed up and the seam of her pantaloons parted to enable them to couple as urgently as the pair they watched. The lewdness of it all was doubly arousing for both. In fact, so hard were the butler's thrusts, the maid was forced to clutch desperately at the window sill for fear of being projected through the opening.

* * *

36

Sated and for the moment content, Melanie relaxed beneath the gardener's now still body. While his dormant shaft lay quiet in its nest, she reached a hand to touch his face. 'I expect you to show me another section of the grounds tomorrow afternoon.'

'Which part would madam like to see?' The return of the subservient speech belied the intimate union of their bodies while rendering the same highly erotic.

An impish smile danced in Melanie's eyes. 'I will let you decide. I am certain you know all the best places.'

So pleasurable were the days which followed, especially the afternoons, Melanie wondered why she had delayed so long before taking up residence in Arlecdon. Though she suspected her liaison with Simmonds was common knowledge among the servants, she did not allow the matter to cause her any concern. Every servant had soon realised Melanie, for all her youthful appearance, was very much mistress of the house. Even the disapproving Mrs Godwin quickly discovered the girl she had labelled a low-bred, gold-digging harlot, knew exactly how to manage a large house and the numerous servants required for the smooth running of such an establishment. By the end of the first week, the majority of those servants avowed to remain unflinchingly loyal to the new mistress.

To the matter of the mysterious grandson and his declared intention of contesting Jeremiah's will, Melanie gave scant thought. Until the day a hired carriage brought an unexpected visitor to Arlecdon.

From the wide eastern terrace of the mansion one was afforded a magnificent view across the valley and over the city to the distant blue water of the harbour. Not unnaturally it became one of Melanie's favourite places to relax. On this particular morning she was studying the latest fashions in *Harpers Bazaar* when the butler glided on to the terrace to inform her a lady had arrived and was now awaiting the mistress in the small morning room.

'Who is she, Carstairs?'

'She would not give her name.' The butler cleared his throat to ease his discomfort at not being able to extract so small a piece of information from the visitor. 'She said she wanted to surprise you, madam.'

'Oh? I wonder –' But before Melanie could say what she wondered the visitor stepped on to the terrace. An unladylike shriek of pure joy erupted from Melanie's lips.

'Dita!' In an instant she was on her feet and rushing to embrace her cousin, both girls laughing with the sheer pleasure of being together again.

'Dear coz,' cried Melanie, 'how wonderful it is to see you again. 'But what are you doing in Sydney? Are you on your own?'

Dita laughed at the impatient questions. 'Oh Melanie. I see you are quite your old self again. You expect to learn in a few words that which may take some time to tell.'

A girlish giggle accepted the fond reproof. 'I have much to tell you also. Carstairs, please inform Mrs Godwin my cousin has arrived. Tell her we would like some refreshments immediately and to set another place for lunch. You will stay to lunch?' she asked Dita.

'Of course I will. Matt is not expecting me to return before late afternoon.'

'Ah.' Melanie's eyes gleamed with satisfaction on receiving the answer to the question she had not yet asked. 'I take it you have resolved your differences.'

Dita's smile held the radiance of a woman who was well and truly loved. 'We have. I wanted to thank you for the part you played in bringing about my present happy state.'

'I had to do something. You, sweet coz, were too mixed up and stubborn to see what was in front of your very nose.'

'So you told me at the time. I was hardly a day back at Edenvale before I realised how right you were.'

'I wondered if you would be angry with me for sending Matt after you. I see you are quite the opposite.'

The joyous peal of Dita's laugh confirmed her cousin's observation. 'Have you been able to resolve your own turmoil as easily? Are you happy?'

'As happy as can be expected.'

'Now that is a leading statement. Yet you look, I don't know, satisfied?'

'I am. Very.' Melanie indicated the man who worked some distance away, where the land began to slope towards the valley. 'He is the reason.'

'A gardener? It must run in the family.' Dita was teasing, her thoughts returning briefly to the virile young gardener she had once known, their uncomplicated carnal relationship balm for her tortured emotions.

Two maids arrived at that moment, one carrying a tray on which were arrayed plates of tempting cakes, the other bearing one which held a jug of iced lemonade and glasses. They knew their mistress's preference on hot summer days.

'You have not yet told me,' Melanie reminded her cousin after they had refreshed themselves with the lemonade, 'why you have returned to Sydney. The last time I saw you, you were declaring you hated the place. I know Matt never has liked cities.'

'Very true. Nor has either of us changed. We will be here for only a few days. On Thursday we board the island schooner.' Her lips quirked at Melanie's gasp of surprise, her eyes twinkling in anticipation to her cousin's reaction to the rest of her news. 'We are going to Paradise Island to be married.'

Melanie was totally bereft of speech: a rare condition which showed just how astonished she was. If Matt Warrender was willing to put his ring on any woman's finger then that woman must know herself the most treasured on earth. Another thought came into her mind.

'There would appear to me, sweet coz, to be an element of *déjà vu* associated with your plan.'

Once again Dita laughed. 'If I am shipwrecked with Matt again I will not mind in the least.'

'What if other interesting people were to be ship-wrecked with you?'

Dita shook her head, momentarily sober. 'My libidinous days of promiscuous indulgence are over. Matt is the only man I want. In truth he was the only one I ever really wanted.'

'Just as you were the only woman he truly desired. I am so happy for you both.'

There was a brief cloud of wistfullness in the green eyes which did not escape Dita's notice. 'Somewhere there is someone special for you too, Melanie. One day you will find him.'

'Perhaps, perhaps not. I believe I am far more flighty and amoral than you ever were.'

'That will change. Believe me,' she added when Melanie cast her a look of disbelief. 'You once told me yourself just how alike in nature we really are. In the meantime you are very comfortably situated. I was quite taken aback by the size of this place.'

'So was I when I first arrived. In fact I am still a little bemused by the knowledge it is mine.' She lapsed into silence, a tiny frown creasing her brow.

Dita studied her, convinced all was not well. 'What is it, Melanie? You are not as content as you would have me believe.'

'Oh I am content enough, dear coz. Only I can not be certain I am going to remain, as you put it, comfortably situated.'

'Why ever should you not? Mr Wilberforce did not leave debts, did he?'

'Heavens no. He was far wealthier than I had even begun to imagine.' She shook her head. 'No, that is not the reason. The problem is an unknown grandson who is contesting the will.'

'Oh dear. You do have a problem. I presume he expected to inherit.'

'So I believe.'

'Have you met this man?'

'No and I hope I never will. He lives in England. Alaric Wilberforce,' Melanie exclaimed in disgust. 'Have you ever heard such a ridiculous name?'

Never having completely accustomed herself to the Aphrodite she had been christened, Dita merely smiled. 'What do you know of him?'

'Very little. Mr Bartlett, Jeremiah's solicitor, is checking his credentials to ascertain if his claim is genuine.'

'You think he may be an imposter?'

'Who knows? There was a grandson who was taken to England when he was a toddler. Oh! It makes me so angry. He probably never cared one iota about Jeremiah. I can just imagine what he must be like. A fat, obsequious toad of a man with spectacles and –' Interrupted by Dita's burst of delighted laughter, Melanie found herself giving a rueful smile. 'With a name like Alaric he would have to be quite horrid. He has had no contact with his grandfather for all those years yet he now expects to sit back and take everything away from me.'

'What has the solicitor advised?'

'Mr Bartlett told me to take up residence in Arlecdon. He seems to think that if the grandson should decide to come to Australia my position is fortified if I am in possession of the house. Otherwise the man might very well move in and refuse to move out.'

When Dita returned to the hotel it was to find Matt pacing restlessly around their small room. His resemblance to a caged beast brought an affectionate smile to Dita's mouth and the glow of love to her heart. Matt hated to be confined within four walls. In persuading him to go to Paradise Island she believed she had made the right decision. Her father would almost certainly offer Matt a partnership in his rubber plantation. She

41

believed Matt would accept. The island life would suit him and Dita had no objections to making Paradise Island their home.

'I missed you,' he said when she entered the room, not even waiting for her to remove her bonnet before he pulled her into his arms to press an ardent kiss on her mouth.

'I have only been gone five hours,' she replied when she was able.

'Which was four hours too long,' declared Matt. 'I had a need for you which I could not satisfy.'

Quelling the onrush of desire his words evoked, Dita turned away to extract the pins from her straw bonnet and lift the flower and ribbon trimmed concoction from her head. Her eyes caught his reflected in the mirror, their ardour sending delicious little shivers quivering between her thighs. 'I suppose you expect me to make it up to you.'

The gleam in his eyes was like sunlight on a frozen lake. 'Naturally.'

'Then help me with my gown, only do not be so impatient that you tear the stitching.'

'I will try not to,' promised Matt who had ruined more than one of Dita's gowns in his eagerness to adore her body. 'I never have been able to understand why women need to wear so many clothes. It is little wonder a man becomes impatient.'

'If you were a gentleman you would restrain yourself.'

'Ah, but I am not a gentleman. Which, my love, is why you like the way I make love to you.'

He did manage to restrain his ardour until she was clad only in her stays and petticoats. Then he pulled her into his arms again, his kiss devouring her mouth, his tongue probing between her teeth. Dita's tongue flexed to meet his in an erotic feint and parry.

Passion, always so easily aroused, trembled between them. One of Matt's hands slid to her buttocks, the other to the middle of her back, his frustration mounting when it encountered the rigid boning of her stays. 'I hope you discard half these layers when we reach the island. I would prefer to have you dressed like the native women.'

'Half naked?' Dita teased.

'Totally naked.'

'I will see what I can manage,' promised Dita who had every intention of wearing the loose shiftlike dresses favoured by her mother. 'Now help me rid myself of the rest of these offending layers.'

For all Matt's professed dislike of unnecessary garments, he took his time. The soft material of her chemise was pushed down to enable him to press kisses against the magnolia swell of her breasts. He suckled gently at her nipples until they became ripe pink peaks of arousal. After admiring the results with an 'Mmm' of approval he carefully covered her breasts over again. Dita, her body alive with desire, awaited his next move.

That was to undo her petticoats and allow them to fall to the floor, then to unfasten the buttons which attached her knickers to her chemise. His hands guided the garment over her hips, down past her thighs and calves to join the jumble of her petticoats around her ankles.

Kneeling on the froth of material, Matt slowly guided his hands up the outsides of her legs and curled them in a circular motion over her buttocks, sweeping down the line of the firm cheeks then around until his thumbs were splayed either side of her pubic mound. He moved them towards each other, through the soft black thatch then forward and down to part the silken folds of feminine flesh.

His head dipped forward, his tongue flicking lightly against the delicate nub he had exposed. An exquisite tremble vibrated to Dita's core. She wanted to spread her legs wide to give him greater access. With her ankles confined in her undergarments, she could not. Matt had done that deliberately, knowing full well the delicate tantalisation and subsequent frustration would be taking the thrill of her arousal to fever pitch.

When he finally allowed her to step free of the tangle of muslin and lace it was to guide her to the bed and seat her on the edge. Once again kneeling before her, Matt unbuttoned first one boot then the other. He drew her stockings down her legs, nibbling gently at her toes when they became exposed.

Dita squirmed and giggled. 'That tickles.'

'Does this?'

Her knees were lifted, her hips pulled forward, Matt's tongue darting at the place he had so recently teased. There was nothing in the least bit ticklish about the needle-sharp darts which pricked Dita's sensitive flesh. Not wanting the special delight to end too soon, Dita wound her hands in the thickness of Matt's hair to pull his mouth away from her pulsing vulva.

He glanced up, saw that her violet eyes were already darkened with passion and, lifting himself to the bed, carried her with him down into the softness of the bedding.

Mouths clinging, arms embracing, legs intertwined, Matt's material-covered thigh pressed between her nakedness. The kiss was more heady than any sexual contact. They were drowning in their passion, rolling over and over. Matt shifted his leg slightly to allow room for his fingers to press into the moistness of her opening. Locked in the kiss, her arms around his back, Dita worked herself against his probing fingers.

In her heightened state of sensuality she soon felt the quickening which heralded the onset of her orgasm. Matt also recognised the signs of her approaching climax but when he would have pulled his hand away she grasped his wrist, holding his fingers in place while she worked herself through a very satisfying orgasm.

When she was quiet, he withdrew his hand, wet with her juices, and curved it gently over her mound. 'I didn't want you to do that. I wanted to be inside you.'

44

'I'll make it up to you,' she promised for the second time.

They undressed completely then, back on the bed, Dita knelt over Matt to pleasure him with her mouth as thoroughly as he could desire to be pleased. She did not take him to his climax, wanting the ultimate pleasure for herself. He lifted her and pulled her over his body, positioning her so that he could slide her on to his throbbing organ. Thus joined, he rolled them both so that she lay beneath him. In the age-old position they celebrated their unity with joyous unbridled passion.

Chapter Three

S ydney Harbour, Delie conceded with ill grace, could be considered to be quite spectacular. Ric, standing beside her on the deck of the vessel that sailed up that magnificent waterway, mocked her peevishness.

'My dear Adeline, you should learn to appreciate new experiences.'

'What makes you think I do not?' Delie was looking away from Ric to watch the sailors, torsos naked, who were scrambling up the ratlines with a fine display of agility and muscles. As always, the sight of their half-naked bodies set up a train of thoughts which had nothing to do with the beauties of the harbour.

Ric's thin lips curled in contempt. 'I was not referring to sex, dear girl. What of natural wonders and exotic cultures? How ever else do you expect to enrich your life?'

'With your inheritance, I hope.' Delie snapped the retort. The fact that it had been her idea to accompany Ric on this voyage to Australia did nothing to lessen her ill humour. There had not been one single person on board she had deemed worthy of her sexual interest. Even if she had not, for the greater part of the journey, been too ill to give thought to that part of her anatomy.

Her sardonic half-brother's unfailing good health, whole-hearted enjoyment of the trip and indifference to her suffering had compounded her misery. There were times when she came close to hating him.

On being treated to an angry glare to accompany the testy riposte, Ric's contemptuous smile widened, the mocking glint in his eyes becoming more pronounced. 'And I thought you came all this way because you could not bear to be parted from me. You only want to make certain I do not decide to remain in Australia and leave you with the Hall falling down around your ears.'

Delie glared at him, lips compressed, refusing to be baited.

'My dear Adeline, I do believe you do not trust me.'

'You are quite right. I do not trust you at all.'

'We do think highly of each other don't we? Whatever happened to sibling affection? Do calm down dear girl,' he mocked, imitating Delie's *sotto voce* blasphemy and tightly clenched hands, 'there will be smoke coming out of your nostrils soon.'

'One of these days I will –'

'Strangle me? That won't be necessary. As much as I have enjoyed the voyage and intend to make the most of the time we spend in Sydney, I have no intention of remaining in the colony any longer than is necessary.'

Twenty-four hours later Delie reminded him of his declaration. In that time Ric had made no attempt to contact old Jeremiah's solicitor. He had found them a suite of rooms in a respectable if somewhat drab hotel then practically dragged her out on a walking explora-tion of the city. Her tart suggestion he should do something only brought a scathing comment on her eagerness to get her hands on the money.

When, on the third morning after their arrival, Ric announced he had an early appointment with Mr Bar-tlett, the solicitor, Delie fumed at him for not allowing her sufficient time to dress.

47

'I never intended that you should accompany me,' Ric told her. 'I am going to the meeting alone.'

'You take delight in being infuriating. You know I thought to go with you.'

'Still anxious to know how much the old boy was worth?'

Delie was very tempted to throw her tea cup at him, along with its content of hot beverage. 'Bastard that you can be at times, in fact most of the time, I do want to see you get what should be yours. How long are you going to be? I will be impatient to hear what the solicitor has to say.'

'Then you must find some activity of interest to counteract your impatience. I doubt I will return before evening.'

After he had met with Mr Bartlett, Ric intended to hire a horse and ride out to Arlecdon. Beyond that his plans were uncertain. Whether or not he presented himself at the house depended a great deal on the outcome of his meeting with the solicitor. He wondered whether the man would be impartial or inclined to lean to either claimant.

What he did not expect was for Mr Bartlett to gape at him slack-jawed and wide-eyed before exclaiming in the utmost astonishment, 'Good grief! Richard.'

Ric's brows drew inward. 'The name is Alaric.'

'Yes, yes, I know.' Mr Bartlett hurried forward to pump Ric's hand, the other resting on the younger man's arm as though to hold him in case he slipped away. 'My dear boy, you are the image of your father.'

'You knew my father?' Ric's spontaneous flare of annoyance at being called anybody's 'dear boy' faded beneath the significance of the statement.

'I knew him very well indeed. Such a sad day when he died. Poor Jeremiah was totally devastated. When your mother took you away to England the pain of losing you as well very nearly killed him. But do take a seat, dear boy, don't keep standing.'

Wincing at the repetitive 'dear boy', Ric took the chair indicated while the solicitor returned to behind his desk. 'I gather he never forgave my mother for leaving Australia.'

'Never. Two weeks after you left he put away your father's portrait plus every photograph and reminder. He blocked out his loneliness with hard work and doubled his wealth in a handful of years. The money he made never meant a great deal. It was just something he did to fill in his life.'

'I knew my grandfather only slightly. He never struck me as being a hard-headed businessman.'

'You never saw that side of him. For all his shrewdness when it came to money and investments, Jeremiah was a sentimentalist. He never ceased to hope that you would one day come back home. I could not count the times he talked about teaching you all you would need to know to be able take over the management of his business interests. When he returned from that last visit to England he was as excited as a child at Christmas because he believed you were coming home at last. He even hung your father's portrait again.' The solicitor paused with a sad, reproachful shake of his head for Ric. 'You should have made the effort. It was such a sad thing to see his excitement and happiness fade a little bit more as each month went by. Eventually he gave up hope and put the portrait away again. I believe he was even lonelier then than in the first years after your mother took you away.'

Whether or not he had intended it to be so, the solicitor had made Ric feel he had been both selfish and heartless. He covered the unfamiliar and decidedly unpleasant notion in the only way he knew, with anger and scorn. 'Is it my fault then, that he fell prey to this gold-digging little tramp?'

The tone of voice and bitter expression on the disturbingly familiar face shocked Mr Bartlett. 'Now, now, my boy, there is no need for saying such things. Mrs

Wilberforce is a charming, well-brought-up young lady whose parents are among the most respectable in the city. I believe she was very fond of Jeremiah. I know she made him happy.'

'So happy that he decided to cut me from his will and leave everything to her.' Ric, barely able to keep the contempt from his voice, quelled the temptation to venture an opinion on exactly what methods the woman had undoubtedly employed to make the old man happy.

Mr Bartlett, in his turn, wore the expression of a person caught out in some wrongdoing. In truth he was torn between loyalty to Jeremiah's grandson and his own fondness for Melanie whom he had known from her early childhood. The fact, which he did not intend to mention, that Melanie had wanted nothing to do with Jeremiah's fortune, and indeed had to be persuaded to move to Arlecdon, convinced Mr Bartlett of the sincerity of her affection for her elderly husband. All that aside, he would have felt a lot happier about the whole affair if Jeremiah had not cut out his grandson entirely.

'I tried to advise him against the new will.' A shake of the head emphasised the futility. 'Jeremiah could be quite stubborn when he chose, which is why he was so successful in business. He was angry with you, my boy. His exact words were that if you wanted to remain in England and waste money on a house that should be left to rot then you would have to find your own money. I am sorry, but that is the way he felt.'

In the brief period of silence which followed, Mr Bartlett saw the nerve which twitched at the corner of Ric's tightly compressed mouth. There was a great deal of anger kept barely in check. He knew the young man would not be easily placated over the matter of his inheritance. While Ric might be the physical image of his father, he possessed none of that reckless young man's *joie de vivre*, nor the gentleness which underlay his grandfather's practical nature. Iron-hard determination would appear to be the only Wilberforce trait Ric had inherited.

Ric glanced up from his studious contemplation of the gloss on his boots. 'What is my position? Can my grandfather's will be declared invalid?'

'Not at all. He was in full mental capacity and under no coercion.'

I bet, thought Ric, the bitch had probably withheld her favours or some such thing. Or else the old man was so besotted with sex he was not thinking clearly. Aloud he said, 'For thirty years, until he married this woman, he intended that I should be his heir. Surely that gives me some claim?'

'Morally, yes. Legally, I am not so certain. I can implement proceedings if you desire but it may take some time to go through the courts.'

'In that case I request you to start proceedings immediately.'

Mr Bartlett's expression indicated he was not at all happy about so doing. 'There is an alternative you would do well to consider.'

'Which is?'

'A personal approach to Mrs Wilberforce. I feel confident she would be willing to sign a portion of the estate over to you.'

'A portion,' Ric scoffed. 'How small a portion, I wonder? Does she imagine I will be satisfied with a few thousand pounds when all should be mine?'

Ric's belligerence was beginning to wear thin with the good solicitor. 'At the risk of being a bore, I will point out that you have only yourself to blame. A legal challenge is going to be both time-consuming and expensive, albeit the estate could bear the cost. The other is a far more sensible option. You should at least meet with Mrs Wilberforce.' When Ric did not respond he continued. 'Of course you are entitled to seek other legal advice.'

'I see no need to do so.'

'I will arrange a meeting with Mrs Wilberforce?' Mr Bartlett's tone was eager.

'Not yet.' Ric rose, the solicitor following suit. 'Thank you for your time, Mr Bartlett. I will be in touch again soon.'

For all Delie was accustomed to Ric's cavalier manner, she was more than a little put out at being left alone in the hotel. She was also beginning to wonder just why she had insisted on accompanying him in the first place. The voyage by ship had been completely horrid and the days since they had landed in Sydney not a great deal better. Delie was bored, both with her own company and the necessity of dealing with her sexual urges alone. If matters did not improve soon she would . . . Delie had no idea what she would do except that it would be something drastic. The very fact that sex had been denied her for several weeks served only to keep her in a heightened state of arousal.

Her hand pressed over her mound, the internal reaction immediate. Oh, hell! If she did not bring herself to a climax without delay she would go mad. With nothing else to occupy her time, she decided she might just as well undress and do the job properly. Unfortunately it took her less than two minutes to orgasm. Legs pressed together to hold her fingers embedded in her hole, she admitted to herself that her climax was only half as satisfying as she wanted it to be. She needed so much more.

Delie began to masturbate again. This time she indulged herself with a fantasy, one she had begun to develop during the voyage. In her fantasy she was once again on a ship manned by half-naked sailors. This ship sailed on calm seas and she was the only woman on board. Always the dominant person in her sexual activities she was, in her fantasy, submissive to the sailors' desires.

They had taken her to the forecastle where she lay in a

hammock of netted rope. Her legs were draped over the sides with all her sex opened to the view of the sailors. The calico trousers of every man were stretched by their erections. A big blond Scandinavian reached out to stroke a finger along her moist crease. Delie writhed in delight, the movement of her hips a silent invitation for him to probe between her folds to the pulsing entrance to her sex.

First he undid his trousers to release his engorged penis. With his middle finger probing her internal warmth in a manner which made her quiver with pleasure, he curled his other hand around his shaft. Soon he had two fingers, then three, inside her, pushing and twisting to raise the level of her pleasure to a sublime degree.

Sailors on either side of her also undressed. Delie reached out to take a hot throbbing rod in each hand. They in return fondled her breasts, kneading the flesh and massaging her nipples to aching hardness. Another sailor came to stand behind her. He tilted her head back then thrust his rigid organ into her mouth. Sexual sensation enveloped her. She hardly knew which part of her body was receiving the greatest thrill. Then she felt yet another sailor slide beneath the hammock to begin licking her buttocks through the mesh. When his tongue worked its way between the fleshy cheeks to lick around her tight rear opening, she began to buck and toss in a sexual frenzy. The sensations created by the stroking tongue magnified those imparted by the thrusting fingers. In response, her mouth worked more avidly on the shaft it pleasured while her hands rapidly pumped the two they held.

Those three, like Delie, were all close to a climax. She was beginning to drown in sensation, her body surrendering to the anticipated flood of ecstasy. When the fingers which were carrying her towards that moment were withdrawn, she would have cried out in protest if her mouth had not been too full. However, she was not left deprived of stimulation for long. The sailor beneath the hammock turned around and guided his shaft through the mesh to press against her hot puffy sex lips. He pushed upward, his rock-hard organ sliding easily into her eager receptacle. With her suspended above him in the hammock, he was able to make each thrust so hard it jolted her body. The sailor who had fingered her to readiness began to play with her clitoris. He rubbed it between thumb and forefinger with sufficient pressure to create an almost unbearable inflammation of desire. Delie lost all control. Unable to cry out her delight or gasp her pleasure, her body convulsed with her orgasm, her frenzy bringing each man to his own.

But they were not yet finished with her. The big Scandinavian lifted her from the hammock to lay her on her back on the wooden floor. Two men, one either side of her, lifted her legs straight in the air, holding them wide, pressed back towards her upper body. Kneeling in front of her exposed sex, the big man took his semi-flaccid shaft in his hand and began to slap it against her vulva. Nerves that were already highly sensitised responded immediately with sharp arrows which pierced back through her pelvis.

Delie moaned. The louder she moaned, the harder he slapped his organ against her soft flesh. His actions were bringing her closer and closer to another climax. Delie could feel the muscle which beat her vulva growing ever harder, the knowledge he was arousing himself adding to her excitement. She began to pant heavily, her small gasps of breath turning into tiny cries of anticipation. In one swift movement he heaved his body over hers, embedding himself deeply before pumping her with a primitive urgency which had Delie screaming with approval.

The shuddering of Delie's body eased as her cries became softer. She lay on the bed, her hand curved over her pulsing mound. That time it had been much better.

But masturbating to fantasies was not what she really needed.

Sydney was proving to be a far more impressive town than Ric had expected. On his ride out to Arlecdon he stopped frequently to admire the magnificent houses and wonderful views. Each time his gaze roved over the town and harbour, a barely discernible emotion stirred in his breast. While it was too faint for him to acknowledge it as a recognition of his birthright, he did wonder why he had been so reluctant to leave England. If he had not, then he would now be riding up the long driveway at Arlecdon instead of peering through the trees at what portion he could see of the house.

Reluctant to make an appearance at the house yet curious to see more, he tethered his horse and walked through the trees to where he could obtain an unhindered view of the massive mansion. The pale stonework gleamed in the sunlight, sparkling windows were thrown open to the warm air, perfect green lawns, colourful flower beds and the fountain centred in the circular drive completing the perfect picture. Astonishment at a grandeur far beyond his imaginings was rapidly surmounted by anger, the greater part of which was directed at himself. Unable to cast the solicitor's words from his mind, he was beginning to think his indifference to his grandfather's wishes had cost him a great deal more than money.

While he stood in the shadows of the trees studying the house where he had been born, he saw a carriage driven from around the side halt at the grand front entrance. A minute later a petite, fashionably dressed woman walked from the house. Even at this distance Ric could see that she was beautiful. He sprinted back through the trees, mounted his horse and cantered it a short distance back down the road before easing it to a steady walk.

As soon as he heard the carriage approaching from

behind, he walked his horse to the edge of the road where he held it in check for the vehicle to pass. When the carriage drew level its sole occupant leant forward to smile at him. Ric inclined his head in acknowledgement, a brief moment of eye contact sending an unfamiliar sensation jolting through his chest.

For a long time he sat on his horse watching the departing carriage. All he really saw was a pair of bright green eyes which had seemed to widen in shock. He wondered if she had recognised him before deciding there was no reason why she should. Unless she was familiar with his father's portrait. Prepared to risk that it might be so, Ric decided he would certainly make the acquaintance of his grandfather's widow. On his own terms.

Determined to find some man, any man, willing to thrust his organ where she desperately needed to feel one being thrust, Delie dressed in her most becoming gown. In a skirt of deep-red merino crepe and bodice of silk damascene in lighter shades, the vibrant colours complemented her dark hair and eyes to give her an almost exotic appearance. Adding a little artificial colour to emphasise the sensual fullness of her lips, Delie made her way to the hotel dining room where luncheon was being served.

A fawning waiter showed her to a small corner table where she was seated in a position to afford her a view of her fellow diners. All were in groups or couples; the only other person who dined alone was an elderly sparrow of a woman who harassed the waiter with what appeared to be an endless number of complaints. In all, they were such an uninteresting assortment that Delie's hopes of finding a lover withered beneath renewed discontent. The undisguised admiration of the obsequious waiter was small compensation. She ordered the soup and briefly contemplated arranging an assignation with the man. While she had no doubt he would be willing, she decided he would be too subservient to satisfy her desires. Delie was seeking a man who would take her as forcefully as the Scandinavian sailor of her fantasy.

There being no such person within the hotel, Delie decided she must finish her lunch quickly and seek diversion elsewhere. She was half-way through her soup when that plan was discarded with the arrival of another diner. Delie studied the man with open interest. Around fifty and slightly overweight, he had a face that managed to convey working-class origins despite the expert tailoring of his morning coat. In her swift appraisal, Delie knew him for a man who enjoyed women. Despite the mediocrity of his physical appearance he possessed a certain something which kindled a spark of recognition in the core of Delie's womanhood.

When he was seated at a table some distance from hers he, too, made a sweeping appraisal of the occupants of the room. He acknowledged Delie with a slight inclination of his head to which she responded with a warm smile. Her gaze held his long enough for the bold message in her eyes to be understood. For a second time he gave the slight inclination of his head then turned his attention to the ordering of his meal.

Delie took her time in finishing her soup. She watched him while he ate and waited for him to make his approach. He beckoned the waiter, spoke briefly with the man, then handed him a card on which he had written something. The waiter carried the card across the room to present it to her with an expression not quite impassive enough to hide his lecherous envy.

According to the gold lettering on the card, Conrad J Irving was an importer of exotic goods from Asia. On turning the card over, Delie discovered he had written a room number on the back. She looked up to find him watching her, awaiting her answer. Delie inclined her head and placed the card in her small bag. When she left the dining room he was just being served his main course.

The door of Room 14 was unlocked. Delie stepped

inside and closed the door behind her. The room had the same anonymity as all hotel rooms and Delie wasted no time in contemplation of its decor. Getting herself out of her gown unaided was going to take time enough. The option of waiting for Conrad J Irving to assist was not even considered. Delie knew exactly how she would be waiting for him when he returned from his lunch.

Thus he opened his door to find her lying naked on the bed, her hands caressing her body with an indolence which suggested she was enjoying their touch rather than attempting to arouse. He neither spoke nor showed any expression either of surprise or pleasure. If not for the lusty gleam in his eyes Delie might have believed she had misinterpreted his message.

While never taking his eyes from Delie's body and the erotic passage of her hands, he removed his own clothing. His naked torso bore a distinct resemblance to a hirsute barrel to which was attached a rampant cock which more than compensated for the hairiness of his body. It was not the longest male organ Delie had encountered but what it lacked in length it made up for in thickness. The mere thought of having it wedged inside her was sufficient to precipitate an eager flow of juices. Delie spread her legs wider and used both hands to part her sex lips so that he could see just how wet and ready her opening was.

Conrad J Irving did not hesitate. He climbed on to the bed and pressed his rod between the inviting pink lips of her sex. The degree to which she was stretched made Delie gasp, the length of time she had been without a man exciting a vibrant response along the length of her canal. Not satisfied to be fully encased he wriggled and pushed against her to force himself even deeper. His wiry pubic hairs rubbed against her labia in their own erotic stimulation.

'Oh yes.' Delie approved. 'That feels so good.'

'Does this?' Taking his weight on his hands with his body held away from hers, he began to rotate his hips.

Delie shrieked. The intense friction of his shaft rubbing the walls of her burning sheath was magnified by the sensation of being stretched even wider. Her climax was building far too rapidly. Delie tried in vain to hold back to prolong her enjoyment. The action of the rotating shaft was too thorough, an increasing tempo carrying her to her climax with the speed of a runaway train. 'Oh yes,' she cried. 'Yes, yes. Keep doing it. Ooh. Oh God!' The final exclamation was wrenched from her when he ceased his circling action to begin pumping in and out. Her second orgasm started almost as soon as her first one faded while the steady rhythm of his piston action suggested he was a long way from his own.

She was beginning to wonder how much more intense sensation she would be able to endure when he suddenly withdrew and lifted himself from the bed. He spoke fully for the first time when he saw Delie's confused gaze on his still rigid organ. 'The Asians know a great deal about sex. One thing I have learnt is how to enjoy sex for a prolonged period without losing my strength from unnecessary ejaculate. I will be able to take you time after time for as long as I wish.'

'Then I hope your wish is for a long time,' said Delie. The prospect of hours of intense sex was almost too good to believe.

A somewhat sly expression entered his eyes. 'You may be worn out long before I am. Are you familiar with these?'

Even though Delie had never seen a dildo, she recognised its purpose immediately. The large bead-like objects in his other hand puzzled her as to their use. Conrad J Irving was coming back to the bed.

'I can tell by your expression you have never learnt these pleasures. I am going to enjoy initiating you.' He handed her the carved wooden phallus then a small bottle of oil. 'Make it slippery so that it does not hurt when inserted.'

The act of rubbing oil over the hard wood and of

feeling the lifelike shape in her hands imparted their own unique sexual thrill. Delie was eager to experience how it would feel to have sex with an inanimate object.

'Not yet,' Conrad J Irving told her when she held the well-oiled phallus out to him. 'I want you to learn the pleasure of the love balls first.'

There were two, the size of small plums, joined by a short length of cord. The surface of each was covered with small protuberances. Delie realised they were made from some type of metal.

First, her sexual tutor bent over her to tongue her sex with an expertise which almost drove anticipation of new experiences fron Delie's mind. When he raised his head it was to insert first one ball into her canal then the other, pushing them as far as they would go. Delie's breathy 'oooh' of delight soon changed to a gasp of delighted shock when he clasped the cord to slowly draw the balls back out. The first one stretched her entrance, the little bumps setting up a vibrant reaction before the ball popped free and her vaginal muscles contracted back to normal only to be stretched again by the second ball.

Time and again he repeated the proceedure before discarding the balls to remount her. Delie was capable of only one coherent thought which was all to do with having sex of a magnitude she had despaired of finding. This time he did not allow her to climax, climbing back off her and giving her time to rest before he took the oiled dildo from her shaking hands.

Though the sensation was not as intense as that given by the love balls, Delie rapidly discovered just how arousing an inanimate phallus could be. Especially when wielded by a man who appeared to know every way to drive a woman into a sexual frenzy. With the phallus left inserted in her pulsing sex, he tipped a little oil on his finger and spread it around the crinkled opening of her rear passage. Delie loved to be stimulated there but had never before had anyone's finger force a way into that virginal passage. The pain of being stretched was soon replaced by pleasure. He worked both phallus and finger with a precision of timing designed to raise sexual sensation to sublime heights.

When he decided she had been pleasured enough he did not, as Delie expected, replace the stimulus of the dildo with his own Herculean organ. Instead he rolled her on to her side and pushed one of her legs to a crooked position to enable him to part her buttocks. He then took up the string of six smaller balls which he carefully inserted into her rear passage one by one. Gasping from a combination of pain and incredible pleasure, Delie waited in almost fearful anticipation for him to draw them back out.

That was not his plan. With the balls left to stretch her anal cavity he once again began to lick the folds and creases of her sex, drawing her to the brink of an orgasm before removing the stimulation and allowing her to rest: as if she could with the continued throbbing in her rear passage.

'Yes,' said Conrad J Irving, watching the passage of emotions across her face, 'I believe we are both ready now.'

For the third time he lifted his body over hers to push his bulky organ deep into her sex canal. This time the balls which stretched her anal passage made the fit even tighter. Delie made little yelping noises, unable to differentiate between pain and exquisite pleasure. The fact that he began to pant for the first time that afternoon indicated the degree to which he, too, was affected by the tightness.

When he had pushed right in, he rolled on to his back to carry Delie over to lie on top. In that position she would normally have taken control. She was given no chance even if she had not been hovering on the brink of a sexual swoon. The man's strength was unbelievable, his hips belting upwards to drive his piston with a force that had Delie lying helpless on his body, unable to do other than to sob from the torturous ecstasy. She thought she had reached the pinnacle of sexual gratification when her orgasm kept building and building to an intensity which tore through her body when it broke. At that precise instant Conrad J Irving grasped the dangling cord to pull out the string of balls with one swift movement.

The abrupt magnification of her orgasm caused Delie's head to jerk up and wrenched a scream from her lips before she collapsed against his body in a near insensible state. Only when, after what seemed an eternity in which the hard piston never ceased driving into her body, her partner began to grunt towards his own climax did she stir herself sufficiently to circle her throbbing sex around the frantic pumping of his shaft to bring him to that state more quickly.

Much later, after she had recovered enough to be able to dress and hobble back to her room, she carried with her some of Conrad J Irving's exotic imports.

Dinner parties given by the Griffiths were always elegant, socially desirable and to Melanie a filial obligation. The days when she had looked forward to her parents' dinner parties with the hope of meeting some interesting young man seemed so very far away. Perhaps in her widowhood she really had grown away from the flighty amoral girl she had been. Her gardener lover satisfied her sexual needs completely. At least he had until she had looked from her carriage into a pair of coal-black eyes.

The image of the unknown man, seated on his horse, would not leave her mind. Even though she had seen him for only a few brief moments, she could recall his face with perfect clarity: the chiselled features, straight dark brows and piercing eyes. His eyes she remembered most clearly of all. Every time she thought of the way they had seemed to look right into her core she experienced the same peculiar reaction. Melanie privately dubbed him her 'dark stranger' with a prayer they would one day meet. When next she had lain with her lover she closed her eyes so that it was her dark stranger's face she saw in her mind. She imagined they were his hands which caressed her body, his tongue which pleasured the pearl of her womanhood and his organ which satisfied her with its ardour.

So obsessed had she become with the man, she would rather have stayed home with her daydreams than peform her social duty. The greys and mauves of half-mourning being quite the worst colours to be teamed with Melanie's vibrant curls, she continued to wear the widow's black. Not that her new gown, copied from the latest fashions in *Harpers Bazaar*, was in the least degree sober. The elaborate creation of black satin with an overskirt of gauze was trimmed with garlands of black roses and frills of the finest pleating. The heart-shaped neckline left her shoulders bare and dipped to a deep cleavage. A clever arrangement of black roses and gauze perched atop her upswept hair style from which a few artfully errant curls were allowed to escape. The only colour apart from the brightness of her hair and eyes was in the emerald pendant which lay against the milkiness of her throat.

Mrs Griffiths greeted her with a mother's pride and affection. 'Melanie, my dear, you look absolutely stunning.'

'Thank you, Mother. You are very elegantly gowned yourself. I do believe everyone will think I am your sister.'

'You flatter me, my dear. Maintaining an appearance of elegance becomes harder each year. And to think I once had a figure equal to yours. Now come with me. Mr Bartlett has brought two extra guests. A couple newly arrived from England.'

Melanie allowed her mother to lead her across the drawing room which was crowded with guests enjoying pre-dinner drinks. 'This would appear to be a very large dinner party tonight. Are you trying to outdo anyone, Mama?'

Mrs Griffiths smiled and tapped her fan against her daughter's arm in mild reproof. 'You know me better than that. There always seem to be so many people who might be offended if they were not invited.'

Melanie's father was a man of less than average height whose greying hair did not yet conceal from which side of the family Melanie had inherited her flamboyant tresses. When Melanie first saw him, he was absorbed in recounting some tale to Mr Bartlett and a tall couple who were standing in such a position Melanie was unable to see their faces.

On turning his head slightly and seeing his wife and daughter he broke off his narration. 'Ah Melanie.'

His companions all turned in her direction. Melanie's step faltered. The queerest sensation threatened her composure. She wondered if she looked as strange as she felt. For all she had dreamt of meeting her dark stranger, she had not expected her reaction to be so intense. There being no hint of concern in her father's welcoming expression, she presumed her appearance remained normal and continued towards the group.

Her father stretched out his hands to grasp both of hers. 'You grow more beautiful every day. Melanie, my dear, I want you to meet our special guests, Mr Richard Liddell and Miss Adeline Liddell. This is my daughter, Mrs Melanie Wilberforce.'

'How do you do.'

'So pleased to meet you, Mrs Wilberforce.'

The exchange of civil greetings was followed by polite small-talk. Melanie smiled, laughed and tried not to stare at Richard Liddell. She wondered if he was as aware of her as she was of him, if any man so suave and self-assured could possibly suffer from churning insides. Having convinced herself it was unlikely she would ever meet her dark-eyed stranger, she found herself to be now in an agony of wondering if he would want to further their acquaintance.

Both brother and sister were seated too far away from her at the dinner table to allow for easy conversation. When the ladies retired to the drawing room to leave the men to their port, Melanie chose a seat beside Delie. The older woman was so very charming, Melanie decided she had imagined what had appeared to be an unfriendly appraisal when they were first introduced. That feeling disturbed Melanie solely because of her interest in the dark-eyed man who was no longer a stranger. Accustomed to her unique beauty arousing the envy of other women, she never allowed their discontent to cause her any worry.

Now, however, the woman appeared more than willing to be friendly. She explained that her brother had suggested they come on a visit to Australia with a view to settling permanently.

'Oh, do you think you might?' Melanie strove to keep the excitement from her voice.

'We have been here but a few days. Ric believes there are many great opportunities for investment in so young a country.'

'There are indeed. Wise investment was what made my late husband his fortune.'

Delie laid a sympathetic hand on Melanie's arm. 'I was sorry to hear of your loss. It is sad to be widowed so young.'

'I am over the worst now. But do not talk about me, I want to hear all about you.'

Delie disclosed only those facts which would give no clue as to Ric's true identity. She also, without making it appear as if she was complaining, told Melanie what a trial it was living in an hotel when one was accustomed to a large house and capable servants. 'We thought to hire a house for the remainder of our visit. Do you know of any which are available?'

The idea which had been hovering in Melanie's mind

since half-way through the meal now sprang to the fore. 'Why not stay with me? I would love for you both to be my guests.'

Delie appeared to be quite overcome by her generosity. 'You are very kind, Mrs Wilberforce, but neither of us would wish to impose.'

'You would not. My house is large, far too large for one person. You will be doing me a favour in providing me with company.'

'I must ask my brother. Ric –' she beckoned him, the men having at that moment entered the drawing-room '– Mrs Wilberforce has invited us to stay with her.'

'That is most generous of you, Mrs Wilberforce.'

'Then you will accept?'

'With the greatest of pleasure.'

Perhaps it was only a reflection of the firelight but the glitter in the black eyes gave Melanie cause to hope there would be a great deal of pleasure indeed.

Chapter Four

Melanie was ringing for her maid before the sun had risen above the tree tops. Unable to sleep, she wanted to be up and about, doing something, anything, to make the hours pass more swiftly. The unexpected meeting with her dark stranger and the joyous anticipation of having him as a guest in her home filled her with a restlessness that would not be quelled.

By the time her flustered maid answered the uncommonly early summons, Melanie was seated at the window gazing with dreamy eyes across the mist-filled valley to the distant pale buildings of the town. He was somewhere down there, in all probability sleeping soundly with no feverish thoughts to disturb his rest. Melanie held no doubt he had accepted her invitation for precisely the same reason it had been extended. Words were not necessary to define the sexual attraction each felt towards the other. A man such as he, whose dark eyes watched the world with cynical amusement, would not suffer any upset of his equilibrium from the prospect of taking a new lover. Goosebumps shivered unexpectedly down Melanie's spine. She had a fatalistic conviction Richard Liddell was going to mean a great deal more to her than she would ever mean to him.

* * *

While Melanie gazed over the mist-shrouded town Ric was not, as she supposed, blissfully asleep. He too had risen from a restless night and had been walking the almost deserted city streets since dawn. The thoughts which occupied his mind were more of a vengeful nature than erotic, Melanie's charm and beauty acting as catalyst to his resentment. If she had been a cheap, tawdry little slut he would have trodden all over her to take back everything she had wheedled out of Jeremiah.

Except the widow was not a bit like the person he had envisaged. Desire for her had flared from the moment their eyes first met. When she gazed up at him the previous evening, the intensification of that desire had been like an iron fist clawing at his groin. Angered that she could affect him so deeply he vowed to have her as many times as was required to get her out of his system. Then, and only then, would he tell her who he was and what it was that he really wanted.

When the carriage, which had been dispatched to collect her guests, trundled up the long driveway to halt at Arlecdon's grand front entrance, Melanie barely gave Carstairs time to open the door before hurrying down the steps to greet brother and sister. Her bright smiling face beamed her pleasure. 'Welcome to Arlecdon. I am so pleased you have arrived at last. I have been impatient with waiting.'

Delie managed to drag her gaze from the mansion's impressive facade to give a sickly half-smile which gained her an unobtrusive warning dig in the ribs from her brother. His own expression was urbane. 'Both Adeline and I are indebted to you for your generous hospitality, Mrs Wilberforce.'

'It is nothing. As you can see my house is large enough to accommodate any number of guests.'

The airy possessiveness sorely tried Ric's self-control. Now that he was walking up the steps of his grandfather's house, a house of which he had kept no childhood memories, his sense of injustice became magnified tenfold.

Delie, who had in no way been prepared by Ric's description of the house as being quite large, managed to find her voice. 'I would call this a mansion equal to any grand manor house.'

'I see you are quite bemused.' Melanie gave a bright little laugh. 'I confess I was equally so when I first came to live here. Especially knowing it was all mine. Even now I frequently pinch myself to make certain everything is real.'

'You have not lived here for long then?' Ric asked with the right degree of civil interest.

'Only a matter of months. But do come inside both of you. I have ordered afternoon tea to be served in the small drawing-room.'

During the course of their tea Melanie happily answered questions, mainly from Ric, about Arlecdon and its estate. She found nothing intrusive or sinister in the questions. To her way of thinking it was perfectly natural someone newly arrived from England would want to make comparisons with his own estate. To Delie, Melanie paid only as much attention as was polite of a hostess. Ric dominated her interest, her gaze feasting on his dark satanic good looks. She wondered how she could arrange for them to be alone together.

'This hour of the afternoon is very pleasant for a stroll through the gardens. Unless you would prefer to see more of the house.'

Although Melanie spoke to both Ric and Delie, all three knew her invitation was meant for Ric. Delie, who was not completely certain of Ric's intentions was nevertheless perfectly willing to give him all the leeway he needed to execute his plans.

'Would you mind very much if I went up to my room, Mrs Wilberforce? I have a slight headache and would like to rest.'

'Oh, you poor thing.' Melanie was immediately

sympathetic. 'Of course you may.' She reached for the bell cord to ring for a maid. 'I feel certain you will find your room quite comfortable but if there is anything you need you must not hesitate to ask.'

'You are very kind, Mrs Wilberforce.'

'Please. You must both call me Melanie. I could not bear it if we are to go around being terribly formal for the duration of your visit.'

'Then you must call me Ric, for I will not answer to Richard.'

'Nor I to Adeline. I much prefer Delie.'

Melanie clapped her hands together in a childlike gesture of delight. 'That is settled then; Ric, Delie. I know we're going to deal famously together. Ah, Kate,' she addressed the maid. 'Please show Miss Liddell to her room.' Then to Delie, 'I hope you are feeling better soon.'

When Delie and the maid had departed, Ric turned to gaze down at Melanie with an intensity which turned the blood in her veins to water. 'So, we are alone at last. You are a very beautiful, extremely desirable woman.'

'You waste no time do you, Ric Liddell,' Melanie declared, playing the coquette. 'You have been in my house less than an hour and already your manner is one of seduction.'

'For what reason, other than the anticipation of being seduced, did you invite me here?' Ric quipped in reply.

'Have you not been told how hospitable we colonials are? If I had not invited you to Arlecdon you would soon have been invited elsewhere.'

'In that case I consider myself fortunate that we met. No other hostess could be near as charming. You were going to show me something of the estate,' he added.

'A small part only. The grounds are so vast they take some time to explore.' Recalling exactly how long it had taken her to explore the grounds and the reason why brought a pink flush to Melanie's cheeks. Despite the fascination she felt for Ric, she was not at all certain she should relegate the gardener to the work for which he was employed. He had been such a strong and satisfying lover. Perhaps that was a matter on which she should keep an open mind. One day Ric would leave to return to England.

While they strolled across the front lawns, between the colourful flower beds, Melanie strove for a composure suitable to someone of her station in life. The presence of the man at her side, the musky masculine scent of him and the way his dark eyes gazed at her, combined to affect her to such a profound degree she feared she was acting like a naive miss who found herself alone with a man for the first time in her life.

They reached the side of the house and Ric looked across at the high hedges. 'Is that a maze?'

'Yes, it is.'

'Fascinating. Shall we explore?'

His lowered tone left Melanie in little doubt as to what thoughts were in his mind. While she was eager to be taken in Ric's arms and to have her body pressed against his, she was reluctant to take him into the maze. To do so would be to drag her feelings for Ric down to the level of the carnal relationship she shared with her gardener. Melanie wanted Ric to mean so much more. In truth she suspected he already did.

'Not now,' she said in answer to his query about the maze. 'Come around to the eastern terrace. There is a spectacular view from there. On a day as clear as today one can see right out to the harbour.'

On reaching the terrace they mounted the shallow flight of steps and walked a little distance along the paved area until Melanie stopped. 'There,' she said, her hand indicating the distant sparkle of water. 'Do you not agree it is quite beautiful?'

'Very beautiful.' Ric was standing directly behind her, the husky cadence of his words touching her like a kiss. In vain she strove to find some light sally with which to respond. Then his hands were on her shoulders and his lips warm and firm against the nape of her neck. 'The

71

more I am with you the greater becomes my desire. When can I make love to you?' His lips traced a path up the side of her neck until his breath was whispering in her ear. One hand moved from her shoulder to curve across her breast and pull her back against his body.

Melanie relaxed in his embrace, savouring the sweetly strange sense of belonging which heightened her own desire.

'Tell me when, Melanie. How soon will I be allowed to adore your body?'

'Tonight,' Melanie managed to whisper, wishing it was night already.

'I doubt I can wait that long. To wake this morning and know I would hold you in my arms before the day was out has been torture of the sweetest kind.'

'It has been the same for me. Oh, Ric, I have dreamt of you since the day my carriage passed you on the road.'

'Do you think I have not dreamt of you? I knew I had to find you.'

Surprise jerked Melanie from his embrace to turn to face him. 'Then it was not by chance you were at my parents' dinner party?'

'Of course not. I wanted to meet you again.'

His head was bending slowly towards her upturned face. Breathless as a virgin, Melanie waited for the moment his lips would brush against hers.

'Your pardon, madam.'

Ric and Melanie moved hastily apart. Melanie spun quickly to face the housekeeper. Ric turned more slowly. Mrs Godwin, her nose wrinkled, began to subject him to one of her disapproving glares. Instead her eyes widened and her jaw gaped in exactly the same manner as had Mr Barrett's. Danger signals flared in Ric's brain. He had not counted on there being any elderly retainers who would remember his father. He inclined his head the slightest degree, his eyes flashing a fierce warning. To the woman's credit and Ric's intense relief Mrs Godwin shut her mouth again.

'What is it, Mrs Godwin?' Melanie's tone was more impatient than she normally used towards her servants. The housekeeper's interruption was most unwelcome.

'I was wondering, madam, if you and your guests will be dining in the formal dining room or if you will continue to use the family dining room.'

'The family room I think. There are only three of us and we would look quite silly seated at a table which seats ten times that number.'

'Very well, madam.'

'One moment, Mrs Godwin. Mr Liddell and Miss Liddell are newly arrived from England. Please instruct the servants they are to do everything possible to ensure my guests enjoy their stay at Arlecdon.'

'Yes, madam.' The woman backed slightly, preparing to take her leave. Before she had fully turned away, she gave Ric a brief questioning stare.

Melanie was intensely disappointed Ric did not return to the point of intimacy at which they had been interrupted. He even appeared to have lost interest in the marvellous view. One could be forgiven for thinking he was somewhat preoccupied.

'I presume you, like most ladies of society, are accustomed to taking a rest in the afternoons.' His tone seemed to suggest he hoped that was her habit.

Melanie's excitement level rose. 'Sometimes.' Was Ric about to suggest he would join her in her rest?

'Then you will not think me rude if I take leave of you to write some letters.'

'Oh.' Disappointment could not be hidden. 'Of course not. I will call a maid to show you up.'

'I thought you might offer to do that yourself,' he said with a gleam in his eyes.

Melanie's excitement level bounced right back up again. She led him through the door Mrs Godwin had used. 'Although the house is large, its design is simple. You will quickly learn your way around.'

They mounted the curving staircase to the first floor.

'That is Delie's room,' she said when they passed one door, 'and this will be yours.' She paused in front of another a little farther along the passageway on the opposite side.

'And yours?'

'My suite is at the other end. I have a corner room with views of both the harbour and the mountains. Would you like to see the view?'

'When I come to your room, Melanie, it will not be the view in which I am interested.' He reached a hand to rub his knuckles lightly across her breast. She felt the caress between her thighs more than where his hand touched.

'When?' Her eyes beseeched him.

'Tonight. That is what you told me. When I make love to you for the first time I have no intention of hurrying the experience. I want many hours in which to prolong the pleasure.'

With so exciting a prospect for the night, Melanie decided she would rest for the remainder of the afternoon. She had a notion she was going to need all her strength to satisfy Ric's demands.

Ric planned to give her at least a half-hour in which to settle before he went in search of the housekeeper. A discreet knock which preceded the woman sidling through his door saved him the bother.

She wasted no time in prevarication. 'You are the master's grandson, Mr Richard's boy, aren't you?'

'Why ask if you recognised me? I believe my resemblance to my father is too strong for me to deny the relationship.'

'Herself doesn't know, does she?' There was a derogatory jerk of her head in the direction of Melanie's room.

Ric's brows drew together in a sternness of expression which could not be ignored, even by a woman who thought her long years of service gave her the right to speak her mind. 'I take it you do not like Mrs Wilberforce?'

Mrs Godwin gave a huffy lift of her shoulders. 'Well it's plain as pikestaff she only married the master for his money. I know her kind and I know what I was interrupting downstairs.'

'Perhaps you do and perhaps you don't.'

'Hmph. She will be taking what she can from you too.'

'There is nothing left to take. The widow has it all.'

'Why not tell her who you are?'

'I have my reasons. Which need not concern you,' he added when he saw the eager curiosity in her eyes. 'Are there any other of the servants who might recognise me?'

'None that I can think of.'

'I believe there was a portrait of my father.'

'That is stored away in a safe place.'

'Then see that it remains there. Mrs Wilberforce has accepted me as Richard Liddell. I trust you will say nothing to make her suspect it is not my true name.'

'She'll not hear anything from me. Though I would like to know why you are being secretive.'

'No doubt you would.'

'I know the master left everything to her, and them married only a few weeks. She used her wiles on him, that's for sure. He always intended everything would be yours.'

'I am well aware of the facts.' The words were snapped with angry emphasis.

A smirk of satisfaction rearranged the creases in the woman's face. 'Aah. Now I understand. You are here for revenge.'

Ric's mouth curled in derision. 'Revenge is petty, Mrs Godwin. Quite simply I am here to take back my inheritance.'

Melanie twirled about her room with her nightgown ballooning out from her body and her arms hugging herself with excitement. Soon Ric would come to her. His gestures, the way he had looked at her throughout their dinner then after, had given her his promise. When she had retired to her room in the afternoon she had quickly fallen asleep to dream of Ric. She had awoken from those dreams with her desire for him considerably heightened.

Her twirling brought her in front of the mirror where she paused to gaze at her reflection. The high-necked, long-sleeved white nightgown was exceedingly demure and had been chosen for the impression of chastity it imparted. On impulse, Melanie blew out the lamps then drew back the curtains of both windows to flood the room with bright moonlight. Perched on the window seat with her knees drawn up to her chin, she gazed out at the blue-washed landscape. When she heard the door open her only movement was to turn her head slightly.

Clad in a long brocade robe, Ric closed the door quietly behind him then stood gazing at the virginal picture she presented. His eyes gleamed with amused appreciation. 'Am I supposed to believe you an innocent who knows nothing of sex?'

Melanie favoured him with an impish smile. 'I am very keen to learn whatever you can teach me.'

'Minx.' Ric chuckled and moved a few paces farther into the room. 'Stand up and take off that ridiculous nightgown. I want to see what you look like.'

Melanie stood, lifted the nightgown over her head then tossed it aside. Sensually naked, she waited.

Ric did not move, though she heard the sharp intake of his breath. 'Turn around, slowly. That's right. Stop there,' he commanded when she was side on to the window. 'Now lift your arms over your head.'

Again, Melanie did exactly as she was bid, raising her arms to curve them over her head. The action lifted her breasts to better define their silhouette in the moonlight.

'Keep turning.'

When she had completed the full circuit and was

facing him again, she lowered her arms to her sides. 'Do I please you?'

'Very much. Your body is every bit as perfect as I imagined.'

'Now it is my turn.'

The robe was the only garment Ric wore. He tossed it aside to fall in a heap on top of Melanie's nightgown. Melanie was momentarily distracted by the erotic image of the dark rich material lying on top of the soft virginal white and thought of Ric's body covering hers.

Feet astride, arms akimbo, he was waiting for her to gaze her fill. A knot formed in Melanie's stomach. All of Ric's skin was of the same swarthiness as his complexion. He was so dark. The firm male nipples were the colour of chocolate, the triangular mat of hairs between them black like those on his head. Melanie's gaze followed the finer line of hairs which reached down to encircle his navel before they continued lower in a sparse scattering to connect with the thickness of the ones at his groin. His manhood, only yet half aroused, seemed to twitch in reponse to her studious assessment. Melanie moistened her lips before her gaze continued its passage down his long slender legs. The finely sculpted muscles promised to be possessed of a strength more than sufficient to drive ecstasy deep into a woman's core.

'Well?' he asked.

Melanie raised her gaze to his face. His eyes were like black diamonds, so bright were they. She walked towards him to stop when their bodies were so close they were almost touching. Her own eyes were jewel bright. 'I believe you will please me quite well.'

He caught her to him then, his mouth covering hers in a kiss all the more wonderful for having been so long anticipated. Melanie lifted her arms to bury her fingers in the crispness of his hair, her lips parting in sensuous invitation. Accepting the invitation, his tongue probed deeply to taste the sweetness of her mouth.

The faintest tremble shivered through Melanie and his

embrace tightened with one hand sliding down to her buttocks. Pressed against him, Melanie delighted in the sensuality of his naked skin touching hers, of her nipples being squashed against the firmness of his chest. She returned his kiss with ardour, her tongue playing against the seductive action of his. Movement against her abdomen told her his manhood was now fully aroused. The hand on her buttocks curved lower to slide between her thighs with his finger coming to rest against the dampness it found there.

Suddenly he scooped her in his arms and carried her back to the window seat where he sat with her in his lap. Using his left arm to support her shoulders, he returned to the task of seducing her with his kiss while his right hand searched between her thighs. Trembling in need of his touch, Melanie opened her legs for him and curved her own hand around the firm column of his arousal.

Clever fingers played gently with her folds in a soft teasing which raised the level of her desire by several degrees. Unable to speak with her mouth still captive to his, Melanie moved her hand from his organ to press his tantalising hand firmly against her quim. There she held it until he slipped a finger between her moist folds to probe the warmth within.

The alternate probing and stroking actions of his fingers remained gentle, the lightness of touch imparting perfect delight which quivered through Melanie's entire body. When the gentle quivers strengthened to a more spasmodical response Ric lifted her from his lap to lay her along the window seat. Shifting his own position to kneel on the floor, he parted her legs wide. One foot he placed on the floor, the other he raised to rest it on the window sill. His fingers toyed briefly with her again before parting the labia to open her to the teasing of his tongue.

All of Melanie's anticipations of Ric's expertise as a lover were being gratified. His tongue he also applied with precisely the degree of pressure necessary to create the most exquisite sensations. Melanie wished she could be caressed in such a manner for ever, even knowing it to be impossible. The myriad little flames of delight, imparted by Ric's tongue, were rapidly fusing together to create a fire which would soon be beyond her ability to control.

Ric moved his thumbs a little higher to push against her flesh and expose the bud of her greatest sensitivity. The instant his tongue made contact, a spear of white hot flame seared to Melanie's core. Her body began to shudder uncontrollably, all thought suspended in sensation. The inferno building in her groin rose to encompass her mind in a swirl of hot bright colours. She was aware only of heat and moisture and Ric's mouth sucking hard on her vulva. Nothing else existed. The rest of her body had dissolved in brilliant colour. All that was left was her burning sex.

Some time later, Melanie had no idea whether it was minutes or hours, Ric raised himself to lean over her and take her mouth in a soft kiss. Melanie tasted her own sharp sweetness on his lips. When he drew back she returned his gaze from wide, emerald bright eyes. 'Oh, Ric,' was all she could manage to say.

'Do you want more?' His gaze was intense.

'I want you.'

Ric lowered his body, the first contact between his glans and her swollen flesh drawing a tiny groan of longing from Melanie. His entry was very slow, as if he wanted to savour the feel of every diminutive cell of that silken sheath brushing gainst his own heated muscle. When he was all the way inside he kissed her hard, crushing her body beneath the weight of his own.

'You feel so beautiful, so perfect.' His voice was husky with desire. A deep groan immediately followed his words. 'I can't wait.'

The urgency of his need set the frenzied tempo of his thrusts. Melanie's fingers clawed at his back, her fingernails digging into his skin. She curled her legs around his body, lifting her hips to meet each penetrating stroke with an ardour more than equal to Ric's. Lust of so frenetic a degree could not last long. Melanie began to climax very quickly with Ric reaching the pinnacle of his compulsion moments later.

They lay side by side on the bed, Melanie in a sated half-sleep in Ric's arms. Twice more they had made love and each time had been more beautiful than the one before. When they were not conjoined in lust they explored and tasted until there was not a thing each did not know about the other's body. So filled with contentment was Melanie, she would have purred if she had been a cat. Instead she snuggled closer to Ric, turning her head to press a kiss on his shoulder. Her hand snaked down towards his recumbent shaft.

Ric gave a mock groan. 'Aren't you satisfied yet?'

'Never.'

'Is that what happened to your husband? Did you wear him into his grave with sex?'

Melanie recoiled as if she had been slapped. Seated back on her knees, she stared at him in disbelief. How could he say such a thing to her after they had made love so ardently. Even through the haze of shock she could see his lips were thinned in a cruel unrepentant line. Realisation that the hurt had been deliberately inflicted had her scrambling off the bed.

Wrenching her nightgown from beneath his robe she pulled it over her head then wrapped her arms protectively around her body. She could not look at him, did not want him to see her tears.

Sounds of movement told her when he left the bed and put on his robe. Hairs on her neck prickled with the knowledge he was standing close behind. Firm hands gripped her shoulders and warm lips pressed against the side of her neck. Without turning around Melanie jerked herself free. Ric pulled her back against his torso with so tight a hold she could not escape the insulting caress of the hand which pressed the material of her nightgown between her thighs.

'Does the truth hurt, Mrs Wilberforce? You should have married someone with the stamina to keep up with your demands. Or weren't there any young men rich enough?'

A sob broke from Melanie, the tears she had been trying to hold back spilling down her cheeks. Pride kept her silent even though her heart ached with hurt and confusion.

'There is no need to cry.' Ric's voice was hatefully mocking. 'You will not wear me out. Just understand that any sex between us will be on my terms.'

A half-minute later Melanie was alone. She went back to the bed, pulled the covers over herself and curled into a shivering ball of misery. It was impossible for her to even begin to work out the reason Ric had spoken in so insulting and hurtful a manner. Especially after the joyous intimacies they had shared. The ardent manner in which Ric had acted, the pleasure he had given with such care, had convinced her that what was between them was far better described as making love than having sex. Apparently she was wrong.

When a fresh flood of tears broke forth, she silently vowed to send both Richard Liddell and his sister away in the morning then knew she could not. Whatever Ric thought of her, Melanie knew very well how she felt about him. She had fallen in love with her dark stranger at first sight. Now she was infatuated. There was no doubting Ric's desire. Could Melanie turn his desire into love?

Tiredness gradually overcame her troubled thoughts. She was almost asleep when she recalled a comment Ric had made earlier in the day about her elderly husband. Was that the problem? Did Ric find it difficult to accept she had been married to a man old enough to have been her grandfather?

Chapter Five

When Melanie entered the breakfast room the next morning, Ric rose quickly from the table to greet her with a warm smile. He held out a chair for her, bending forward as she seated herself until his lips were brushing lightly against her ear. 'You were wonderful last night.'

The emotive cadence of his voice made Melanie recall just how wonderful a lover Ric had been. Her anxiety over meeting him, which had been with her since she woke, slipped away. When he spoke in such a tone and his dark eyes gleamed with desire she could easily forget his hateful remarks about Jeremiah.

'Delie is not up yet?' she asked, simply because she could think of nothing else to say and felt the need to speak. From the manner in which Ric was looking at her he appeared almost ready to have sex with her in the middle of their breakfast. Not that Melanie would try to prevent him if he did.

'My half-sister is a lazy creature. I doubt she will stir for another hour or more.'

'Should we wait to consult Delie or is there anything in particular you would like to do today?'

His eyes gleamed even more brightly. 'Have sex with you again.'

Melanie cast him a pert smile. 'Apart from that.'

'I would like to ride around the estate with you as my guide. You do ride, don't you?'

'A little.'

'Then I can think of no better way to spend the morning.'

'We could make a day of it and ride to the Hog and Hound. A small inn on the western road,' she explained in answer to a querying lift of Ric's eyebrows. 'They serve a simple but quite excellent meal.'

'That sounds delightful.'

An hour later, knowing how lovely she looked in a velvet riding habit which matched exactly the colour of her eyes, Melanie hurried out to the stables. Ric was already there, waiting. He held the bridle of a big bay gelding while the groom finished saddling a smaller roan mare. Ric assisted Melanie to mount before swinging lightly on to the gelding's back.

Side by side they rode out of the yard, down past the kitchen garden to the orchard. The groom, who was entirely devoted to his good-natured mistress, watched them go and thought what a grand couple they made. Simmonds, Melanie's gardener lover, watched them approach with a similar thought in his mind. He realised why the mistress had not sought his company in recent days. They had almost reached him before he stepped into full view. Melanie was smiling at something the man had said, her joy in his company visible on her face. The man's expression was intimate.

Simmonds clenched his fists in anger and took another pace forward. 'Good morning, ma'am.'

'Oh, good morning, Simmonds.' Melanie gave him the briefest acknowledgement before returning her attention to Ric.

Ric, however, had noted the man's surliness and the resentful glare which had been directed more at him than Melanie. 'Quite a sullen fellow. Is he upset for some reason?' He spoke in a tone low enough for only Melanie to hear.

Automatically looking back she saw that Simmonds stood as he had been, glowering after them. With a toss of her head she turned back to Ric. 'Do not mind him, he is only the second gardener.'

If Melanie's words did not carry clearly back to Simmonds, the toss of her head certainly gave him their meaning. Humiliation and rage sent a dull flush of colour rising from his neck to suffuse his face. He might only be a gardener but his amoral mistress was going to discover he was not a man to be toyed with.

Sexual arousal, for Delie, was synonymous with waking up. No morning went by when she did not pleasure herself before rising from her bed. Before her meeting with Conrad J Irving her skillful fingers had served her well. The wooden phallus was now more frequently used. Delie kept it, the oil and her other sex toys in a small camphor-wood box. The box was always placed within easy reach of her bed.

Stretching with a sensual languor, Delie kicked off the bedcovers and began to run her hands lightly over her naked flesh in preparation for a more sexual caress. She then took the dildo from its box and began to oil it carefully. During that process she thought, as she always did when her fingers thrilled to the shape of the wood, what a great pity it was that Conrad J Irving had to leave town the day after their meeting. Delie would have liked several repeat performances of his brand of sex.

For the past few days the novelty of her toys had kept her amused if not wholly satisfied. Delie was so highly sexed she craved almost constant stimulation. Within the very near future she would need to find herself a lover. One with a shaft as hard as the imitation one she slid between her thighs. Oh, but it did feel good. She could easily close her eyes and pretend more than one man pumped her with his rigid organ and rubbed his finger over her sensitive nub. Delie climaxed very quickly.

Not long afterwards she rang for the maid, took breakfast in bed and, on learning Ric and Melanie had gone riding, decided to employ her time in search of a lover. Why should Ric be the only one having fun? Delie was well aware her brother had spent the greater part of the night in Melanie's room.

When Delie dressed she shocked the maid by dispensing with both undergarments and stays. Delie brushed aside the girl's remonstrances with haughty impatience. Obviously this particular maid was going to be no fun at all. Delie wondered if there was another, more open-minded, with whom this scandalised creature might be replaced. Someone like Annie who had been more than willing to do anything Delie asked.

For over an hour Delie roamed through the elegant house, her resentment of Melanie increasing more with each room she entered. The luxury at Arlecdon emphasised by contrast the shabbiness of Liddell Hall. But her beloved home would not, Delie vowed, remain in such a deplorable state for long. As soon as Ric had tired of the widow and claimed his own, Delie would make certain none but the best of furnishings were used to refurbish the Hall.

During the course of her exploration Delie encountered a few of the maids, each of whom bobbed a quick curtsey before hurrying about her work. Not one appealed to Delie, who was adept at judging a person's sexual potential at a glance. Therefore, the scene she came upon on entering the upstairs sitting room pleased her immensely even if it did give her an initial start of surprise.

Whoever would have thought the supercilious butler would be such a randy buck. He had one of the maids tipped over the back of a sofa with her skirts bunched up around her waist. His hands rested on her buttocks while he, with an expression of carnal gratification twisting his face, pumped his rod into her with an energy which was apparently equally satisfying to the maid.

Since Delie made no attempt to enter the room unobtrusively they became aware of her immediately. Two faces registered guilty shock at being discovered in the act. The maid's expression was fearful, the butler's showing his conflict between an instinct to pull free and the need to keep driving to the release which was imminent.

'Do keep going,' said Delie, providing the solution to his dilemma. 'I like to watch people enjoying themselves.'

Carstairs was too far gone in his sexual thrall to wonder about the woman's unusual statement. He renewed the energy of his thrusts, ignoring Delie who had come to stand beside him to watch his well-lubricated shaft slide in and out with voyeuristic delight. But he could not ignore her presence when she began, in a low lecherous tone, to both describe what she was seeing and tell him what he should be doing. His pumping became more frantic, his breath a series of loud grunts. The maid was also panting with the approach of her climax. Delie slid a hand beneath the girl's body to rub at her rigid nub. A cry of astonished pleasure broke from the maid's lips. The butler's rhythm changed to long deep thrusts which carried him to his own release.

Only then, with their lust sated, did both servants begin to consider the ramifications of the situation. Carstairs pulled his throbbing cock out of the maid who wriggled to push down her skirts and stand upright. Delie moved faster than either. Kneeling in front of the butler she grasped his rod and sucked it fully into her mouth before it had time to relax. She worked quickly, sliding her mouth back and forth and sucking him deeply into her throat. There was not a man alive who could resist such expert fellation. Carstairs shot his second load into Delie's mouth, something he had never before done with a woman. His ecstatic gasps indicated just how much he enjoyed the experience. Unable to believe her eyes, the maid stared and felt herself growing all wet again.

Delie rose and smiled regally at them both. Her words were addressed to the girl. 'Come to my room this afternoon. I would like you for my maid.'

She then turned and walked from the room to leave butler and maid totally bemused and highly aroused. They looked at each other. Carstairs tipped the maid back over the sofa to begin humping her even more vigourously than before.

Melanie rode at Ric's side through the quiet bush, delighted by his interest in everything he saw. Laughter bubbled from her lips until a different kind of laughter, harsh and manic, echoed suddenly through the treetops. She had not thought a man as self-possessed as Ric could possibly be so startled. He reined his horse to stare around them.

'What on earth was that?'

'Him.' Melanie pointed to a high tree branch slightly ahead of them.

'The bird?' Ric was disbelieving.

'Watch. There comes his mate.' Another large brown and white bird landed next to the first. Both birds threw back their heads, opened their strong beaks and emitted more of the same raucous laughter. 'We call them Laughing Jackasses. Their real name is the Kookaburra.'

'Quite incredible.'

'They are, aren't they? Wait until you see one catch a snake for its supper. It will fly into a tree with the reptile in its beak and beat it against the branch until it is quite dead.'

'Have you seen that?'

'Once.'

Ric gave a slight shake of his head, an almost bemused expression on his face.

'What is the matter,' demanded Melanie. 'Don't you believe me?'

87

'Of course I do. It is just that . . .' Ric stopped speaking.

'What?'

'Nothing. There is a good clear patch ahead. Will we give the horses a canter?'

Though the gelding could easily have outstripped the mare, Ric allowed Melanie to go ahead. She rode well, wheeling her horse just before the trees closed in again. In her bright green gown, with teasing laughter on her face she presented an appealing image of girlish happiness. Ric could not collate the typification of innocence with either the sensual woman whose body he had adored or the avaricious schemer he believed her to be. Her knowledge of, and interest in, the flora and fauna of the bush did not sit easily with his concept of a woman who would use her sex in a mercenary and heartless manner.

These contradictions, as Ric perceived them, in her nature had the effect of smudging the clarity of his own plans. On accepting Melanie's invitation to Arlecdon he did so with the clear-cut intention of taking his pleasure with her before he revealed his true identity. The latter he planned to do in as belittling a manner as possible. That had still been his intention when he left her crying in her room. Having proved to his satisfaction just how much of a little slut she was, he anticipated with cruel delight the moment of revelation.

But that had been last night. The moment Melanie walked into the breakfast room, her eyes wide and uncertain, he had known his lust was not yet sated. The beautiful widow would know him as Richard Liddell for a little while longer.

The Hog and Hound was crowded with customers when Ric and Melanie arrived at the inn. Two stagecoaches were in, their passengers taking their lunch while the horse teams were changed. A waggon, a buggy, one private carriage plus a number of horses had brought other customers to the popular public house.

'I had not thought there would be so many people here,' Melanie said almost in apology to Ric when they entered the crowded dining room. 'I doubt there are any tables left.'

A number of the diners looked up when the couple entered, with cursory glances quickly transformed to stares of appreciation. The tall dark man and his lady companion were so obviously from the upper echelons of society that the landlord wasted no time in hurrying over to them. Wiping his hands on his apron he welcomed them to his inn and assured them he would find them a suitable table.

They were given a table in a relatively quiet corner, after two of the coach passengers had been persuaded to move elsewhere, then served with a promptness they might have expected if they had been the only diners. The meal lived up to Melanie's promise of tasty simple fare; the wine the landlord produced was a smooth mellow red. It warmed the blood in Melanie's veins and evoked a memory of the previous night when Ric and she had sat naked on her bed toasting each other's sexual prowess with a similar wine. When she looked across at Ric she believed he knew her thoughts. He was watching her with a sexual intensity which directed all the alcohol-induced warmth in her veins to between her thighs.

'Have you finished?' he asked, on draining the last of his wine. 'Then let us go.' When he held out her chair he whispered in her ear, 'I want to be alone with you.'

Melanie guided them back towards Arlecdon by a different route. One which took them up to a grassy knoll strewn with granite boulders. From there they were able to look down on Arlecdon. In an unspoken agreement Ric dismounted then lifted Melanie from her mare. His hands rested on her waist with his lips brushing briefly against her before he led the horses a short distance to tether them where they could graze.

'I have only ever been up here once before,' Melanie told him when he came back to stand beside her. 'To look down on Arlecdon like this and realise how grand an estate it is fills me with the most disturbing emotions. I find it very difficult to believe it is mine.'

'You made a fortunate marriage.'

Melanie stiffened. Memory of Ric's parting insults returned. 'I was fortunate to marry a good kind man who saw me as other than an object of sex.'

'Now that I do not believe.'

'Why not?' Melanie, on the defensive, swung around to face him.

Ric was smiling, albeit there was more of the sardonic than pleasure in his smile. 'Because you, my dear, are the most ravishing woman I know. There would not be a man alive who could resist your body. I know that I can not. Nor am I going to wait until tonight. I want you now.'

'A riding habit is not the easiest garment for a lady to remove without the help of a maid.'

'You will not need to remove it unaided. I am more than willing to assist.'

Assist her he did until she was clad only in her undergarments; her breasts, with their covering of fine cambric, were pressed upward by her stays.

'You have no need of that lacing,' said Ric, even while his eyes appreciated what he beheld. 'Your body is perfect without. Yet you look so damned irresistible.'

Moistening her lips with her tongue, Melanie pouted up at him. 'You appear to be resisting very well.'

'That's what you think.' Ric caught her hand to drag her to him, his lips hungry upon hers.

Melanie swayed against him, welcoming the kiss which had the power to stir her so deeply. In her deepest being her body cried out for him to take her, to fill her with the hardness she could feel pressed against her abdomen.

Easing his embrace only slightly, Ric guided her over to the nearest cluster of rocks. There he lifted her to seat her on one of the granite boulders. Again he dipped his head to capture her mouth in a kiss. This time his hands were occupied with the fastening of his trousers.

Well aware of what he was doing, Melanie began to tremble with anticipation. A trembling which intensified when Ric pushed her knees apart and spread the open seam of her pantaloons. Expecting to feel the touch of his fingers, Melanie felt instead the hardness of his manhood pressed between her thighs. Firm hands grasped her legs to pull her slightly forward. At his command, Melanie leant back with her hands braced behind her on the rock. With her body arched back she was positioned to receive the full depth of Ric's thrust.

An elongated 'ooh' of pleasure sighed from Melanie's lips, the eroticism of her position heightening her response. To be like this, half dressed, seated on a rock to receive a man's organ had to be the most arousing of her many and varied sexual experiences. Greater eroticism was yet to come.

Ric hooked her legs around his waist thus freeing his hands to pull down her camisole. With her breasts exposed to his caress he cupped a hand around each to roll the soft mounds in circular movements towards each other. The pads of his thumbs rubbed over her nipples. Nor were Melanie's breasts all he circled. The movement of his hips being restricted by having her legs clasped around his waist, he began to supplement his short strokes with circular gyrations of his pelvis. The multiple action touched every sensitive nerve ending in Melanie's sheath.

Her lips parted, eyes closed, Melanie allowed her head to hang back. Every thought was shut out, everything cleared from her mind except recognition of the wonderful sensations Ric was creating in her body. The ecstasy she was experiencing was plainly visible on her face.

'You do like sex don't you.'

The almost sarcastic observation brought Melanie's eyes wide open. Ric's eyes gleamed with an emotion she could not understand. His eyes were too dark for his thoughts to be easily read. There was certainly nothing of anger in the way his rod caressed the silken walls of her sheath nor the manner in which his hands massaged her breasts.

He gave a mocking smile for her puzzlement. 'I want you to show me how good you are at pleasing a man.'

Holding himself motionless within her he grasped her arms to pull her upright against his body. His kiss was an oral seduction in which his tongue became a second penis delving into her mouth. Clinging to him in monkey fashion with her arms around his neck and legs around his waist, Melanie began to clench and relax her internal muscles over his stationary organ.

Ric turned carefully around until his back was resting against the rock on which Melanie had sat. With it to provide support he slid slowly to the ground taking Melanie, still connected, with him. From there Melanie took control. With her hands on Ric's shoulders to give her support, she raised herself enough to be able to reposition her legs in a kneeling position either side of his hips.

She then began, without lowering herself any farther, to rotate her hips. Her intention was of teasing Ric with an erotic stimulation of the most sensitive portion of his manhood. In so doing she was tantalising herself to an almost unbearable degree. The little sounds which her-alded the approach of an orgasm began to issue from her lips, building in intensity to equal the burning within until the latter could no longer be born and she pushed herself down to fill the burning cavity with all of Ric's hardness.

Her desire to hold herself pressed down against his groin until the hot flood subsided made no allowances for Ric's need. Strong hands grasped her hips to lift her up and down, her body simulating manly thrusts to create a friction which rendered her orgasm even more wonderful. Her thigh muscles were aching from the repetitive motion, that pain mingling with the other, more intense, physical reaction.

'Oh stop, please.'

But her plea was not heeded. Ric continued to pump her body up and down until, with a loud grunt, he pulled her down as hard against his groin as she had been before. With her hands pressed on the aching muscles of her thighs, Melanie clenched herself around Ric's pulsating shaft. By using her internal muscles to grip him tightly again and again she heightened the pleasure of his climax. Then, when Ric's features began to relax from their contortion of ecstasy, she began to circle her hips.

'Was that good enough for you, Mr Liddell?'

'Very good.'

'Do you want more?'

'I can see that you do.'

'You are not complaining I hope?'

'Never. But this rock is not the most comfortable of back rests.'

'Then we must find a better position.'

Melanie lifted from Ric's lap and turned on to her hands and knees with her buttocks pointed towards him. She gave a coquettish glance over her shoulder. 'Will this do?'

Ric quickly proved the suitability of the new position. The physical pleasure of being united, of having his flesh brushing against hers, was soon inflamed by rising desire. With the tempo of Ric's thrust increasing, Melanie jerked back to meet each one. The pressure of his hand on her buttocks stilled her actions so that he could pull free. Ric then began to rub the head of his shaft along her burning crease. Every two or three strokes were taken low enough to rub across her sensitive peak of pleasure. Tiny arrows of delight pinged through to Melanie's core. She moaned both her approval and demand for more. Ric gave all his attention to her clitoris to drive her into a lustful frenzy. Her orgasm was imminent and she wanted him inside her. She cried out to him, begging him to give it to her hard.

'You should have been a whore,' he said. 'You've already sold your body once. Men would pay a fortune to fuck a woman like you.'

He belted into her to breach the dam of her desire so totally that Melanie felt as though she was drowning in the ensuing flood of feeling. Nor did it take long for Ric to reach the pinnacle of his own gratification.

Later, dressed in her riding habit once more, Melanie gazed down on Arlecdon with clouded eyes. Bathed in the afternoon sunlight it was like a golden castle set amidst beautiful gardens surrounded by natural bushland. She knew she was already developing a possessive love for the house but she did wonder if her late husband's wealth was more likely to bring her unhappiness.

When Ric brought the horses over, she turned to search his face for some clue to his true feelings. 'Why do you say such hateful things to me?'

Ric's expression revealed nothing. 'I have never said anything which was not the truth.'

'How could you know what is, or is not, the truth? You have only just arrived from England.'

'I have been here long enough to hear the story of a beautiful young lady who married a very rich old man.'

'You think I married Jeremiah for his money. I would not have thought you a person to give credence to gossips.'

'Why else would a woman as lovely and as highly sexed as you marry a man old enough to be her grandfather, if not great grandfather?'

'He was kind and gentle and very lonely. Believe it or not I was exceedingly fond of him.'

'And very soon a wealthy widow.'

'There was no one else to whom he could have left his estate.'

'Did he have no relatives?'

'No. No one.'

Distressed by the conversation Melanie turned away and in so doing missed the flash of raw anger which flared uncontrolled on Ric's face.

How right he had been all along, and how wrong poor deluded Bartlett. There would be no benefit from appealing to this avaricious little whore's sense of moral right.

Throughout the ride back to Arlecdon he was silent. A dark brooding silence which Melanie made no attempt to break. There were thoughts enough to occupy her own mind. Her dark stranger was something of an enigma. He could be making love to her with his body while at the same time insulting her with words. Yet she knew, no matter what he said or how he acted, he need only look at her with that dark piercing gaze and her body would be his.

Not for one moment did Delie doubt the maid would obey her command. Therefore she was ready and waiting when the young woman presented herself at the guest bedroom.

'What is your name?' Delie asked.

'Mary, miss.'

'Very well, Mary. The maid I have been assigned does not suit me in the least. On the other hand I believe you might suit very well.'

'If you think so, miss.'

'Oh I do. Tell me, Mary, have you ever had sex with another woman?' Delie was loosening her robe as she spoke to reveal she was naked underneath. The expression in the maid's eyes would have been answer enough.

'Once or twice, miss.'

'Is that all?' Delie feigned disappointment. 'Then you

will need to prove that you know enough to please me, and I can not be pleased unless you are naked too.'

While the maid hastened to undress, Delie reclined on the bed.

She had no intention of taking any action herself. Her body would be passive to the maid's ministrations. The girl had a pleasantly voluptuous body, her thatch more coppery in colour than the light brown of her hair. Her very large, very dark, nipples drew Delie's lustful gaze. Time enough, she told herself. Later she would suck those nipples. First the girl must pleasure her mistress. Now that the maid was undressed she appeared uncertain of what to do next.

'I am waiting,' said Delie in a tone which indicated she was not prepared to wait for long.

Suspecting that Delie might become vindictive if thwarted, Mary hurried over to the bed. Though she preferred to use her mouth to pleasure a man she knew perfectly well how to do the same for a woman.

Before long Delie was gasping her approval of the maid's ability to apply her tongue with erotic precision. 'Ooh, you are good. Now fuck me with this.' She handed the maid the dildo she had earlier oiled in readiness.

Mary took the phallus and gazed at it in fearful fascination. 'Won't I hurt you with this?'

'Only with pleasure.'

Rather nervously the maid pushed the wooden instrument into Delie's love hole, her cautious action becoming more confident when Delie's eyes began to glaze with sexual contentment. Growing even more daring, Mary began to twist the phallus in addition to working it back and forth. The other woman's rising excitement found a reciprocal response in her own body.

Mary shifted her position to enable her to slide her fingers into her own moist sex. The faster she worked on Delie the faster she masturbated herself until both of them were experiencing the ultimate sensation. Except Mary had a conviction Delie's was far more satisfying than her own. She wished she had a cock, wooden or otherwise, planted where her fingers were tightly pressed.

Her wish was soon answered. Delie took the phallus herself and plunged it into the maid. With a cry of disbelieving delight, Mary began to orgasm almost immediately. Delie pushed the dildo a little deeper. 'Leave it there inside you and suck me again.'

The throbbing effect of having so rigid a stimulant implanted deeply in her sex hole made the maid even more creative in the use of her tongue. The residual taste of Delie's first orgasm gave the incentive to bring her to another.

When that occurred, Delie grasped the girl's hair, holding her head down to make her suck harder. Then as her orgasm began to fade she pulled the wooden phallus out of the maid's wet canal and slid it into her own mouth to relish their combined tastes.

'You may get dressed,' Delie said when finally she allowed the gasping maid to raise her head. Her dark eyes glazed with lust, she continued to suck on the dildo while she watched the maid's shaky efforts to restore her appearance to its proper neatness. 'I believe you might, with a little more training, be even better than the maid I had in England.'

'Thank you, miss.'

'There is just one other matter before you go.'

'Yes, miss?'

'A man. Your butler's cock was very tasty, however he does not appeal to me as a lover. Who else is there who might be able to fulfil my needs?'

'I can think of no one, miss.'

'Then you must think harder. Who does your mistress take to her bed?'

Mary appeared uncomfortable. Delie was waiting for her answer. 'The servants talk about one of the gardeners.'

'What is his name?'

'Simmonds. He is a married man, miss.'

'Since when did that make any difference? Wake me in time to dress for dinner, Mary.'

'Yes, miss.'

Delie did not even watch the maid depart. She pushed the dildo back into her still throbbing sex and rolled on to her side. With that instrument of sexual pleasure to keep her both aroused and satisfied she would soon fall asleep.

Chapter Six

'*F*or how long do you intend to amuse yourself with our widow? I would have thought two nights would be sufficient to jade your interest.'

Ric responded to Delie's query in his customary sardonic manner. 'Do I detect a hint of disgruntlement, dear sister? Is there no one in the house to keep you amused?'

'Not as amused as you appear to have been. Really, the way you watch the woman one could be forgiven for thinking you have become as besotted as some callow youth who has had his first taste of sex.'

To Delie's great annoyance, Ric laughed. 'Our widow, as you call her, is very beautiful and extremely sexual. Even you must be attracted by her rather unique quality of desirability.'

'Huh! She is not one to enjoy sex with another woman. If she was you would not be the only Liddell to frequent her bedroom.'

Ric's thin lips curled in a malicious sneer. His sister's sexual predilections were neither unknown nor approved. However, he did not interfere unless her behaviour was contrary to his own interests. 'Poor Adeline. Is that the reason you are out of sorts? Do you lust after the widow too?'

'Oh, get fu–'

'No crass language, dear girl.' Ric hastily interrupted. 'Do try to remember you are supposed to be a lady.'

'Well you stop being so damned infuriating,' Delie retaliated with considerable heat. 'I have a right to know how long you intend to continue with this deception. You told me you were going to sort out your inheritance quickly so that we could return home.'

'Ah, there you have the crux of the matter. You see, this is my home although I had no memory of it. I was born in this house.'

'Which is all the more reason why it should be yours.'

'Patience, dear Adeline. One day Arlecdon will be mine, you may rest assured of that. For the time being however I intend to continue fucking our ravishing widow.'

'And you criticise my language,' Delie scorned.

Ric merely laughed. The night he had spent with Melanie had done nothing to slake his lust. If anything he desired her more now than he had in the beginning. Her ability to make love with whorish wantonness while retaining an almost innocent girlish insouciance, he found completely disarming. His grandfather's widow was so very different from the person he had expected her to be that he had developed a desire to know her better, to understand her mind and her emotions. Ric needed to know for certain the real reason she had married Jeremiah. He wanted to find out if she had in any way influenced the old man to change his will. Most of all Ric needed to know if she was, with other men, the way she was with him. For reasons to which he would not fully admit he wanted to assure himself that sex between them was as special to Melanie as she declared it to be.

'Are you both ready?' Melanie's bright entry into the room brought Ric to his feet and Delie from her envious perusal of a valuable antique clock.

'We are,' confirmed Ric, his dark eyes resting on Melanie with appreciation.

Melanie acknowledged his unspoken compliment with a little smile. 'I believe Grimes is bringing the carriage around now. Shall we go?'

During the drive into the city Ric derived considerable sardonic amusement from the ingratiating charm of Delie's manner. He made a mental note to tell his half-sister her talents for acting and sex would earn her a fortune in the theatre. Next time she harped on the need for money to repair her ancestral home he would suggest she earn her own by utilising her talents. Ric's interest in the restoration of Liddell Hall had faded considerably since he set foot in the land of his birth.

The two women were engaged in earnest discussion of the latest fashions.

'You must tell me if you consider our shops equal to those in London,' Melanie was saying. 'We do try to keep up with the latest trends but even copies of *Harpers Bazaar* are months out of date before they reach us.'

'Why do you women consider it so important to be draped in the most fashionable frills and fabrics?' Ric's voice was a mixture of amusement and bewilderment.

'Why does the female of any species preen herself in front of the male?' Delie was quick to retort.

Melanie's light happy laugh was a reflection of her mood. She had not felt so very happy for a long time. Ric's loving the night before possessed an ardour which suggested his feelings for her went beyond sex. Nor had he made any of the hurtful remarks which had previously spoilt her pleasure. She smiled across at him. 'You do not mind that we are to go shopping and leave you to your own devices?'

'Not at all. There are places I want to see and things I want to do. You two go off and enjoy yourselves.'

* * *

Both Melanie and Delie enjoyed themselves a great deal. Delie expressed surprise and delight over the elegance of the merchandising establishments and the quality and variety of ladies' apparel which was available. Her greater surprise, which she did not mention, came with a discovery of how much she enjoyed Melanie's company. Drawn as were all who knew her by Melanie's special brand of charm, Delie began to wonder if her brother was not more attracted than he admitted.

They were to meet Ric at one of the higher-class hotels for lunch and duly made their way to the place a little before the appointed time. Ric was not yet there and the two women were shown to their table by a bowing waiter.

'This is quite unlike Ric not to be punctual,' said Delie after Melanie had requested the waiter to bring them each a glass of madeira with which to refresh themselves while they waited.

'We are a trifle early,' Melanie replied. 'He no doubt expects us to still be absorbed in our shopping with no thought for the time.'

Delie agreed with a laugh. 'You are probably right. Melanie –' she leant forward and lowered her voice '– who are that couple who keep staring at us?'

'Which couple?' Melanie cast a curious glance around the dining room.

'They are seated almost directly behind you, several tables away.'

Melanie turned to recognise the couple instantly. Her normally pleasant expression transformed to one of cool disdain.

'They are not people with whom I associate,' she said on turning back to Delie.

'They appear to desire association with you. They are coming over to our table.'

Melanie allowed herself the luxury of some inward fuming during the brief time it took the couple to reach their table.

102

'How are you, Melanie?' greeted the woman. 'It has been so very long since we have seen you.'

'Yes,' agreed Melanie, wishing it was even longer, 'it has.'

That Melanie's manner should border so nearly on rudeness had Delie greatly intrigued. She cast a questioning glance from Melanie to the couple who were looking at her with friendly smiles.

'We would like to be introduced to your lovely companion, Melanie.'

A flush of annoyance stained Melanie's cheeks. She discovered she disliked Jonathon as heartily as ever. 'Miss Adeline Liddell, Jonathon and Emily Grimshaw.' Melanie made the introduction as brief as possible.

'Are you newly arrived in the colony, Miss Liddell?' Jonathon was all suave charm.

'I have been here a little over a week,' replied Delie who was becoming even more curious as to why Melanie disliked the fair handsome man and his fashionably dressed, slightly older, wife.

'I do not suppose you have met many people?' the woman was asking.

'I have been to one dinner party given by Melanie's parents.'

'Then we must invite you to one of ours. Where are you staying?'

'At Arlecdon, with Melanie.'

'I have heard it is a very beautiful house. Melanie made a fortunate marriage.'

'No more fortunate than yours, Emily,' Melanie was quick to retort, annoyed by the manner in which the conversation was being carried on as if she was not present.

Emily merely responded with a supercilious smile. She spoke to Delie. 'We really would like you to come to one of our evenings. Can we send you an invitation in a day or two?'

'I would like that very much.'

The Grimshaws then took their leave and Delie wasted no time in questioning Melanie. 'Why do you dislike those people?'

'A number of reasons. Jonathon Grimshaw was once betrothed to my cousin. He treated her shamefully. That woman to whom he is now married was a spinster school teacher who ingratiated herself into a certain section of society by dispensing sexual favours.'

'She would not be the first woman to have made use of her natural talents.'

'Nor will she be the last. Except that Emily's talents are neither confined to her husband nor the opposite sex. Not that Jonathon objects, if the gossip is to be believed. I cannot tell you not to accept their invitation but I must warn you that their evenings, as Emily calls them, are reputed to be little better than orgies.'

Which piece of information only served to make Delie hope the promised invitation was not long in arriving.

Melanie strolled along the narrow path which twisted through the natural bushland. Her objective was a small pavilion, sited to allow a person to relax and enjoy a view more spectacular than the one from the side terrace. On their return from town Delie had retired to her room to rest. Ric, after sharing their lunch, had stated a wish to stay longer in the town and urged the two women to return to Arlecdon. He turned aside Melanie's insistence on sending the carriage back for him with the declaration he would find himself a cab when he was ready.

Too restless to lie in her room, Melanie walked the grounds thinking about Ric. He had been so evasive about what business kept him in town that she was unable to rid herself of a conviction it was in some way connected with her. Not for the first time she wished he was an easier man to understand.

Absorbed in her thoughts, Melanie did not hear anyone behind her until her arm was caught in a rough

104

grasp and she was pulled around to be confonted by a glowering Simmonds. The ferocity of the gardener's expression sent a fearful little thrill down her spine.

Melanie jerked her arm free. 'What do you think you are doing?' she demanded.

'I want to know what you are doing for sex. Am I no longer good enough for you now that you have a gentleman to share your bed?'

'How do you know that he does share my bed?'

'Because you have not come to me for over a week. The only other times you have stayed away so long is when you are bleeding and I know it is not that time of month for you now.'

'What I do is no concern of yours. Do not forget I am your mistress.' Melanie turned to walk away.

He allowed her several paces before rushing after her. This time he held both her hands low behind her back to pull her forward against the bulge at his groin. 'You were eager enough to have this before.'

The responsive tingle between Melanie's thighs told her she was not uneager now. However, she objected to being handled in a rough manner. 'Why do you complain, Simmonds? I seem to recall you were prompt to remind me you have a wife.'

Angry purple colour suffused the gardener's face. 'So I have. A good gentle woman who deserves a faithful husband. But you, madam, have ensnared me with your pale scented body. I am obsessed by the need to have sex with you.' He pulled her harder against his arousal, moving his hips in a coupling action. 'You will not do this to me, madam, then cast me aside.'

Transferring the grasp of her wrists to one large hand he began to pull at the bodice of her gown.

'Stop it,' cried Melanie. 'You will tear my clothes.'

'Then you had better take them off because I am going to have you whether you are willing or not.'

He dragged her by the arm the remaining short distance to the pavilion, Melanie almost stumbling to keep up with his angry strides. His near primitive behaviour both thrilled and aroused her. Not that she was going to let him know how ready she was to surrender her body to his mastery.

They undressed with equal speed, then he pulled her down to lie on their discarded clothing. His hands moved over her body in a manner Melanie was certain would leave bruises. 'You were the one to start this, madam, but I will be the one to say when it ends. I am not ready to be finished with you yet.'

The vehemence of his words thrilled Melanie to her core. 'I never said I wanted to be finished with you. You were the one to make that assumption. Put your hand between my thighs and you will know I speak the truth. See,' she said when Simmonds' hand probed her moist inner warmth. 'I am wet and ready for you.'

'I hope you are ready for this.' Positioning himself in a seated kneel he grasped her legs to pull her hips over his thighs and raise her feminine opening towards his rampant organ.

His fingers toyed with her again, to coax greater evidence of her arousal. With a forefinger of each hand on either side of her labia he trapped the tiny peak of sensitivity then rubbed his fingers up and down in opposing motion. Melanie gasped. The action was painful to a degree far more arousing than his internal probing. Simmonds maintained the rubbing action until the shudders of her body became uncontrolled.

At that point he reached for her hand to guide it to his heated shaft. 'Pleasure yourself. Use my cock to make yourself come.'

His erection was so strong that there was considerable resistance to Melanie's effort to pull the head down to the level of her pulsing sex. Her lover parted the folds of flesh to enable Melanie to stroke the swollen glans against her silken inner folds. Nerve endings already highly stimulated quivered in delight. At first Melanie kept her hand placed halfway down his shaft to guide the head in long strokes up and down her crease. The expression on the gardener's face told her his pleasure was equal to that which she gave herself.

Melanie shifted her hand to take the head between thumb and forefinger, just above the roll of his foreskin. Holding him thus she brought the extremity against her own swollen nub. The intensity of the instantaneous reaction made her cry out in delight. She began to quickly rub her lover's glans against her clitoris until she was seconds away from her climax. 'Now. Now!' she cried, guiding the hot head to her burning opening.

Simmonds pushed hard, at the same time pulling her hips upward and rising to a full kneel. He held himself deep until her orgasm began to flow, his hands sliding beneath her buttocks to support them in the air. Only her head and shoulders remained on the ground, her semi-inverted position magnifying sexual sensation. The angle of his penetration stimulated places not normally subjected to the friction of masculine thrusts. Uable to move her hips to reciprocate his piston action, Melanie could only moan her pleasure.

She felt his fingers bruising her buttocks with a grip which prevented her from being jerked backward by the savage force of each inward plunge. At the moment of his climax his fingers dug even more deeply into her flesh as he gave the hardest thrust of all. He kept his shaft deeply bedded with only short pulses to complete his satisfaction.

'You must come here to me again tomorrow,' the gardener told her when they were dressed.

Melanie gazed at him with a coolness of expression in complete contrast to her recent ecstasy. 'I will be here if I choose. If not you must satisfy yourself with your wife.'

Before he could answer she turned and walked away, knowing he would let her go. Both his lust and hers had been satisfied for now. Sex was all there was between them. Not once had he ever kissed her, nor would she allow him to do so if he tried. Melanie intended to keep their relationship one of mutual orgiastic gratification.

Neither Melanie nor her lover was aware that Delie had watched every carnal minute.

Delie did not immediately waylay the gardener. She waited until he walked a little distance into the trees to relieve himself before moving from her place of concealment. His surprise rapidly turned to wariness. Delie gave him a smile of reassurance. 'I will tell no one what I saw if you will also satisfy me with that wonderful organ of yours.'

'You ask the impossible, miss. I am not some circus animal to perform on cue.'

'I am very good at coaxing a man to perform.'

The gardener's expression was as haughty as that of some royal personage. 'I must desire a woman before I can have sex with her.'

'Are you telling me that you do not find me desirable? If so I must remedy that situation.' Delie placed a hand on the crotch of the man's trousers as she spoke, her eyes gleaming in triumph when she felt movement beneath the fabric. Her hands moved deftly to free the twitching muscle. Before Simmonds had time to react, she sank to her knees to take the rising shaft into her mouth.

When it came to imparting oral pleasure, Delie was a woman without comparison. Before long the gardener was sporting an erection equal to the one that had pleasured Melanie. Delie became impatient to feel its hardness driving deep into her sex canal. While her mouth made certain the great organ maintained its hardness, her hands undid the waist button of her skirt and the tape of her petticoat. Underneath she was entirely naked.

She rose swiftly to her feet and clasped her hands behind the man's head to plant a lush kiss on his mouth. 'Fuck me,' she commanded. Being tall, her pelvis was on a level with his. By lifting to the balls of her feet she was able to position her opening over the head of the man's organ.

'Very well, lady,' Simmonds replied to her demand. He curved a hand around her right thigh to lift her leg high, thus opening her to receive the full strength of his upward thrust.

'Oh, yes!' cried Delie, delighted after so many days to have a man's hard cock banging into her. She began to wriggle her hips to magnify her pleasure and exhort the gardener to greater energy.

He was quick to respond. 'I know your type, lady. You are not like the mistress. I bet you enjoy this too.'

A finger was plunged into her anal opening, the action so rapid that Delie gave a cry of pained surprise which turned almost immediately into a long groan of pleasure. The finger which wriggled in her rear passage magnified the effect of the organ banging into her love hole.

'Oh yes,' she cried. 'Yes. Harder, harder. Oh God yes. I'm coming.' Her fingers clawed at his shoulders, her cries of ecstasy completely uninhibited, her pelvic thrusts as frantic as the man's. 'Oh yes,' she declared when the tumultuous joy eased to a steady throb, 'I did enjoy that. And you are still so strong inside me.'

'I am not yet finished, lady. You did a good job of arousing me.'

'I can take more,' said Delie, gyrating her pelvis around his shaft.

'My way,' declared Simmonds. He lifted her free from his shaft and turned her to face away from him. His hands pushed her body forward until it was at right angles to her legs and she was obliged to brace her hands against her thighs to prevent herself from toppling over. The gardener's fingers delved into her love canal to draw out the juice of her orgasm and smear it around her anus and even inside the narrow passage. 'You liked having my finger in your arse. How about my cock?'

He was forcing his way in even as he spoke, stretching that tight tube to a degree Delie found almost unbearable. The incredible stimulation was what she found hard to bear. An agonised sob of delight broke from her lips. She wished she had her dildo with her so that she could plunge it into her love canal to fill both places with hardness. The thought was sufficient to make her orgasm again, the tightness which gripped his shaft rapidly doing the same for the man.

With only a token knock to herald her arrival, Delie walked into her brother's room when he was in the last stages of dressing for dinner. 'Well?' she demanded.

'Well what?' responded Ric, simply to annoy.

'You went to see your grandfather's solicitor, didn't you?'

'I did, and I presume you are impatient to know if and when I am to become rich.'

'When, is what I want to hear. I trust there is no "if" about the matter.'

'You quite like Melanie, don't you?' Ric surprised her by asking.

'Well enough. I would like her a lot more if she had not cheated you out of your inheritance.'

'Do you think you could tolerate having her as a sister-in-law?'

'What? Are you mad?' Ric's expression told Delie he was perfectly serious. 'Good heavens. You have not fallen in love with the woman, have you?'

Ric gave a twisted grin. 'Considering the number of times you have declared me to be quite heartless, I find that a completely superfluous question.'

'Then why ask me such a strange one?'

'Not so strange if you will stop to think. Grandfather's will was legal and can not be contested without a great deal of trouble and expense. On the other hand, a wife's property immediately becomes that of her husband.'

Delie's eyes widened and her mouth gaped before she gave a small gloating laugh. 'I always knew you were a devious devil. There is just one small detail you appear to have overlooked.'

'Enlighten me.'

'How can you be certain our widow will want to marry you? Especially when she discovers your true identity.'

'I have no intention of allowing her to know my full name until after we are married. As to the other, she has already shown her eagerness to have me in her bed.'

'But not you alone.'

Ric turned to stare at his sister. 'What do you mean?'

Anyone less accustomed to him might have been intimidated by the ferocity of his expression. Delie simply gave a light shrug of her shoulders. 'While you were in town this afternoon Melanie entertained herself in a quite lusty manner with one of the gardeners.'

'How do you know that?'

'I saw them together. In fact I watched the entire thing fron start to finish. Our widow was on fire for her randy servant.'

'Were you spying on Melanie?' Ric's tone was as cold as his expression.

'Only by accident. You see I had thought to make the acquaintance of the gardener myself.'

'Did you?'

'Now that is something I do not intend to tell you.'

Ric discovered he did not like the thought of Melanie having sex with another man, especially as he entertained a strong suspicion as to which gardener Delie referred. He had wondered about the man they had seen in the orchard. A mental image of Melanie naked in the gardener's arms was so unpleasant that he dismissed it from his mind to anticipate instead the night ahead. Melanie appeared so very pleased to see him and gave every indication she was impatient for the hours to pass until they could be together.

When Ric did enter her room she rushed into his arms,

raising her face for his kiss. 'I have missed you today,' she whispered.

Ric held her close, delighting in the feel of her naked body beneath the fine fabric of her nightgown. His hands moved in sensual patterns on her back. 'Do I mean so much to you?'

'You know you do. Ever since we met I have had this feeling that I exist only for you.'

'Such an ardent declaration, dear Melanie. Do you flatter all your lovers with similar words?'

Melanie eased slightly away to gaze at him with earnest eyes. 'There has been no other lover I have cared for so much. With you it is all so special. Don't you feel it too?'

Despite a resolve to admit to no such thing, Ric was swept by such a surge of emotion he pulled her back against him to kiss her with the ardour of a lover. He felt her tremble in his arms and pressed her hips closer. His own desire was manifested in the aching rigidity of his manhood. The intensity of his need brought the proposal of marriage hovering to his lips. He was thinking not of material gain but of the delight of having this woman always in his bed.

'I believe I am obsessed by you,' he whispered, only to wonder why she should stiffen briefly in his arms. He did not know another man had uttered almost identical words to her a handful of hours earlier.

'Come to the bed,' she begged. 'I need you so very much.'

They lay as lovers, on their sides, facing each other while they kissed and caressed. Ric scattered kisses on every feature of her beautiful face, on her throat, then on the rosy aureoles of her breasts. The way she thrust her breasts upward to meet his lips filled him with the urge to give her the most intimate kiss of all.

He slid backward along the bed, trailing his lips over her satiny skin to her navel, then lower, across the firm plane of her abdomen and down to the triangle of red-gold curls. Melanie spread her legs wide for him and Ric's lips touched those other soft sweet ones. Her taste was akin to ambrosia. Ric teased her gently, taking delight in her soft moans of pleasure. He was in no hurry to bring her to a climax for he enjoyed adoring her in this manner.

Wanting to open her even more to his oral caress he slid his hands beneath her buttocks to raise them slightly from the bed. The sharp cry of pain Melanie gave brought his head up to stare at her in surprise. 'What is the matter?'

'You hurt me.'

'How could I? I barely touched you.'

Ric pressed his hand against her soft flesh and this time her gasp of pain was not to be ignored. In one swift action he rolled her on to her abdomen. Revelation of the cause of her pain fired him with rage. Melanie's buttocks were covered in bruises. Darker patches showed Ric where a man's fingers had dug into her tender flesh. Those fingers had not been his.

The rage in him flared out of control. Ric raised his hand to bring the palm down against the bruises with stinging force. Melanie's scream of pain afforded him considerable satisfaction. 'I could forgive you for being a deceitful slut if you had not tried to pretend I was someone special.'

Again his hand descended in a forceful slap. This time Melanie's scream of pain ended with a sob. 'You are special.'

'Then who did this to you? And this?' The questions were accompanied by a slap first on one bruised buttock then the other. To have her face-down and sobbing on the bed destroyed the last of his self-control. With savage actions he lifted her buttocks high enough to be able to drive his angry organ into her depths. An altered tone to her cries and the moistness which enveloped his penetration told him how much she had been aroused by the infliction of pain.

113

The knowledge angered him afresh and he used her savagely, calling her every foul name which came to mind. He felt the warm flow of her orgasm but still he was driven by his anger. 'Whores get treated like whores,' he said.

Pulling free, he flipped her on to her back, straddled her body and thrust his rod, salved with her juices, against her breastbone. Ric gripped her breasts to push them together to form a casing for his shaft. He renewed his thrusts, his fingers bruising her breasts as painfully as the gardener's had bruised her buttocks.

When his shaft pulsed with his climax and the warm ejaculate spurted on her throat, the anger in his expression was replaced with one of contempt. He climbed from the bed and stared down at her, soiled with the product of his lust. 'Now you really look like a whore.'

Convinced she was thoroughly belittled, he tied on his robe and walked to the door.

'Ric.' Her voice halted him. He turned to stare back at where she lay in the same position. With her gaze holding his, Melanie scooped a finger along the creamy trail then sucked it into her mouth.

Chapter Seven

There was a time, mused Melanie who was inspecting the bruising on her breasts and buttocks by the light of day, when sex had been simple good fun. She was not at all certain she relished being plunged into the rôle of a *femme fatale* over whom men were driven wild with obsessive lust.

True enough, she had enjoyed her gardener's mastery and even the savage manner in which Ric had taken her. By words and actions he had sought to degrade her, to prove his lust for her was equalled only by his contempt. In her initial shock at the abrupt change from seductive adoration to rough handling, Melanie had almost hated him for the insulting manner in which he sought his climax. But Melanie had the last laugh, so to speak. Ric's expression had been absolutely livid when he stormed from her room.

Melanie rang for her maid to prepare a bath for her then sent the girl away to evade curiosity over the bruises and subsequent speculation in the servant's quarters. After adding several drops of lavender oil she sank neck deep in the warm water to relax. Before she dressed to go downstairs, before she faced Ric, she needed to compose her thoughts and if possible her emotions. Of one thing she was becoming increasingly certain: Simmonds would have to go.

The more thought she gave to the matter, the more Melanie became convinced Ric's rage had been occasioned by jealousy. To Melanie this suggested his interest in her went deeper than the purely sexual.

Those conclusions reached and her good spirits restored, Melanie dressed in a becoming day dress with a simple frilled skirt and front-buttoned tunic bodice. The restrained style of the outfit was intended to steer Ric's thoughts away from her sexuality to other aspects of her nature he might find endearing.

Ric, however, had taken the gelding and ridden to town. Of which fact Delie enlightened her when Melanie found the other girl in the upstairs sitting room idly turning the pages of a magazine.

'Do you have any plans for today, Melanie?'

'My business manager will be arriving shortly. I meet with both him and the estate manager every Friday morning. Mr Brown always stays on for lunch.'

'Oh?' Delie perked up with interest. 'Is Mr Brown what one might call eligible?'

'Hardly.' Melanie laughed. 'He is middle-aged, married, and not by any stretch of the imagination to be considered a Prince Charming. Since you ask such a question I realise I am not being a good hostess. I must arrange a dinner party for you both.'

A discreet knock, sounding on the door before Melanie finished speaking, heralded the arrival of the butler. He bore in his hand a small silver letter tray. 'Excuse me, madam. This letter has just arrived for Miss Liddell.'

The man addressed himself to Melanie. He could never look at the other woman without recalling what had happened in this very room, over the sofa on which she now reclined. The things Mary told him about what she did with her mistress always gave him an incredible hard-on. Which was, of course, Mary's intention since she was the one who then received all the pleasure. Be

116

that as it may, Carstairs was becoming obsessed with the idea of concealing himself in a position from which he could watch the two women.

When Delie commanded he carry the letter across to her he did so with the greatest reluctance and fervent wish his manhood could be schooled into neutrality as easily as his facial expression.

'It is an invitation from the Grimshaws,' Delie declared on opening the letter. 'For dinner this evening. They will send their carriage for me. How nice of them.' She looked up at Melanie whose face was as impassive as the recently departed butler's had been. 'You do not mind do you? The invitation does not appear to include you.'

'I would not accept if it did. You do whatever you wish, Delie. I have told you what I know of the Grimshaws.'

An almost feline smile curved Delie's mouth. 'Do not worry, Melanie. I am perfectly capable of taking care of myself in any situation.'

Poor Mr Bartlett was shocked to the tips of his toes. He pulled a handkerchief from his coat pocket and used it to mop the sweat from his brow while he tried several times to clear his throat. Jeremiah's seething grandson paced back and forth in the small office with all the mannerisms of a caged tiger. Mr Bartlett found him almost as menacing. In a vain hope he attempted to restore their meeting to a semblance of civility. 'Please sit down so that we may discuss this matter in a rational manner.'

'There is nothing to discuss.' Ric paused in his pacing to glower at the solicitor. 'I have told you what I require you to do. You have my grandfather's original will. How difficult will it be to make that stand up in court?'

The older man's expression was pained, his face florid with embarrassment. 'I do not think you will be able to prove a case of coercion.'

'Sexual coercion.' Ric corrected the solicitor. 'Whatever opinion you hold of the young widow I know her for what she is. I am now in absolutely no doubt as to how she persuaded my grandfather to change his will.'

'You will need proof.' Mr Bartlett was beginning to wish himself anywhere but in his office with this angry young man.

'I will obtain all the proof that is necessary.'

'May I ask how?'

Ric sneered. 'There are ways of dealing with such a woman. Would witnesses and a signed confession be sufficient?'

'I suppose so.' The reply was grudging. Mr Bartlett felt very unhappy about the entire situation. More especially because he had believed, less than 24 hours earlier, that the matter of Jeremiah's will was going to be resolved in a manner satisfactory to all concerned. 'You were of a different mind yesterday,' he reminded Ric now.

'This is today. Yesterday she still had me fooled.'

Mr Bartlett sighed. Such a very angry young man. He could not even begin to imagine what Melanie might have done to evoke such ire. 'I take it you intend to move back to your hotel.'

'I most certainly do not. If anyone moves out of Arlecdon it will be the conniving little widow.'

All this irascibility and flinging about of insults was beginning to wear thin with the good solicitor. 'Have you revealed your identity to Mrs Wilberforce?'

'No. Nor will I do so until it suits my purpose.'

'Then if I were you, young man, I would take a good look at myself before I branded another person deceitful.'

The pertinent criticism hit Ric with the force of a blow. He drew himself even taller, a cold expressionless mask settling over his face. Only his eyes burnt with emotion and a nerve pulsed at the side of his neck.

Mr Bartlett rose stiffly to his feet in a gesture of dismissal. 'I am sorry, Ric, but given the circumstances I am unwilling to proceed as you request. If you want to drag this matter through the courts then you must engage another lawyer.'

Ric did not argue. Still holding himself with the rigidity of a tin soldier he bade the solicitor a curt good morning.

When he strode from Mr Bartlett's office Ric had every intention of seeking the services of another man of law. The suggestion that his own behaviour was less than circumspect cut into his pride. Cynical he might be, low-handed he was not. By the time he walked two street blocks he was in so black a humour he was wishing he had wrung Melanie's neck instead of giving her a beating. Corporal punishment had not produced the intended result. He was remembering, with a resurgence of anger, how her hot wet sheath had welcomed his invading shaft when a small hand caught at his arm.

Ric spun around with such a ferocity of expression that the unknown woman dropped her hand from his arm and took a fearful step backward. After a muttered, 'I beg your pardon, sir,' she would have hurried away if Ric had not caught her by the hand.

'Wait,' he said. 'How much?'

'Two shillings, sir.'

'Are you clean?'

'As clean as yourself, sir. I don't carry the pox.'

'Very well then.'

The woman led the way down a side street to a shabby tenement house. In contrast to the less than salubrious nature of the neighbourhood, the woman's flat came as a pleasant surprise. The old and worn furniture had been made to look as presentable as possible and the sheets on the bed were redolent with rosemary.

'You appear surprised,' she said.

'I assumed you came from a brothel.'

'Not I. I am particular about the men I take. My body is for sale only because I have no other means of supporting myself.'

'Why not? Your speech is that of a woman with education.'

The woman, who had called herself Sarah, gave a slight lift of her shoulders. 'My story is no different from that of many a woman raised to a life of leisure only to suddenly find herself in impoverished circumstances.'

While she spoke she had undressed, the task completed quickly with clothing chosen for that purpose. Ric saw that her figure was full and shapely with a tendency to plumpness. When she moved close to him he could smell the scented cleanliness of her body.

Eager to lie with her, Ric shed his coat and shirt, her fingers splaying across his chest in an erotic caress while he fumbled with his trouser fastening.

'Hadn't you better take off your shoes?' Her voice was husky and slightly amused.

Ric directed a startled glance down at his leather-shod feet. He had been so absorbed in the need to exorcise his demons he had been impatient for the sexual act.

'I can see you need help.' Sarah guided him to sit on the bed so that she could remove his shoes. After Ric had eased his trousers and underpants past his hips she drew them the remainder of the way down his legs. Her gaze feasted on his rearing manhood. 'Mm. I like the look of you.'

Such blatant appreciation was a salve to Ric's battered pride. He stretched back on the bed with his hands pillowed beneath his head. 'Make me forget my troubles for an hour or two.'

The woman rose to lean over him with one knee resting on the bed. 'For two shillings all I will do is lie on my back and allow you the use of my body for a quick release. To do as you ask will require all my skill. I am very good.'

'I will pay you well, Sarah.'

'I will pleasure you well, sir.'

From the manner in which she had appraised his manhood, Ric expected Sarah to give immediate attention to that part of his anatomy. Instead she knelt beside him on the bed and ran her fingers lightly over his torso, feathering her touch in a way he found totally sensual. 'You are far too tense to enjoy true pleasure,' she told him. 'Move down the bed a little.'

When Ric had eased his body far enough down the bed for her to be satisfied, Sarah shifted to kneel behind his head. Fingers buried in his hair began to massage his scalp until he closed his eyes. All his angry thoughts were melting out through her fingertips. 'You will put me to sleep,' he murmured.

'You will be relaxed but you will most definitely not be asleep.' Her hands shifted to massage the strain from his shoulders then moved down over his chest with circular stroking actions.

On opening his eyes, Ric discovered Sarah's breasts were hanging above his face, their dark tips too tempting to resist. His tongue stretched up to flick against the tantalising peaks and render Sarah's massage of his masculine breasts all the more erotic.

'Better.' She approved his response. 'But you are still too tense.' Stepping from the bed she walked down to the end where she began to massage Ric's legs. Once again she used the lightest of touches which feathered all the way up his legs until he was aching for her to brush them over his aching sex parts. Her smile told him she knew the precise effect her hands were having and he begged her to caress his balls and shaft. Instead she ordered him to roll on to his front, her massage then going all the way up the backs of his legs to his buttocks.

Ric groaned. 'I thought your intention was to make me relax. You have done quite the opposite.'

'Have I indeed? Perhaps I should see.' Sarah's hands urged him to roll back. Ric's throbbing organ rose in a rigid projection from his groin. 'Mmm. I think more massage is needed.'

Her fingers ran lightly down the length of his engorged muscle and feathered over the heavy sac before working back up to the helmeted head. One forefinger drew the lightest of circles over the tiny opening.

For a second time Ric groaned. If Sarah could do that with her hands he wondered what she could do with her mouth. He was soon to find out.

Her tongue took the place of her finger to give little flicks at the sensitised hole then all around the helmet. The movements were lighter and even more tantalising than those made by her fingers. When that portion of his manhood had been magnificently pleasured she ran her tongue in several long licking movements up and down the column before teasing around his sac. She took his balls in her mouth. Considerate of their tender sensitivity she sucked and rolled them with her tongue to impart unbelievable pleasure without any hint of pain. Finally she took the entire organ into the warm cavity of her mouth, her tongue and lips continuing their caress as she worked up and down the shaft.

Shudders of ecstasy racked Ric's body. The woman had a mouth like an angel. Very soon he was going to explode into that mouth if she did not stop. He did not want to climax in that manner, nor did he want the wonderful sensations to stop.

Sarah, however, was as expert as she declared herself to be. Just when Ric thought he could no longer hold back, she swung a leg over his hips. Back to him, hands braced on his thighs she lowered herself down to encompass him completely in the silken glove of her sex. Ric's orgasm exploded, its intensity aided by Sarah bouncing herself up and down. Nor did she stop, her actions keeping him hard until she, too, reached the pinnacle of pleasure.

Ric stretched his arms up to cup her breasts with his hands. 'You really are very good. So good you can name your price.'

Sarah lifted herself free and sat back on her heels to

face him. 'A crown, sir, is all I ask. The pleasure was very much mine.'

Luncheon seemed to go on for ever. Melanie's business manager was never in a hurry to leave the luxury of Arlecdon or rush his enjoyment of the excellent food and fine wine. All this was supplemented by his appreciation of the company of the beautiful young widow. Add to that a second attractive woman and Mr Brown became extremely reluctant to take his leave. Eventually his departure could be delayed no longer. A sigh of relief passed Melanie's lips when the front door closed behind the man.

'I did not think he was ever going to go.'

'The man appears to be quite infatuated with you.' Delie was highly amused by Mr Brown's unctuous flattery of both Melanie and herself. All delivered in a manner which suggested the rotund little man with the heavy jowls and florid complexion thought himself to be physically irresistible.

A quick smile acknowledged Delie's amusement. 'Mr Brown always carries on his little flirtations. He means nothing by it and I take no offence. He has a wife and several children and is extremely good in his handling of all my business affairs. If not for his help and clear explanations I would still be without a clue as to how things should be managed. However, I do find his company trying at meal times.'

'You are the most unlikely business woman, Melanie. No offence,' Delie hastened to assure. 'You are so petite and feminine.'

'What is your image of a woman of business?'

'You know, tall, strident voiced.'

Laughter gurgled from Melanie. 'I have known one or two women who could fit your description. To be honest I was never much interested in financial matters until recently. After my husband died I wanted nothing to do

123

with his affairs. Now I feel I owe it to him to take good care of the business empire he worked so hard to create.'

'This is no concern of mine, I know, but I have heard your husband had a grandson who thinks he should have inherited.'

'Where did you hear such a thing?' Both Melanie's glance and her question were sharp.

Delie realised she had made a mistake and attempted to pass it off with a shrug of her shoulders. 'Servants always gossip.'

'I was not aware any of the servants knew of the matter.'

'So it is true?'

This time it was Melanie who gave the shrug. 'Mr Bartlett did receive a letter from some person who claimed to be a grandson. I have heard nothing more so must assume the man was an imposter as we thought.'

'What would you do if you found out he did exist?'

Melanie looked at her in surprise. 'Why are you so interested?'

'I am merely being inquisitive. Take no notice of my rudeness.'

'I do not think you rude. Since you ask I will tell you that this Alaric Wilberforce, if he is real, will get nothing. He did not care for his grandfather when Jeremiah was alive so I do not believe he has a right to anything now.'

Which adamant declaration told Delie precisely what she wished to know. Melanie had no idea Ric was the grandson. It also appeared Ric's plan of marriage was the only way either of them were going to get their hands on any of the old man's money. Having made the necessary discoveries Delie fluttered her hand over a small yawn. 'I must have my afternoon rest or I will be falling asleep at the Grimshaws' tonight.'

Melanie gave a hard little smile. 'I doubt you will be given the chance.

*   *   *

124

After Delie had retired to her room Melanie quietly left the house to meet her gardener as arranged. He was not at the pavilion when she arrived and, forced to wait several minutes, she became increasingly nervous. She was not so much concerned by what he might be angered enough to do to her but whether or not he would accept his dismissal. Things might become awkward if he refused to leave Arlecdon. Not that Melanie had any intention of changing her mind. Simmonds had become a complication in her life.

'So you came.' The voice so close behind her gave Melanie a start. She spun around, hand pressed to her chest. For a man of such solid build he could move very quietly.

'You startled me.' Melanie stated the obvious, his sudden appearance having exacerbated her nervousness. Already he was unbuttoning his shirt. 'No, wait. I did not come for that'.

'I came for this.' He rubbed his hand over his bulging groin. 'Will I need to use force, mistress?'

Melanie swallowed, her gaze fastened on the suggestive action of his hand. An undeniable moistness was beginning to pool between her thighs. Why not, she thought. After Simmonds was physically satisfied he might be more amenable.

'My body is already too bruised to enjoy force.' She hurriedly stripped off her lower garments then turned her back to him. 'See what you did to me yesterday.'

'You brought that upon yourself. My need for you was too great.'

At the calm statement of fact Melanie looked back at him over her shoulder. 'I trust you are more in control today.'

'Totally in control.' He stepped close behind her to lightly rest his hands on her naked buttocks. 'I am sorry that I marked your lovely body. Today I will make it up to you.'

He knelt where he was behind Melanie, his hands

sliding forward around her hips to come to rest on her inner thighs with the fingers barely touching the outer swell of her sex. Warm lips pressed a kiss on her tender buttocks, the action so wonderfully erotic it was more than a balm to her bruised flesh. The kisses continued to trail over Melanie's buttocks, arousing her so greatly she wished he would move his fingers closer together.

On being asked to spread her legs, Melanie did so eagerly, only it was his tongue, not his fingers which eased her aching anticipation. The pleasurable relief of having her moist folds caressed changed rapidly to panting urgency as the deft tongue set her nerve endings reacting with hammering little pin-pricks.

As soon as Melanie began to gasp, the gardener slid from beneath her, stood and turned her around. 'Not yet, mistress. I want you naked.'

'I want you now,' Melanie half-begged, half-commanded. Not only had he left her hovering on the brink of an orgasm, she was reluctant to remove her bodice.

Simmonds shook his head, totally implacable. 'Take off the rest, or I will do so for you.'

At the unspoken suggestion he might be less than gentle if compelled to complete her disrobing, Melanie hastened to remove her bodice and the short chemise to which her knickerbockers had been buttoned. Simmonds' gaze, as she knew it would, went immediately to the purple marks on her breasts.

'I did not give you those bruises.'

'You caused them. It was because of the ones you inflicted that I suffered these.'

'Was your gentleman lover angered to discover he is not the only one to receive your favours?' His eyes narrowed at her telltale flush. 'Take care, mistress. You too easily arouse the passions of men.'

'I see that your passion is well aroused.'

The gardener curved his hand around his rampant member. 'My organ is hard and strong. I want you to sit over him.' He reached out to grasp Melanie under the armpits and lift her from her feet. Realising his intention, Melanie placed her hands on his shoulders to take some of her weight until her vulva was positioned against the head of his organ. He then allowed her to slide down until she was seated against his pelvis, morticed to the tenon of his shaft.

Melanie curled her legs around his thick waist and would have slid her arms around his shoulders if his hands had not urged her to lean back until her body was angled to his the length of her outstretched arms. His strong hands against the small of her back and her grasp of his shoulders kept her supported. There was nothing to support her head which lolled back the first time Simmonds flexed his knees to ease out then deeply thrust his organ.

The intensity of the sensations imparted by the action permeated every cell of Melanie's body. Only a man with Simmonds' great strength could support a woman in such a position yet be able to drive himself into her with such wonderful force. Carnally helpless against his lust, Melanie revelled in the build-up of her internal tension, savoured the way the tiny pin-pricks of arousal became as knives of desire then the flaming swords of a perfect climax. He pulled her forward so that she could rest her head on his shoulders while her convulsions gripped his organ and his hands gripped her waist to pull her down against his own urgency.

Spent, clinging limply to his body, Melanie wondered if she was doing the right thing in sending this man away. She was uncertain of Ric, and her gardener's sexual prowess might be difficult to replace. By the time they had dressed her resolve had been restrengthened. There had been other great lovers in her past. Ric was the one she wanted now but if she did lose him she held no doubt she could find other great lovers for the future.

'Now that I have had what I came for, what was it that you wanted, mistress?'

Melanie faced him squarely, unflinching. 'You warned

me before I should take care where I dispense my sexual favours. That is a conclusion I had already reached. You are an excellent gardener and your services, in all ways, have been appreciated.' She paused, noting the dull flush of colour rise from his neck and the sullen light of understanding come into his eyes. 'None of your services are required any longer at Arlecdon.'

'And if I will not go willingly, without fuss?'

'I think you will.' Melanie took a piece of paper from her pocket and held it out to him. 'I am not so callous I would evict you and your wife from your home without prospects for your future.'

Giving her a stare of curiosity, the gardener took the paper. On unfolding it the colour in his face deepened and his eyes blazed with anger. 'Do you think to buy me off? I am not such a man.' He made as if to tear the paper in half.

'No! Stop.' Melanie caught his wrist in her hand. 'I do not mean it as an insult. Forget your stupid pride for a minute and think. What could you do with that amount of money?'

The man stared down at the bank draft. With two thousand pounds he would be able to buy twenty or thirty acres to start his own small farm. He could build a nice cottage for Bess, himself and the children for whom they continued to hope. He recalled the way it had been between them the previous night. Surely a child had been conceived from so much passion. His libido having been so thoroughly aroused by both his mistress and the other lady, he had done things to, and with, his gentle wife he would never before have dreamt of doing. Not only had she both surprised and pleased him with her response, she had confessed she had always forced herself to lie quietly on her back because she believed that was what was expected of a wife.

When her gardener raised his eyes to look back at Melanie she gave an inward sigh of relief.

'You have been generous, mistress. When do you want me to leave?'

'The sooner the better, don't you think?'

Simmonds inclined his head. 'I willl tell my wife to start packing immediately.

The heavy folds in which the drapes hung when drawn back from the window provided perfect concealment. Carstairs had slipped behind them the moment they heard Delie's footsteps in the passageway. Mary, who was busy turning down the bed when Delie entered the room, left that task to help her mistress undress. 'Do you want me to stay with you this afternoon, miss?'

'For a little while. I am going out this evening and will need to have some sleep. I always do sleep better if my body is pleasured first.'

'Shall I undress, miss?'

'If you wish. I want you to pleasure me with your mouth but I may get the urge to do the same for you.'

Because she very much hoped that Delie would, Mary not only undressed completely, she positioned herself on the bed with her buttocks pointed towards Delie's face. Her secret knowledge of Carstair's watching everything from behind the curtain excited her to such a degree that her vulva was already pulsing. For the butler's explicit benefit she parted Delie's folds with her fingers and held them wide to expose the red inner lips of her sex and the small protuberance above.

Mary's tongue worked more assiduously than ever before. It was plunged deeply into Delie's receptive opening then drawn out to waggle along the crease. Delie's moans and the way she lifted her quim to Mary's mouth proved the effectiveness of the maid's tongue. Several repeats of the action brought Mary her reward when Delie pulled the girl's moist quim to her own mouth.

Behind the curtain, Carstairs fumbled to undo his trousers to release his straining organ to the comfort of his hands. To have Mary describe what she did with the lady had been highly arousing. To actually watch them licking and sucking each other with undeniable enjoyment had made him so hard he thought the skin of his penis would split from the strain. Eyes agog, he watched the women twisting and writhing on the bed. There was no doubt each was bringing the other to a climax. The butler began to work his hand up and down his throbbing organ, his breathing becoming more laboured, louder.

Delie heard the panting immediately and lifted her mouth away from its feast of the maid. 'What was that?' Moving quickly and quietly she crossed the room to pull back the curtain at the precise moment Carstairs gave a great groan and spurted his seed into the air.

With her hand still holding back the curtain and taking no heed of the drops which had landed on her breasts, Delie murmured, 'Well, well. So you enjoy a little voyeurism do you, Carstairs?' Looking back at Mary she saw her crouched on the bed in an attitude of fear. 'You knew he was here, didn't you? Stop.' She turned her head quickly to order the butler who was attempting to stuff his shaft back into his trousers. 'You have had your little bit of voyeuristic fun, now I want mine. Get undressed.'

Without waiting to see if he obeyed the command, Delie walked back to the bed. There she took the dildo from her box and began to oil it in readiness. Both servants watched without speaking. Mary was eagerly waiting to see what Delie intended to do with that wonderful instrument. The butler, who had never before seen anything of the like, was wondering the same.

Delie spoke to Carstairs. 'I want to watch you banging hard into Mary. Unfortunately you wasted your strength. I can not allow poor Mary to suffer while she waits.'

Understanding Delie's intention, Mary lay back on the

130

bed and spread her legs in readiness, eager for Delie to pleasure her with the wooden phallus.

Nor did it take long for Carstairs' spent manhood to begin jerking upright. He stepped nearer the bed so that he could see how the wood glistened with the maid's juices. Another step brought him right to the edge of the bed. Mary propped herself on one elbow.

'Go on,' Delie urged, though neither needed any encouragement for the butler to thrust his hardening shaft into Mary's willing mouth. Delie appreciated the way her maid's pink lips slid up and down the man's darker muscle. 'You do that so well Mary that I need to be satisfied too.'

She lifted her buttocks and spread her knees to present her moist opening to Carstairs. He wasted no time in pushing two fingers precisely where Delie wanted them to be. With the three thus connected, the stimulative attention to each person's sex organs exhorted the recipient to impart a greater degree of the same.

Though she was enjoying herself immensely in the sexual triangle, Delie commanded they change. Now that Carstairs was as hard as he had been before, she wanted Mary on all fours on the floor so that the butler could take her from behind.

Mary positioned herself then gazed imploringly at Delie. 'Can I have the love beads?'

For answer Delie stroked the slippery phallus against Mary's anus. The girl quivered. 'Mary likes to be pleasured in her rear passage,' she told the butler. 'Do not disappoint her.'

Carstairs had always wanted to try anal sex. He pressed urgently against the crinkled opening. 'Go carefully,' warned Delie. 'Use this oil first.' The man dipped his finger in the oil then worked the digit into the narrow opening until it was stretched and ready. His organ then entered the gasping maid's virginal passage with ease.

'Oooh,' cried Mary.

'Aaah,' gasped the butler.

'You need these too,' said Delie, sliding underneath the maid to insert the twin love balls into the maid's vagina.

Carstairs felt their stimulation as intensely as Mary. Before long both man and woman were screaming and shouting through unbelievable orgasms.

'Now it is my turn to be pleasured.' Delie handed Carstairs the phallus and Mary the anal beads. 'Make certain my climax is as satisfactory as was yours.'

The Grimshaw's carriage arrived for Delie just before six o'clock. An hour later, an anxious Melanie sat down to dinner with Ric. She had seen him only briefly on his return from town when his manner had been cool and withdrawn. Now she had no idea what to say to him. Idle conversation would be wasted on someone so brooding and uncommunicative. For perhaps the hundredth time since he had arrived at Arlecdon, Melanie wished she knew what went on in Ric's mind. There was nothing in his manner to indicate whether he would or would not come to her room this night. Nor, in light of what had occurred the previous night, did she feel confident enough to ask.

They were waiting for the soup plates to be cleared away and the main course to be served when Carstairs approached Melanie. 'Excuse me, madam. There is a man just arrived who wishes to speak with you.'

'At this hour?' Melanie was rightfully astonished. 'What is his business?'

'He says he is an old friend from Cape Town, madam.'

'Cape Town?' Melanie repeated. 'But I do not know any ...' Her voice trailed off and the colour drained from her face. She cast a quick glance at Ric who was watching with a hard interest. 'You had best show the man in, Carstairs.'

On the departure of the butler, Melanie took up her glass to sip at the wine. Anything to keep from looking at Ric while her frantic thoughts dealt with this disturbing turn of events. She did not raise her head until Carstairs reopened the door.

Looking every bit as tall, golden and gorgeous as she remembered him, Pieter van Heuren approached across the room with outstretched arms. 'Melanie, my love. Are you suitably surprised?

Chapter Eight

*B*efore Melanie could say whether she was, or was not, surprised Pieter had reached her chair and bent down to kiss her firmly on the mouth. 'I have been so looking forward to being able to taste your lovely lips again. A lifetime seems to have passed since I last kissed you.' The warmth of his tone and the gleam in his eyes, combined with the possessive manner in which he held her hand, suggested he was referring to more than kisses.

With not inconsiderable effort Melanie regained her scattered composure. 'You have taken me totally by surprise Pieter. What are you doing here, and at this hour? Have you dined yet?' she added as an afterthought.

'I have not dined,' Pieter confessed. 'Though it was not to beg a meal my arrival was so timed.'

'You will join us just the same. Set another place, Kate.' Melanie turned aside to give the order to the maid and her gaze fell on Ric who, she realised, had half risen when Pieter entered the room only to sit back down again. 'Oh, Ric, forgive me. I am forgetting my manners in my confusion. Richard Liddell, Pieter van Heuren. Ric and his sister Delie are my guests,' she told Pieter, then thinking perhaps Ric deserved some explanation turned back to him. 'Pieter and I met in Cape Town.'

The men exchanged formal nods and when both were seated Ric questioned Melanie. 'You have been back to Cape Town since your husband died, I presume?'

Colour flooded Melanie's cheeks, Ric's cool supposition being even more startling than Pieter's arrival. She wished she had never told Ric when and where Jeremiah had died.

Pieter came to her rescue when she began to stammer a reply. 'If Melanie had come back to Cape Town she would not be sitting here now. I had no intention of letting her go once she returned. However I became impatient with waiting so I have come here instead.'

Which declaration, while saving Melanie the necessity of answering Ric, confused her totally. As far as she was aware there had never been any question of her returning to Cape Town, nor had she ever expected to see Pieter van Heuren again. In the distressing days while she awaited a return passage to Australia she had regretted ever meeting him in the first place. Those were facts she had made very plain to Pieter when, after reading in the paper of Jeremiah's death, he had visited her at her Cape Town hotel.

'You have not explained why you are here,' she reminded him now.

'I thought I did. I have come to see you, my dear Melanie. The actual timing of my arrival was beyond my control. We were delayed in docking then there were a few minor problems with immigration officials which had to be sorted out before anyone was allowed to disembark. I hired the first cab I could find to bring me straight here.'

'Would it not have been more seemly to wait until morning?' Ric was at his most sardonic. However, Pieter's smile assured Melanie he had not taken offence.

'Perhaps it would. Only I was far too impatient to see Melanie again. The instant I set foot on Australian soil I knew I could delay no longer the delight of seeing her in the flesh.'

Melanie gave a small, somewhat nervous laugh. 'So much flattery Pieter. I will soon be believing you really did make the journey just to see me when I did not think you would even remember me.'

'Not remember you? Darling Melanie, as if I could ever forget.' His voice deepened to husky suggestiveness. 'You left me a memento of your visit.'

The frown of incomprehension which started to draw Melanie's brows together vanished when she remembered the torn silk drawers. Bright colour flared in her cheeks only to drain rapidly away. She wished Pieter, whose bright blue eyes held lascivious amusement, had not mentioned the matter in Ric's presence. That man's eyes had grown darker, his entire mien more uncompromising than ever.

Fortunately for Melanie's composure, Pieter changed the subject to an appreciation of what he had seen of Arlecdon and his impressions of the town and harbour. Somehow the remainder of the dinner passed amiably enough with the two men treating each other with civility if not friendship. By the end of the meal Pieter had cunningly engineered an invitation from Melanie to avail himself of the hospitality of Arlecdon.

'I did not expect you to provide me with a place to stay, Melanie.' Pieter dissembled with the greatest of charm. 'I feel certain there are any number of comfortable hotels in which I can secure a room.'

'I insist you stay with us. Your presence will even our number for we are imbalanced at the moment. You will like Delie. It is such a pity she is not able to meet you tonight.'

'I will be charmed to meet her, of course, but you are the one who commands all my attention.'

Melanie was hoping Delie might distract Pieter's attention away from herself. She was not even certain why she had insisted he stay at Arlecdon. After having taken the necessary action to ensure Simmonds was no longer a threat to her relationship with Ric, she perceived a greater one in Pieter. Not the least part being her increasingly vivid recollections of his sexual prowess.

A cynical smile curled about Ric's lips. He knew Delie well enough to be able to predict her reaction to the blond South African. 'My dear sister will most certainly be charmed to make your acquaintance. How fortunate you are, with your arrival being completely unexpected, that Melanie does not have a house full of guests.'

If Melanie did not consider it strange for Pieter to have brought with him a case holding sufficient to see him through the night, Ric most certainly did. There was something about the unexpected appearance of the man which had Ric's mind working rapidly. He felt an antipathy towards van Heuren which had nothing to do with the overt attentions the man was paying Melanie. Melanie herself had been discomposed by the unexpected arrival. Even though she was now at ease with him, Ric felt certain Melanie would have been far happier if Pieter van Heuren had not appeared at Arlecdon, despite the invitation for him to remain as her guest.

All things considered, Ric decided to wait another day before proceeding with any of his own plans. Thanks to Sarah's skill he had returned to Arlecdon in a far better frame of mind than when he had left it in the morning. It was not only Sarah's sexual expertise which had helped, but also her ability to listen. To his intense surprise Ric had found himself telling her why he had been in such an ill-humour. Sarah had made them tea and listened while he talked, now and then asking a question or making a remark which helped him to put his feelings in perspective. Afterwards he had sex with her again, using all his skill to ensure Sarah was the one receiving the greater pleasure. Her pleasure naturally enhanced his own.

When he left her tiny flat Sarah was three guineas richer and Ric was again considering the advantages of marriage to Melanie.

Regaining his inheritance was, he told himself, the primary benefit. Her delectable body was another. He wondered if Melanie would be a faithful wife and was surprised to discover how much that mattered. Ric was willing to bet his inheritance that Pieter van Heuren had been an infidelity when she was married to Jeremiah. What bothered him now was whether Melanie had invited her former lover to stay for precisely the same reason he had been invited. Ric had already made the decision not to have any sexual contact with Melanie in order to discover if any of his feelings for her, and hers towards himself, were of a nobler kind than lust. Now he was not at all certain if he should stay away from her that night. Might it be a case of which one of them got to her room first? Which thought was sufficient for Ric to tell himself he was not going to demean himself by becoming involved in some kind of sexual one-upmanship with Pieter van Heuren.

Melanie spent the night alone. The choice, in the end, had been her own. Or so she believed. She had no idea whether Ric or Pieter had tried the handle of her locked door.

Emily Grimshaw greeted Delie with effusive warmth. 'I am so pleased you accepted our invitation. I promise you an extremely enjoyable evening.'

'I am very pleased to be invited.' Delie, who was attempting to match her hostess' manner was distracted by the loose flowing silk robe Emily was wearing. When she moved, the material brushed against her body in a manner which indicated she wore nothing underneath. Delie's own gown, chosen to display the fullness of her breasts and the sensual curve of her hips, was rather elaborate.

'Yes,' agreed Emily, apparently reading Delie's mind. 'You are a little overdressed. Come with me and I will fit you out with something more suitable before dinner.'

Emily led Delie to a bedroom on the first floor where she opened a wardrobe and brought out a garment similar to the one she was wearing. While Emily's was in shimmering shades of turquoise the one she chose for Delie was a vivid red. Emily held it up in front of Delie. 'This colour will suit you perfectly. I will help you to change.'

For reasons Delie was unable to define she had been becoming more and more sexually excited since stepping foot inside this house. The sexual aura emanating from Emily combined with Melanie's warnings to raise her anticipation of exotic pleasures. Now, while Emily assisted her to undress, Delie carefully judged the other woman's reaction to her nudity. Her only interest seemed to be in Delie's thick black mat of pubic hair which she studied with a thoughtful expression. The appraisal evoked the familiar tingling awareness in Delie's sex. However Emily neither said anything nor attempted to touch Delie, not even when she helped her to slide the robe over her head. Her only question was to ask Delie how long her hair was.

'Almost to my waist.'

'Then you must wear it down.'

The confining pins were removed from Delie's hair. Emily took up a hair brush to sweep the black tresses in a shining swathe over Delie's left shoulder. She stood back to admire the effect. 'Very good. Now we will go down to meet the others before we go in to dinner.'

The others were five men and two women, one of whom was definitely Asian. The dark hair and olive complexion of the other girl suggested she was of Middle Eastern or Mediterranean extraction. Jonathon, Emily's husband, Delie had already met. Emily introduced the two women first. 'This is Bianca and Mai Lee. Jonathon you know. Edgar and Crispin are twins so they count as one. This is Harry and last but by no means least, Rufus. Everyone, I would like you to meet Delie, our special guest.'

They all exchanged greetings, with each one of the group overtly studying Delie. She was finding it extremely difficult not to stare at Rufus. A tall muscular islander who wore a sailor's cut-off trouser and tight shirt was the last person she would have expected to meet at a dinner party. Mai Lee and Bianca wore loose robes while the other men were attired in formal dinner suits. The collective effect was somewhat bizare and immensely intriguing.

At dinner, Delie found herself seated between the twins with Rufus and Mai Lee opposite. Though she did not know what might occur she was surprised when the dinner progressed exactly in the manner of any semi-formal dinner party. The polite small talk and observance of social manners, when most of them were dressed in such informal attire, rendered the entire situation more erotic than if there had been suggestive conversation.

After the meal the women arose according to custom to retire to the drawing-room and leave the men to enjoy their port. Only this drawing-room was unlike any Delie had seen before. Mirrors set between the tall windows were matched by ones exactly opposite. More mirrors on the ceiling reflected back the light of the large chandelier to illumine with spotlight clarity a low padded dais in the centre of the room. The only other furniture consisted of various types of chairs, two sofas and numerous cushions of all shapes and sizes which were scattered on the floor. There was also one small sideboard.

'Now,' said Emily, 'we must prepare you.'

'Prepare me for what?' Delie's question held more eager anticipation than trepidation. All three women were smiling at her in a way which suggested they were all going to enjoy what was about to take place.

'You will have realised we are a unique company. One of which you will enjoy being a part. If I had for even a moment doubted you are a woman to embrace all manner of sensual pleasures you would not have been invited. However, if you wish to be invited again, you must pass our tests.'

'What do I have to do?'

'Everything that is asked of you. Now take of your robe, please, and lie on your back on the dais.'

Delie did as she was asked, the lush velvet cover on the dais pleasantly sensual against her skin. Bianca and Mai Lee positioned themselves one on either side of the dais while Emily stood at the foot. Emily leant over to finger Delie's pubic thatch.

'First you must be shaved. You will find it is so much nicer. Show Delie how appealing she will look.'

The latter being addressed to Mai Lee and Bianca, the two women lifted their robes over their heads and stood with their legs slightly parted. From her position on the dais Delie obtained an unrestricted view of their naked genitals. Their erotic appeal had her moistening her lips with her tongue. How she would like to lick them both. The two women were smiling down at her with what Delie took to be encouragement. She simultaneously raised both hands to stroke her fingers along the tempting creases. Emily, smiling her approval, did the same to Delie.

Delie arched her hips towards Emily's clever fingers and probed her own deeper into Mai Lee and Bianca. Both girls began to caress their own breasts and to rotate their quims over Delie's fingers. Their pleasure in her caress enhanced her enjoyment of Emily's attention to her own intimate places. When she looked up at the ceiling she discovered she could watch what Emily was doing. Delie was becoming so aroused she knew, if she allowed herself to, she would reach the zenith of pleasure very quickly. But Delie, who knew from experience that to delay an orgasm made it all the more intense, was enjoying herself far too much to want a climax this early in the evening. She was certain she would be having more than one fabulous orgasm before the night was over. Therefore, when Emily removed her fingers and said, 'Enough', Delie was in a way relieved.

The women then set about the task of shaving Delie. A towel was placed beneath her buttocks and Mai Lee and Bianca each grasped one of her legs to hold them wide. The immediate result of being so opened carried her straight back to her former level of arousal. Emily apparently realised because she ran the dry shaving brush gently from base to top of Delie's folds, the bristles tickling all her sensitive nerve ends to vibrant life. When Emily continued to brush in sweeping strokes the length of Delie's crease she knew she would not be able to withhold her orgasm again. The burning was building deep within and she moaned and tossed her head from side to side. At the final crucial moment the stimulus was removed. Delie cried out in protest. Mai Lee and Bianca tightened their grip on her legs.

Emily gave her a reassuring smile. 'The girls will hold you steady so that you do not twitch. This is a delicate procedure and I would not like the razor to slip.'

Not being too keen on that possibility either, Delie lay perfectly motionless, which was not easy considering the degree to which she had already been aroused. The warm water, lather, Emily's fingers pulling her flesh taut and the feel of the razor whisking away her pubic hair were all highly erotic sensations. If not for her fear of being cut, Delie would have climaxed before Emily had finished her task.

At last it was done. Emily carefully wiped all of Delie's folds and creases then fetched a small mirror to angle it between Delie's thighs. 'There. What do you think?'

Delie gazed at the reflection in fascination. Though she had studied the most intimate details of other women's sex parts she had never before looked upon her own. Emily used her free hand to part Delie's naked outer labia so that she could see the rosy inner lips and even the hooded nub of pleasure. Again Delie looked at the mirror above to see the wonders of her body reflected

142

from a different angle. 'I think I will stay like this always.'

'I knew you would.' Emily was triumphant. 'I felt exactly the same the first time I saw myself shaven. Now we must finish preparing you for the men.'

Kneeling at the foot of the dais, Emily discarded her robe. Mai Lee brought a cushion which Bianca helped position under Delie's buttocks to raise her hips and open her even more. Emily's fingers again parted the outer labia and she began to flick her tongue against the sensitive inner flesh to send delicious shivers deep into Delie's body.

Bianca and Mai Lee also knelt on either side of Delie to begin licking around her breasts. The expert stimulus to both erogenous zones filled Delie with delight. She soon realised the oral attention was intended to provide sensual stimulus without arousing her to the point of losing control. Stretching her arms beyond her head to clasp the top edge of the dais, Delie gave herself up to exquisite pleasure. With eyes half closed she was not even aware of the men coming into the room until Jonathon spoke.

'I congratulate you, Emily. You have chosen well, as usual.'

Opening her eyes, Delie discovered the men were arranged around the dais watching her with libidinous interest. Although they were still fully clothed she could see that each one was sporting a healthy erection. Recalling what Emily had said about preparing her for the men, Delie wondered if she was to have sex with all of them. She certainly hoped she would soon be allowed to view the organ that caused such a distention to the material of Rufus' trousers. Delie could not tear her gaze away.

Jonathon laughed and slapped Rufus on the back. 'I would say you are the lucky first tonight. Delie appears fascinated by you.'

Even as Jonathon spoke, Rufus began to peel off his

shirt. The three women moved away from Delie. Wide eyed, dry mouthed and very wet between her thighs, Delie waited for Rufus to remove his trousers. When he did, her breath caught in her throat. At the sight of the huge darkly-purpled organ her body began to secrete additional lubrication in anticipation of having to accommodate so much length and thickness.

Rufus took Emily's place at the foot of the dais and it became the head of his hard organ which stroked between her moist folds. Her nerve endings jumped with a thrill of delight which sent a *frisson* right through her body. At first she was content to enjoy the feel of him stroking her cleft but as the intensity of her arousal increased she strained towards him in an endeavour to push herself on to the marvellous organ.

Her attempts were frustrated by Rufus keeping his body at a distance which allowed for only the extreme end of his organ to be touching her. The frustration heightened Delie's arousal to such a degree that she was ready to beg Rufus to fill her with his bulk. Then she had other things to occupy her mind. The twins had undressed and now knelt either side of her to push their own hard erections towards her mouth.

Delie did not know which one to take first. Crispin solved her dilemma by pressing his shaft against her lips. They opened to accept him eagerly then closed around the glans to hold him in her mouth with little sucking actions. After she had pleasured him for a few moments he pulled back to allow his brother to take his turn. All the while Rufus continued to stroke his shaft along her crease. Delie could feel how swollen her labia had become. Inside she was burning with need. Again she strove to push herself on to that teasing organ.

This time Rufus placed his hands on her thighs to prevent her from moving. He rested his thumbs on her vulva and used them to massage the puffy flesh and draw it open. Now he rubbed against her with the entire length of his organ, sliding up and down the moist valley with an action which curved to drag over her clitoris on each ascent and descent. The burning friction on so sensitive a peak quickly carried her to the verge of her climax. Already twice delayed, the release could not possibly be held back a third time. Yet it was. Just when Delie thought heaven would be hers, all sources of stimulation were removed. Delie sobbed her frustration. She had been so very near.

When Rufus pulled the cushion from beneath her hips and told her to roll over she did so, eager to be given her satisfaction embedded on his shaft. With her view of the room changed she saw that everyone was now naked and engaged in various sexual acts.

Mai Lee was continuing what Delie had started with the twins. Harry and Bianca were giving each other oral pleasure. What really surprised Delie was the spectacle of Jonathon being bound to a straight-backed chair by his wife. Before she could wonder too much about the bondage scene, Rufus again began to stroke his glans against her vulva.

Determined not to be frustrated again Delie pushed back then sighed with relief when she felt the head slide between her sex-lips. Another inch and she was groaning her satisfaction and approval. Inch by inch Rufus pushed deep then even deeper, stretching the soft casing as he went until Delie wondered if she would be split internally by so much bulk. To have the wondrous size of him filling her to such a degree triggered the onset of the thrice-delayed climax.

Rufus had felt her muscles tense. 'Hold it back,' he ordered. 'You musn't let it go yet.'

'I have to,' cried Delie in near despair.

'You cannot,' said Emily, turning to look at her. 'You must do everything that is asked of you, including not having an orgasm.'

The fear of never being invited to return was incentive enough for Delie to strive for control.

'Now you can take all of me,' said Rufus.

145

Delie thought she already had until she felt that great organ press even more deeply inside her body. Unfortunately the degree of concentration necessary to prevent herself from having an orgasm took the edge off her pleasure.

'I did not think you would be so tight,' Rufus declared in a tone which could have indicated either approval or annoyance. 'If I move I might hurt you. I want you to clench me.'

Because she was so tightly stretched Delie did not think she was going to be able to obey the instruction. Concentrating her mind wholly on the union of their bodies, she contracted her vaginal muscles as strongly as she was able. A flame of pleasure seared through her and she heard Rufus groan. Again and again she clenched and released. Without being told, she knew she would be allowed to orgasm when she had brought Rufus near to his own. She hoped that would be soon because she could not hold out for very much longer.

Then Rufus curved over her back, using one hand to pinch and pull her nipples and the other to locate and rub her engorged clitoris. The sharp, almost painful sear of sensation was too much for Delie's body. Her orgasm exploded with such intensity that she came near to swooning with the combination of ecstasy and relief. And when she felt the flood seep out to where they were joined, Rufus took hold of her hips and began to pump.

The orgasmic lubrication in her passage enabled him to move easily, the long measured strokes gradually increasing in force until each one seemed to bang right through to her heart. Delie's body was being jerked back and forth so vigorously she was no longer able to hold up her head. Strong fingers twisted in her hair and she gasped even louder when the grip on her hair was used to pull her head up. Harry's shaft was pushed into her mouth.

There was no action Delie needed to take, other than to close her lips around the rigid column. The force of

Rufus belting into her from behind drove her mouth up and down Harry's organ. With Harry's hands gripping her hair and Rufus gripping her hips, Delie found herself see-sawing back and forth on two throbbing organs. Her own great orgasm had barely begun to fade before it boiled up and exploded a second glorious time. Her inability to be able to cry out her pleasure was an exquisite torture of its own kind. An increase in the speed and urgency of Rufus' thrust meant Delie's mouth moved faster over Harry's organ. Then Rufus began to grunt loudly with his orgasm and Harry's warm ejaculate shot into her throat.

When both men drew away Delie collapsed on the dais to lie face down sapped of strength. When no one appeared to take any notice of her, she rolled over and looked around the room. Mai Lee was still occupied with Edgar and Crispin though she was now the one being pleasured. Emily had taken Harry's place with Bianca. Harry and Rufus were refreshing themselves with wine. Only Jonathon was on his own.

Securely strapped to the chair with his hands tied behind the back-rest and a leg to each front leg of the chair there was nowhere he could move. A cushion had been placed behind his back so that his pelvis was pushed forward. His erection jutted stiffly upward, the expression on his face one of lascivious excitement.

Delie immediately understood Jonathon's twisted desires. Climbing from the dais, she walked over to the chair, stepped across Jonathon's lap and slowly lowered herself over the stiff projection. Having been so stretched by Rufus she barely felt Jonathon inside her at all – what sensation there was more pleasurable than arousing.

Jonathon, highly aroused by all he had been compelled to watch while bound and unable to participate, was far more excited than Delie. He strained against his bonds in an endeavour to create movement. 'Help me, please.'

The agony in his expression gave Delie the sense of sexual power she loved. With not one of the company apparently interested in telling her what to do, Delie relished her chance to take command. She would be in no hurry to give Jonathon complete satisfaction. This time she would control the timing of his orgasm as well as her own.

Using her leg muscles to raise herself to a position where only a short portion of Jonathon's shaft remained encased in her warmth, she cupped her breasts in her hands and lifted them within reach of Jonathon's mouth. He stretched his neck forward, straining at his bonds, to flick at her nipples with his tongue. Soon they were straining forward of their own volition, two brown peaks eager to be licked. When Jonathon's mouth closed over one breast and his teeth grazed her nipple, Delie gasped in delight. She then began to move, just the tiniest degree, over the partly embedded shaft.

'Ye-es.' Jonathon exhaled, his eyes beginning to glaze with sensual appreciation.

Because she wanted him to continue sucking her breasts, Delie leant forward a little more and began to rotate and gyrate her pelvis with more energy. Now that she had recovered from Rufus she was eager for another orgasm. The very fact that Jonathon did not fill her to anywhere near the same degree held its own unique appeal. To ensure every part of her inner sex was stimulated she found it necessary to rotate her hips in their fullest circle.

Emily had come to stand beside the chair. Delie glanced briefly at her hostess, her concentration now on what she was doing. 'Ah, Delie. You are very good. But I think you need a little help if you are to orgasm again.'

Taking one of Delie's hands Emily guided it between her thighs. From the slipperiness she encountered Delie knew Emily had already enjoyed at least one climax. Excited by the knowledge, she pushed three fingers into the other woman's opening and moved them in a manner correspondent to the circling of her hips. The gyrations of her body pulled her breasts to magnify the pressure of Jonathon's sucking mouth.

Delie was becoming more excited. She deliberately increased the twisting of her upper body so that the grazing of Jonathon's teeth on her nipples imparted an arousing degree of pain. Emily's hand, which had begun to caress her buttocks, stroked down to the small crinkled opening. 'Yes, please,' cried Delie and Emily pushed her finger into the anal passage. It pressed forward against the front wall so that both Delie and Jonathon received stimulation. Jonathon climaxed first, his loud scream of ecstasy precipitating Delie to her own.

When Delie climbed off Jonathon's lap, Emily knelt down to take his shrinking shaft in her mouth to bring it back to life. Harry joined them. Kneeling behind Emily he began to play with her labia, drawing out her secretions to spread them around her anus. First he inserted a finger to stretch the opening, then he pushed slowly but steadily into her rear passage. All the time Emily did not pause once in her oral manipulation of Jonathon who craned his neck to watch everything Harry did. After he was fully embedded, Harry curved his arms around Emily's hips to push the fingers of one hand into her front passage and to use the others to stimulate her clitoris.

Watching as avidly as Jonathon, Delie saw the way Emily's eyes became glazed with sexual rapture. Delie wished somebody would do the same to her. She began to stroke herself while she looked about to see what everyone else was doing. Rufus, Mai Lee and Bianca were in a wonderful tangle of arms, legs, cushions and pulsing sex organs. Edgar reclined on the dais with his twin standing near by. They beckoned Delie to join them.

If Edgar had climaxed yet that night it had made no difference to his virility. His rod stood straight and tall. Crispin told her she was to position herself over Edgar but not to encompass him yet. To have the velvet head of Edgar's shaft just brushing her swollen sex lips created a delightful tease. This became magnified by Edgar massaging her outer labia with his thumbs. In the mirror Delie saw that Crispin had produced a small bottle of oil.

'We do everything together,' he said when he began to smear it around her anus. When the outer skin was well lubricated he tipped more oil on his finger then carefully inserted it into the opening. While he lubricated her internally he told her she could now lower herself over Edgar. This Delie did eagerly. To have a hard organ in her front passage and an erotic finger in her rear was unbelievably exciting. Better was yet to come.

Crispin knelt behind Delie and Edgar pulled her forward. She watched in the mirror when Crispin pulled his finger out then parted her buttocks before he pressed his hard rod into her anal passage. Delie's first gasp was followed by a series of rapidly exhaled groans. To feel Crispin easing in, to be fulfilling a long-held desire to be impaled by two men at the same time, was sufficiently arousing without the added stimulus of being able to see herself thus sandwiched. Not once were they reflected but over and over in never-ending series with each mirror throwing back the images in the others. Every member of the group was also reflected, the attention of each now fully focused on Delie.

'Circle your hips like you did with Jonathon,' Edgar instructed.

The moment Delie began to rotate her hips, Crispin began to pump, each action raising the stimulus imparted by the other. The sensations Delie experienced were beyond comprehension, the building of orgasmic tension almost unbearable. Her entire body seemed to be on fire. She was being consumed in flames. All she could see was a sheet of blazing reds and orange. Then there was pain. A searing, wet, flooding pain. Delie was screaming, mindless with the intensity of her orgasm, the cries of the twins joining her in a chorus of excitation.

Emily, Jonathon, Rufus, Harry, Mai Lee and Bianca,

responding to such magnificent carnal joy, all experienced spontaneous orgasms of their own.

A little while later Emily sat beside Delie on the dais. She drew the other woman into an embrace and kissed her fully on the mouth. 'Welcome to our little group, Delie. Will anybody worry if you do not return home tonight?'

Chapter Nine

Melanie might just as well have saved herself the bother of locking her door. Her maid had barely departed after awakening her in the morning before Pieter came into her bedroom.

'Don't you believe in knocking?' Melanie demanded, the nightgown she had been lifting over her head instinctively held in front of her nakedness.

Pieter was unabashed. 'Why so coy, my love? I have seen all of your charms before. Remember?'

Of course she remembered. Far too well. First sight of Pieter had been sufficient to evoke vivid recollections of the one and only time they had been lovers. The way her body reacted with all the familiar sexual signals was proof it was eager to relive the experience even if her mind and heart were not. Her mind for once being stronger than her voluptuous flesh, she had thought to protect herself from her own weakness by locking her door.

An audible click told her Pieter had just done the same thing. He smiled at the indignant widening of her eyes. 'We do not want our reunion to be disturbed, do we Melanie?'

'I do not want any reunion. I locked my door last night. Remember?' She taunted him with his own words.

'And made me suffer a night of agony dreaming about you instead of being with you. I was very tempted to break down the door. Nor would you have stopped me. Your eyes betray your lust, my dear.'

'Pieter, please. I am in love with Ric.'

'If you are, I doubt the sentiment is reciprocated. In fact I gathered you are not exactly his favourite person.'

'We had an argument. I was hoping we would make up last night.'

'Only I arrived to spoil things for you.' Pieter's smile was not in the least repentant.

'I do not know why I asked you to stay. Your arrival was inopportune and unwelcome.'

'Inopportune maybe. Unwelcome never. You might be telling me you love Ric but your body sends out different signals. You want me to make love to you. I saw it in your eyes last night and I see it now.' He moved right up to her to take the nightgown from her unresisting fingers and throw it aside. 'My memory has not done you justice. You are even more exquisite than the image I carried in my mind. Why did you not let me in last night? I want to adore every inch of your body, taste all of your sweetness.'

In all the time he was speaking he neither touched her with his hands nor his gaze. His bright blue eyes stared into Melanie's wide and wondering green orbs. Even so she felt the moisture welling between her thighs.

'Have you forgotten what I look like, Melanie, or do you remember how much you admired my body?'

His conceit was forgiven when he shed the few garments he wore to present her with a visual reminder of his physical beauty. As he had done in Cape Town, he stood a little away from her to allow her eyes to drink their fill of his golden godlike physique and magnificent purpled phallus. An uncontrolled shudder ran through Melanie from head to foot.

Pieter gave her a triumphant smile, stepped forward to scoop her into his arms and carried her to the bed.

There he set her gently on her back and began, as he declared he would, to adore her entire body. He lifted both her arms above her head to hold her wrists captive against the pillows with one hand. Her breasts were stretched so taut that the fine marbling of bluish veins were stark against the transparent whiteness of her skin. Except for the small patches of yellow discoloration.

Knowing he must recognise the fading bruises for what they were, Melanie held her breath. Pieter made no comment though his gaze lingered for so long that Melanie found herself arching her chest upward in an increasing desire to feel his mouth on her breasts.

When Pieter did lower his head it was to lick the underside of her breasts then swirl his tongue around the perimeter of each cone in turn until Melanie was aching so fiercely for the caress to reach her nipples that most of the ache became centred much farther down her body. At last the moist circling of his tongue on her right breast worked up to the peak until it traced the darker hue of her aureole but only brushed the outer edge of her nipple. Melanie felt it tighten and strain upwards. Her breath was suspended, waiting for Pieter's tongue to caress the yearning peak. He moved to her left breast and repeated the entire procedure.

Only then, when Melanie began to plead, did he turn his attention to her nipples. He took each one in his mouth, wetting it thoroughly with his saliva. Then he pulled it through his teeth with sufficient pressure to make Melanie gasp but not to cause unpleasant pain. Finally he blew upon the straining peak, the soft cooling brush of air on the wet skin drying the nipple to aching rigidity.

Pieter lifted his head to admire the results of his work. 'Mm, I wonder if I can do the same with the other little peak.' He slid his hand between Melanie's thighs to hold the palm curved over her vulva.

Melanie's body reacted instantly to the contact. She longed for him to touch her more intimately. His warm, sensual lips were now trailing down her body in a series of light kisses, his tongue coming back into play to tease the indentation of her navel then circle around the hollow. Once again he made the area completely wet then blew upon it to cool and dry it. The sensation was unbelievably arousing, spreading from her navel to her womb and down to the soft flesh that pulsed against Pieter's hand.

Releasing her wrists, Pieter took hold of her legs to turn her across the bed. Her hips were aligned with the edge, her legs hanging over the side. Eager to be pleasured by his tongue, Melanie opened her legs wide to enable Pieter to kneel on the floor between her thighs. His fingers parted the outer lips of her vulva to expose the silky inner parts to his tongue. The wedged tip made several long stroking passes up and down.

Melanie sighed with pleasure. 'Oh Pieter. That feels so wonderful.'

'And you taste delicious. I want to lick out all your sweetness.' He placed a hand on each of her knees to bend her legs up then moved his hands to her inner thighs to press them wide apart. The strain on her groin pulled on Melanie's vulva to open her completely to the probing of Pieter's tongue. Her anal opening and the sensitive tissue between the two orifices were equally vulnerable to his caress.

Long licking movements travelled from the apex of her cleft down to the crinkled hole where it teased so expertly that Melanie discovered the area was a far more erogenous zone than she had ever believed it could be. The clever tongue returned to probe into her sex opening and thrust in an imitation coital action. Every part of Melanie's genital area was tingling with ecstasy, except the tiny peak to which he had referred. Soon she was begging for the ultimate caress.

'How badly do you want me to taste your little rose bud?'

'Please, Pieter. Don't tease. I cannot bear it.'

So aroused was she, so aching for release, his tongue

barely touched her aching bud before her body convulsed with the onset of her orgasm.

Pieter moved quickly. Hands placed on either side of her body, feet braced against the floor, he thrust so swiftly and deeply that she cried out loud with the joy of his possession and continued to cry out until Pieter reached his own climax and his fierce pumping eased to a more leisurely stroking.

On the other side of the bedroom door stood a grim faced Ric, his resolve to take every penny of his grandfather's fortune away from the whoring widow reinforced tenfold. If there was only one way to do so then marry her he would. But she would remain his wife for no longer than it took to transfer everything to his name. After he returned to England she could carry on with her amoral life. When he moved silently away from the door, away from the audible evidence of her lustful enjoyment, he wisely ignored the sickened curling in his stomach.

If he had remained in the passage a few minutes longer he would have realised his plan might not be so easy to execute.

Pieter had altered their positions so that Melanie lay on top of him, responding to the gentle movement of his hips with ones of her own. For now she thought of no one but Pieter. Her body had been sublimely pleasured but not yet sated. She wanted to continue to feel him move inside her. Already he was growing stronger. Without really knowing why, Melanie raised her head to kiss Pieter on the lips. His hands cupped her face, his mouth taking the kiss to deepen it to one of sensuality.

When he held her head away his bright eyes were gleaming. 'I am going to marry you, Melanie. You will not be able to say no.' He began to thrust into her again with such urgency that Melanie was incapable of saying anything.

* * *

Not having any idea Ric knew of Pieter's morning visit, Melanie endeavoured to glean from him some indication of her importance in his life. While she had not agreed to marry Pieter, her refusal had by no means been adamant. Ric, however, remained as unfathomable as ever and every degree as sardonic.

Melanie was crossing the hall, having come down from checking to see whether or not Delie had returned, when she was waylaid by Mrs Godwin who appeared ready to pick a bone with someone. With a sinking heart, Melanie realised she was going to be that person. The woman's small mouth was pinched in disapproval, her dislike of her mistress barely concealed. She wasted no time in coming to the point. 'The servants are concerned ma'am. They want to know how many of them are going to be dismissed.'

'Why on earth should they think they will be?' Melanie's shock was audible in her question. 'I have never given a single one of the servants any reason to believe I was less than satisfied with their service.'

'You dismissed Simmonds, ma'am. He was a very good gardener. With a wife,' she added, in pointed inference.

The colour which rushed to Melanie's cheeks was rapidly followed by a surge of annoyance. If anyone was going to be dismissed it would be Mrs Godwin. Nor would that be too far in the future. Melanie was becoming tired of the woman's brusque manner and ill-concealed disapproval. She did not even see why she should explain herself to the odious housekeeper except to put the minds of the other servants at rest.

'Simmonds was not dismissed out of hand, Mrs Godwin. He was perfectly happy to leave Arlecdon. Now I am sure there are duties which require your attention.' Thus saying, she swept past the housekeeper to continue on to the study.

Ric followed her into the room. His expression was thoughtful. 'Why was Simmonds dismissed?'

Melanie took a deep breath before she answered. 'Will you believe it was because of you?'

'I won't and even if it was, you wasted your time.'

'Why? You were angry with me. I thought I had to make my choice.'

'My dear girl, do you really expect me to believe you? You dismiss one lover in the afternoon then welcome another the same night.'

Melanie had the grace to blush. 'I did not ask Pieter to come here, Ric.'

'Nor did you send him away. In fact you made him very welcome.'

This time Melanie paled. 'You know?'

'Do not look so distressed. I really don't give a damn how many men you take to your bed. I had my fun.'

The words hurt. Ric could be downright malicious and yet . . . 'Don't you want me any more?'

'What I want, my whoring little Melanie, is –'.

But whatever Ric wanted Melanie was not destined to hear. Delie came bursting into the room closely followed by Pieter.

'I hope you were not worried about me.' She spoke to both Melanie and Ric. 'I stayed the night at the Grimshaws'.'

'I take it they kept you entertained,' Ric observed with a sarcasm Delie ignored.

She gave Melanie a conspiratorial smile. 'I had a wonderful time. You were so right about Emily and Jonathon. They have the most interesting circle of friends.'

'I am glad you enjoyed yourself, Delie.' While Melanie would never consent to participate in any activity organised by the licentious Grimshaws, she was not about to condemn Delie for being more sexually adventurous. Nor had she any right to do so. Delie was not beholden to Melanie any more than her infuriating brother. Secretly comparing Ric with Pieter, the one so dark, the other so fair, she could not decide whether either one could be considered more handsome than the other. They both knew how to pleasure her body. Why then should she feel herself drawn to Ric? He liked to hurt her, with words if not actions. Pieter would never be violent. Perhaps she would be wiser to send Ric and Delie on their way and marry Pieter. Except she could not bear the thought of Ric going out of her life.

Delie's surprise on first encountering Pieter van Heuren was quickly surmounted by two other emotions. The first was a surge of lust, the second a fear that his presence at Arlecdon might jeopardise Ric's plans for regaining his inheritance. She wasted no time in getting her brother on his own, dragging him into the library where she believed they would not be disturbed.

'Who is this Pieter van Heuren?'

'Yet another of our widow's many lovers. I suspect she was indulging her rapacious sexual appetite with him while my poor grandfather lay dying.'

The offhand cynicism caught Delie's attention. 'Are you jealous?'

'Good God, no. Whatever gives you that impression?'

'You have changed again. I thought you were beginning to like Melanie. Now you speak in exactly the manner you used before we came to Australia, when we did not know her. What happened to your plans to marry her?'

'They, my dear Adeline, have not changed. At least not entirely. I will marry the widow then discard her as soon as I have what should have been mine.'

'Will we return to England?'

'Of course. I will even indulge you in the restoration of Liddell Hall.'

'There is a condition, of course?' Delie knew her half-brother too well.

'Keep our South African occupied until I have secured Melanie. I fear she likes him too much for safety.'

Delie chuckled. 'That is about the nicest thing you

159

have ever asked of me. Rest assured, dear brother, I will keep our blond charmer very well entertained. I have a few tricks that will take his mind off Melanie.'

Their entire conversation had provided Pieter with a great deal of entertainment. He moved silently away from his position outside the library window, thanking the providential timing which had enabled him to hear all that had been said. Brother and sister had given him a great deal of food for thought while he continued his interrupted stroll around the perimeter of the house.

Ric Liddell was not the only one keen to get his hands on Melanie's fortune. Marriage to a wealthy wife was the only way Pieter was going to be able to continue living the life to which he was accustomed. His uncle had not only cut him off without a cent, he had banished him from his home and refused to pay a single one of his creditors. An angry scowl erased every trace of charm from his handsome face.

The greater part of his misfortune could be attributed to the charming, deceitful young thing who had fallen eagerly into his arms only to sob and wail of forceful seduction when they were discovered together in the cottage. Pieter declared himself willing to marry the girl, her father being attractively wealthy. The scorn with which his gallantry was received still cut him to the core. A young man without prospects of inheritance or employment was not to be compared with the English lord to whom the girl was betrothed.

Pieter had vowed to be revenged though he had no idea how until he remembered Melanie. A few discreet enquiries had sown the seeds of vengeance. With such great wealth at his disposal he would be in a position to engineer the financial downfall of both his uncle and the girl's socially ambitious parents. Nothing and no one was going to deflect him from his purpose. Not even Ric Liddell or his lecherous sister.

Pieter's assault on Melanie's fortune had been carefully

planned. The surprise visit had thrown her off balance as intended and secured him the invitation to stay at Arlecdon. From that point his intention had been to woo her both with his sexual expertise and charm before proposing marriage. The presence of another man and Melanie's locked door had prompted him to act more quickly. He knew, when she refused him after responding so ardently to him sexually, he had a rival in the other man. Now he knew how to get rid of Ric Liddell.

As for Delie keeping him entertained, Pieter was perfectly willing to avail himself of any hedonism she offered. A woman who oozed so much sexuality was to be taken for all the pleasure she could give. He doubted she knew any sexual tricks which would deflect him from his purpose. In fact he believed he could raise her to such heights of passion that she would willingly clarify certain details of brother and sister's relationship to Melanie's deceased husband.

What Pieter did not realise was the extent of Delie's loyalty to her brother. He also misjudged her aptitude to take unbridled enjoyment from sex while never being carried away on a tide of passion. Even in the throes of a mindless orgasm one part of her mind always knew what she was doing. Pieter's other mistake was in thinking there was nothing she knew about sex which would have him so inflamed with lust he would forget all about Melanie.

Throughout luncheon Pieter made certain everyone, including Melanie, understood that he considered himself the most important person in her life. Her lack of enthusiasm caused him no great concern. Before long she would be eager to accept his hand in marriage. However, he did consider he might be prudent to secure her affections a little more before availing himself of what Delie was so blatantly offering.

When he went searching for Melanie after lunch, he discovered she had gone riding. On ascertaining that Ric was still in the house, Pieter decided he might as well take his pleasure with Delie. He would use the afternoon to discover the best way of exposing Ric's deceit to Melanie.

Delie bade him enter when he knocked lightly on her door. He found her seated at her dressing table, her maid standing behind. The robe Delie wore gaped open at the front to reveal a considerable portion of voluptuous breasts. Her welcoming smile held a hint of mocking challenge.

Pieter knew exactly what had been going on prior to his arrival. The knowledge Delie allowed her maid to fondle her breasts aroused him immediately. He wondered what other services the woman performed. When he looked at the maid fully for the first time, he saw the raw sexual hunger in her eyes and the pleading when she turned her gaze away from him to look at Delie in the mirror.

'You may go, Mary.' Delie dismissed her maid without a qualm. The girl could go off somewhere and masturbate, or find the butler to satisfy her urges. Pieter van Heuren was a man Delie wanted all to herself.

Only the minimum time required for him to shed his clothing elapsed before both were lying naked on the bed. Pieter sought to be the dominant partner, to have Delie twisting and moaning in response to the things he planned to do to her. Instead he found himself lying on his back, subjugated to Delie's will.

Her attention went directly to his swollen manhood. She moistened the tender skin with her tongue before her lips made tiny sucking actions along the length of the shaft from his tender swelling sac to his sensitive swollen glans. The passage of her lips created such pleasurable sensations that Pieter decided to remain subservient for a while and allow her to do as she wished.

He soon realised she was an expert in the art of imparting oral pleasure. The sucking action was followed by her tongue licking him up and down then swirling in a circle around the ridge of his circumcision. When she had aroused him to a point where his breath was rasping, her mouth closed over the soft helmet of his shaft to suck at the clear fluid of his arousal.

Absorbed in the exquisite things Delie's mouth was doing to his organ, Pieter took no heed of what she was doing with her hands until he felt her oiled finger rubbing against the tight crinkling of his anus. His instictive tensing relaxed when he discovered her caress was highly stimulating. Pleasure superseded shock. The combined effects of Delie's finger rubbing gently around his anus while she sucked on his glans made his erection even stronger. But when Delie pushed her finger into his anal passage he cried out in protest.

She lifted her head to gaze down at him, her eyes glowing like black diamonds. 'Don't you like what I am doing to you?' Her finger twisting in his anus and her mouth closing over his penis successfully forestalled any protest he might have been going to make.

Never before having known the unique pleasure of anal stimulation, he groaned in protest again when she removed her finger.

'If you liked my finger inside you then you will certainly like these.'

Pieter lifted his head to see a string of beads in her hand. Each was the size of a hazelnut and joined to the next by a short length of cord. Delie was coating them with oil from a small bottle and the realisation of what she intended to do brought a sharp protest to his lips.

'You have never known true pleasure if you have not experienced the sensual delight of the beads,' Delie told him.

'I think it is an experience I am willing to forego.'

'Nonsense.' Shifting her position, Delie knelt across

his chest so that her shaven sex was presented for his attention.

The nakedness fascinated Pieter; he found the exposure of every crease and fold highly erotic. Delie had returned to sucking on his organ and fingering his anal opening. All the wonderful sensations being created in the lower half of Pieter's body rendered the rose-pink genital lips, presented for his delectation, totally irresistible. He stretched out his tongue to lick at Delie's quim and at the same time she again probed her finger into his rear passage. She rotated her finger to ease and stretch the opening but, because she also rotated her pelvis, Pieter became more concerned with catching the tantalising naked sex with his mouth.

Soon her finger was removed and he felt the first of the wooden beads being pushed into the opening. It stretched him so painfully that he reciprocated by closing his teeth on Delie's labia. He felt the shock go through her body and heard her gasp. Then the second bead was pushed after the first. Once again Pieter bit gently, the increased flow of secretions indicating the degree to which she was becoming aroused. Four more times the process was repeated. Each time his anus was stretched to receive a bead, Pieter felt his erection become increasingly harder. When his sphincter muscles closed behind the last bead, he discovered their presence in his rectum was not unpleasant.

Taking his shaft in both hands, Delie returned to caressing the head with her lips and tongue. Despite the unbelievable intensity of the stimulus he realised, with a pleasant surprise, he was nowhere near ready to orgasm.

Pieter began to work more diligently on arousing Delie. His tongue alternated between dipping into her hole and stroking the length of the crease or flicking over her swelling nub. She began to move her hips up and down, exhorting him by her action to carry her through to her climax. Pieter was more than willing. When her abdominal muscles tensed, he nibbled at her engorged bud until he toppled her over the edge into her orgasm. His teeth were pressed against her inner labia, his mouth sucking hard enough to create a stimulating degree of pain.

Forgetting all about what she was doing to him, Delie flung up her head. For the intense duration of her orgasm her concentration was on her own pleasure. When her climax began to fade, she moved down his body, lying against his abdomen to trap his organ between her breasts. Pieter immediately began to thrust between the soft enclosure until Delie dipped her head to take one of his balls into her mouth. At the same time she pulled the cord which dangled from his anus.

Pieter's body arched in shock, the sudden withdrawing of the wooden ball stretching his anus far more painfully than when it had been inserted. When she did the same with the second ball, while continuing to suck on his ever tightening sac, his organ jerked with the imminence of ejaculation. Delie quickly slid a hand between their bodies to grip the base of his shaft and apply gentle pressure until his ragged breathing steadied. Then she pulled out the third bead, maintaining pressure on the base of his sperm channel so that he was unable to orgasm. The build-up of pressure was the nearest thing Pieter had ever felt to torture. He tried to remember how many beads she had inserted in his rectum. Three more. Would he be able to stand the agony? The woman had sexual torment down to a fine art.

His only salvation lay in retaliating with some painful antics of his own. He pinched her clitoris hard between a thumb and forefinger. Delie's body jerked against the unexpected stab of pain and she pulled out two beads in quick succession. Pieter's eyes smarted. His penis was throbbing, his anus ached. All his mind could think about was his overpowering need for release. He was not going to risk pinching her again.

Delie ceased sucking on his balls to ease her body back

and slide her lips back up the length of his shaft. Her mouth closed over the throbbing head then slid down until he was fully encompassed. She released the pressure on the base of his shaft simultaneously pulling out the final bead. Pieter climaxed, his body convulsing. So great was the exquisite agony of release he continued to buck his hips, thrusting into Delie's mouth with a force which would have perturbed a less experienced woman.

When he gave the final thrust, she released him from her mouth and slid along his body to press her warm sheath over the organ before it had time to relax. Pieter stretched his aching legs out straight and Delie took her weight forward to rest her hands on either side of his legs. From there she began to move back and forth, holding him to a full erection. Soon she began to rotate her hips, pressing down on his pubic bone. Pieter knew she was working herself to another climax. Nor was he far from reaching the same state, the unusual position and altered angle of penetration adding to the stimulus. They came almost simultaneously, both gasping from the sexual euphoria they were experiencing.

Before Delie's orgasm had ceased, Pieter pushed her forward to free his shaft. He quickly pulled himself from beneath her and knelt behind her. From there he entered her again, grabbing her hips to pull her up to take his thrust. The protestations Delie had been making since he pushed her away changed in one breath to sounds of approval.

The things Delie had done to him had Pieter so aroused he was in no danger of losing his sexual strength. Now Delie was going to feel just what she had done to him. If she did not like it – too bad. Though he had a feeling she would. While he pumped with a steady rhythm, he sucked on his thumb to wet it with his saliva before he pushed it into her anal passage. The other hand he curved under her body to rub at her already over-stimulated nub. Both actions were greeted with cries of delight which excited him to bang into her more vigorously while increasing the stimulation at both clitoris and anus.

Delie's breath came in short gasps intermittent with loud cries of pleasure. Before long she had climaxed for the third time. However, Pieter was now in a state where he could go for a long time before reaching an orgasmic peak. And he had no intention of easing a single one of his actions until he did. By then Delie had succumbed to a series of small orgasms. She became so exhausted that her arms did not have the strength to support her body. Her chest and face lay against the bed, her cries of pleasure now whimpering responses to so great an excess of sexual stimulation.

Perhaps the grassy knoll, which held such memories of sex with Ric, was not the wisest of destinations. Yet it was there that Melanie rode. She dismounted, tethered her mare, then stood for several minutes gazing down at Arlecdon. A surprising thought came into her mind. If Jeremiah were still alive, she would be living there quite happily being adored by her husband and able to satisfy her sexual urges with a discreet choice of lovers. Instead her choice was between two sexually powerful men. Pieter was a far different kettle of fish to Simmonds. Between Melanie and the gardener there had been mutual carnal lust. With Ric there was lust overlaid with an aching need to be told she was loved. Now Pieter had arrived to woo her body with his sexual adoration and her emotions with an offer of marriage.

With a sigh, Melanie turned away, found a boulder against which she could rest and drew her cousin's letter from her pocket. The greater part of Dita's letter described life on Paradise Island with colourful accounts of her father's rubber plantation and the friendly islanders. Through it all ran an unbroken thread of happiness although Dita made only brief reference to her marriage to Matt.

Melanie folded the letter to return it to her pocket.

Dita's lively communication had not cheered her at all. She could remember perfectly the time when her dear cousin had been the one confused and unhappy over matters of the heart. Then it was Melanie who had given advice and done all she could to bring Dita and Matt to a reconciliation. Now their situations were reversed. Melanie would have given anything to have Dita to confide in. She so desperately needed someone understanding to help her sort out her life. If only she knew how Ric really felt about her. In spite of what he had said to her that morning, she had not given up hope. She wished she knew what he had been going to say before they were interrupted by Delie.

Fifteen minutes later, Melanie's thoughts were still going around in the same confused circles. About to remount to ride back home, she heard another horse approaching. Ric rode on to the knoll. He showed no surprise on seeing her there.

'Did you follow me?' she asked as he dismounted.

'Naturally.'

'Why?' Melanie awaited his reply with suspended heartbeats. His face as usual told her nothing.

'You really should have been a whore, Melanie, you know how to drive men crazy with lust. I heard the way you cried out your delight with your lover this morning –' he ignored Melanie's gasp of shock '– and I find I want to hear you doing the same again for me.'

'You were spying on me.' That was the one thing which fastened in Melanie's mind.

'Not intentionally. You see I had the same idea as your Pieter, except he got in first. Now take your clothes off, Melanie, so that I can have my share now.'

'No.'

'Refusing sex? That is not like you at all, my dear. You don't care who the man is, just as long as he is hard enough.'

'But I do care.' Melanie was close to tears. 'The point is that you do not. You call me names and treat me with

168

contempt. Pieter could give you lessons on how to be a real lover. Even Simmonds had more consideration.'

'He gave you bruises.' The remark was snapped out.

'Yes, and I enjoyed what he was doing to me.' Her voice rising with emotion, Melanie took no notice of the angry pulse beating at the side of Ric's neck. 'I did not enjoy the things you did.'

'I did not give you bruises.'

'You bruised my breasts.'

'Show me.'

'Why? So that you can gloat? Oh, go away and leave me alone. I wish I had never invited you to Arlecdon.' Angry tears on her cheeks, Melanie turned to walk away.

Ric sprang after her, caught her arm and pulled her back to face him. Upset beyond endurance, Melanie hit out, flailing with clenched fists. Ric's attempts to parry her blows and her increased struggles sent them both crashing to the ground, rolling over to finish with Ric lying heavily on top of her.

She could feel the hardness of his arousal pressing against her abdomen while the fury in his eyes both frightened and excited. He lifted himself from her to push her skirt up then his weight was on her again, one arm across her chest pinning her down until he freed his organ from his trousers. Her undergarment was shredded in one vicious movement. The next instant he thrust into her without even bothering to touch her first. The force of the penetration was brutal yet, when he reached his fullest depth, Melanie arched her hips to meet him.

His eyes blazed down at her then his mouth was upon hers, hard, passionate, possessive. Melanie's hands clawed in his hair, her legs curled around his waist, her hips lifted to welcome the wild urgency of his thrusts. She could no more get enough of him than he could of her. Even after she climaxed she continued to arch to meet him, her hands moving down to his buttocks to pull him deeper and urge him to soar to his own climax.

When he did, she pulled him hard into her and ground

herself against the base of his shaft, never wanting for them to be separated. Ric rolled on to his back carrying her over to lie on top. He took her face between his hands to kiss her again, more tenderly this time but with no less passion. Then he curved his arms around her shoulders and held her cradled to his chest. She lay there content, feeling his shaft relax slowly from its nest within her body.

Ric's hands began to move gently over her back. His lips were pressed close to her ear. 'Will you marry me?'

Melanie's only reaction was to stiffen slightly, uncertain whether or not she had heard correctly. Only when he repeated the question did she raise herself to look down at him. 'Pieter has already asked me that.'

Quite suddenly she found herself sitting on her bottom on the grass, tossed away from Ric without the least bit of ceremony. He sat up and, to Melanie's intense surprise, propped his elbows on crooked knees with his head in his hands. She scrambled over to kneel beside him, her hand reaching a tentative touch to his arm.

'I never said I had accepted him.'

'Will you?'

'Not now,' she said, at the same time surprising herself by thinking what a pity it was that bigamy was illegal. Not that she could imagine either Ric or Pieter agreeing to such a ménage. 'Ric. Why do want to marry me? You always act like you hold me in contempt.'

Ric lifted his head, his gaze not turning to Melanie but down over Arlecdon. 'I never intended to speak to you in such a manner. I rode after you with the intention of making love to you, and of asking you to marry me. The trouble was, all the way up the hill I kept thinking about you enjoying yourself with Pieter this morning.'

'You were jealous.' Melanie was triumphant. 'Just like you were jealous of Simmonds. Oh Ric, you really do care.'

He looked at her. 'I think we both proved that a few minutes ago.'

170

'Then I will marry you.'

'I want it to be soon. I cannot wait.' His eagerness and the expression of relief in his eyes Melanie attributed to love.

'Neither can I. I do love you, Ric.'

'Do not tell anyone yet. I think we could wait until after the event.'

'I should tell Pieter.'

'I suppose you should. If only to keep him out of your room.'

'Do you want me to send him away?'

'That is up to you. I am going to learn to trust you, my dear, like I hope you trust in me.'

'I do, I do.'

Some time later Ric and Melanie rode back to Arlecdon together, both elated by the prospect of their marriage. Melanie because she believed her love was reciprocated, Ric because he was now so much closer to his inheritance. There was only one niggling cause for disquiet. Melanie's ardent declaration of love had almost disarmed him. He was still shaken by the force of the passion which had overtaken them both. Despite his vow to abandon Melanie the minute everything was legally his, he could not erase from his mind a surprisingly pleasant image of them living together at Arlecdon as man and wife.

Chapter Ten

Not until long after he left Delie did Pieter remember the other reason he had been eager to avail himself of her company. By the time he emerged from his state of sexual bemusement to a more rational frame of mind he realised he had, as far as Delie was concerned, missed his chance.

Realising how imperative it was for him to have some proof of Ric's identity before denouncing him to Melanie, Pieter pondered over the problem of where to obtain such proof. He was roaming about the house in the hope of enlightenment when he happened upon the elderly housekeeper. Pieter's cunning mind went quickly to work. By exerting every ounce of the gentlemanly charm which he could produce at will and which rarely failed to gain him whatever he wanted, he soon discovered Mrs Godwin had been in Jeremiah Wilberforce's employ for nigh on forty years. From that point it was not too difficult for Pieter to extract the entire family history, such as it was.

'How very sad,' Pieter remarked, 'that Mr Wilberforce should lose his only son and not even have a portrait or photograph to remember him by.'

'Oh no, Mr van Heuren, there is a very fine portrait

indeed. The master couldn't bear to look upon it and ordered it put away in the attic. Such a fine likeness too. I would like to see it hung again, especially now the young master is here. Only he doesn't want herself to know who he is.'

'You mean Ric, of course. I thought there was some relationship.'

'Oh no. I didn't mean ...' Mrs Godwin, totally flustered at having spoken out of turn sought for words with which to retract her careless disclosure.

The van Heuren charm was turned on in full force. 'Do not stress yourself, Mrs Godwin. I will not repeat anything you have told me. In fact I will forget all about it the moment we go our separate ways. I confess I suspected something of the truth. Now that you have told me the family story I find myself somewhat surprised Ric was not his grandfather's heir.'

'It's not my place to say what the master was thinking of, especially when he married herself. To my mind it should have been Mr Ric who got everything, him being so like his father and all.'

'You mentioned the portrait being a great likeness. I am something of a connoisseur of portraiture, Mrs Godwin. Would it be possible for me to see this one?'

The housekeeper's prevarication was merely token. Together they went up to the attic where the portrait was propped against the wall. The instant he saw it, Pieter knew exactly what he was going to do.

That was even before Melanie told him she would not accept his offer of marriage.

They were in her private sitting room, Melanie having sent one of the maids to fetch Pieter. Misunderstanding the reason he had been summoned, he immediately sought to take her in his arms. Melanie twisted away. 'No, Pieter. I only want to talk.'

'We could make love while we talk or, better still, leave the talking until later.' He had managed to retain a grasp of her hand. His thumb traced sensuous messages on her palm, his eyes wooing her with a suggestive smile. There was scarcely a woman alive who could resist such potent sexual flattery. Certainly not Melanie.

She snatched her hand away and moved to place some distance between them. 'This morning you asked me to marry you.'

'Have you decided to say yes?'

'This afternoon Ric asked me to marry him.'

'I see.'

Silence stretched between them with Melanie searching Pieter's face for some clue to his thoughts. He nodded his head, seeming to come to some decision, the smile he gave her rueful. 'It would seem I delayed too long in leaving Cape Town.'

'You are not angry then?'

'I could never be angry with you, darling Melanie. I am disappointed, yes. I thought you had some feeling for me.'

'I do. What I feel for Ric is quite different.'

'In what way is it different? You were not pretending to enjoy the pleasures we shared this morning.'

'I am not talking about sex, Pieter.'

'But I am. If I was to take you now, adore your body, you would not be so certain you want to marry Ric.'

'Nothing would change,' Melanie declared. Unfortunately her voice sounded nowhere near as decisive as she intended to be.

Pieter was smiling. 'Are you willing to put it to the test?'

Melanie hastily shook her head and took another pace backward.

'I have no intention of forcing myself upon you, Melanie. Not that I believe you would ever be unwilling. You have made your choice and I respect that. Will you just allow me to hold you one more time?'

'What is the point?'

'My dear Melanie, I did come halfway across the

world to see you again. What harm is there in another kiss?'

'Just one kiss, Pieter.'

'Only one,' he agreed, his conception of what the embrace would entail totally different from Melanie's.

She found her body crushed against his, held firm by a hand splayed across her shoulder blades and another on her buttocks. Warm lips forced hers open to receive the erotic entry of his tongue, which probed her mouth with an action imitative of coital movement. When Melanie would have pulled away, the hand on her back shifted to hold her head. Captured in the embrace, Melanie attempted to hold herself stiff, to deny any response to so sexually suggestive a kiss. She thought she was succeeding until Pieter began to move his pelvis against hers, coupling with her while they were both still fully clothed.

The effect was devastating on her senses. Not even the greatest exertion of willpower could prevent the moist response between her thighs, the wish there were not several layers of material between their bodies. In arousing her desires, Pieter had aroused his own; the hard column of his erection pressed temptingly against her abdomen. Melanie cursed her weak and willing flesh. Pieter had no need to force her at all.

'Oh, I'm sorry.' Delie walked into the room and Pieter and Melanie broke apart, Melanie wondering why nobody in her house ever seemed to bother knocking on doors.

'I thought you were alone, Melanie,' was Delie's only suggestion of an apology. 'I certainly did not expect you to be here, Pieter.'

'Do not concern yourself, Delie,' said Pieter, keeping his annoyance under perfect control. 'I was on the point of leaving. We will continue with our discussion later, Melanie dear.' He departed with a warm smile for Melanie and a brief nod for Delie.

Her expression was none too pleased when she turned

from gazing after him to regard Melanie. 'I actually came to congratulate you. Ric told me you are to be married yet I find you in a very intimate embrace, kissing Pieter.'

'He was kissing me. You won't tell Ric, will you?' Melanie recognised Delie's displeasure with a tiny lurch of fear. 'I promised he could trust me and I would hate for him to change his mind about marrying me.'

Delie gave a short laugh. 'You may rest assured he will never do that. You can not begin to imagine how badly he wants to make you his wife.'

Dinner that evening assumed the air of a celebration when Pieter raised his glass in a toast to the betrothed couple. The gesture pleased Melanie, surprised Delie, and made Ric wonder what ulterior motive the other man might have for being so generous. No man who had spent hours enjoying sex with a woman to whom he then proposed marriage could possibly accept with equable humour his rejection in favour of another. Nevertheless, the meal progressed with a great deal of good-natured talk about weddings, blushing brides and honeymoons, by the end of which Melanie was convinced of Ric's love.

They had adjourned to the small drawing-room for coffee before Pieter showed his hand. Even then the conversation began innocently enough with Pieter declaring the more he saw of Arlecdon the more impressed he became with its beauty.

'Your late husband was a man of excellent taste Melanie and, crass though the mention of such matters may be, fortunate to have the financial ability to indulge his appreciation of quality.'

'Jeremiah worked very hard for his money. I am only just beginning to understand how much hard work the running of a business empire entails.'

'Well I don't suppose you will have to worry your pretty head over such matters after you are married.' He turned to Ric with the air of asking a perfectly innocuous question. 'I presume you will take over control of your grandfather's businesses, Ric, keep a Wilberforce at the helm, so to speak.'

Silence, so thick it could be cut with a knife, descended on the room. Pieter glanced at each of three stunned faces and his eyebrows rose in mild surprise. 'Did I say something wrong?'

Melanie found her voice first. Or at least a faint part of its normal audibility. 'What do you mean, Pieter? About keeping a Wilberforce at the helm?'

'Nothing.' Pieter managed to look even more surprised. 'With Ric being Jeremiah's grandson I naturally assumed he would be taking charge of everything after you were married.'

The tight strained face, dominated by shocked green eyes, was turned towards the man who had spoken no word to refute Pieter's claim. 'Is that true, Ric? Are you Jeremiah's grandson?'

'Do you mean to tell me you did not know?' Pieter forestalled Ric's response by addressing his question to Melanie. 'How could you not when Ric so resembles his father he might have posed for that wonderful portrait.'

'What portrait?' Melanie's attention immediately jerked back to Pieter.

'Do not tell me you have never seen it? The artist who painted Richard Wilberforce was a genius indeed.'

'I was not aware any portrait existed.' Melanie looked at Ric's stony expression and Delie's shocked, angry one. Ric – Alaric. How could she have been so gullible? She turned back to Pieter. 'Will you show me where this portrait is?'

'That is easily done. I thought it such a shame for a work of that quality to be hidden away I took the liberty of bringing it down to the library where I could study it in a better light.'

Melanie was on her feet before Pieter finished speaking. The others followed her agitated dash across the hall, almost colliding with her when she stopped abruptly just inside the library door. The portrait of Richard Wilberforce had been propped against a bookcase in a position where it was fully illuminated. Even Ric was stunned by his resemblance to his long-dead father.

Very slowly Melanie turned around to face him, her colour gone, her eyes green pools of pain. Her voice was low with controlled fury. 'And you dared to talk to me of trust.'

The nervous pulse beat at the side of Ric's neck. 'I was going to tell you.'

'When? After we were married? I may be many things but I am not a fool. I am well aware of the laws concerning a wife's property, Mr Alaric Wilberforce. You thought it would be easier to marry me than to contest the will. There is no way now that you will ever get your hands on a single penny of Jeremiah's money.'

'You are naturally upset.' Ric had also gone pale beneath the swarthiness of his skin. 'We will talk about this quietly. Just the two of us.'

'There is nothing to talk about. Now if you will all excuse me I have lost my desire for company tonight.'

For several moments after Melanie swept past them and out of the room nobody spoke. Delie broke the silence, casting a venemous glare at Pieter. 'You bastard.'

Pieter gave a deprecatory shrug of his shoulders. 'How was I to know you were here under false pretences?'

'I would like to know how you discovered the truth.'

'Mm. I bet you do. Unfortunately for you I am going to leave you to figure that out. Right now Melanie will be in need of consolation.'

Fear of Pieter causing further problems goaded Delie to protest. 'You leave her alone. You care no more for Melanie than you do for me.'

'There, my dear Delie, you are quite wrong. You are much better at sex than Melanie but, you see, she is the one who has all the money.' He reached a hand forward to press through her dress to the junction of her thighs. 'I like what you do with that. I will be coming back for more. After I have consoled Melanie.'

'Ric.' Delie appealed to her brother for help.

Ric, however, had not heard a single word of their exchange. He had moved across the room to stare at his father's likeness. The portrait seemed almost alive, the artist having captured the devil-may-care nature in the smiling mouth and laughing eyes. Unfamiliar emotions stirred in Ric's breast. He found himself wishing he had known the man who sired him, or at least held some memories of the years when he was alive. Mingled with that regret was another. If it was possible to turn back the clock of time, Melanie would have known from the beginning he was Jeremiah's grandson. Now he would have to work hard to win back her trust – and her love. He could only hope he was able to convince her his feelings for her were genuine.

'Ric.' The impatience in Delie's voice and her hand shaking at his arm brought him out of his reverie. He gazed at her with a cynical quirk to his mouth.

'So, my dear Adeline, the cat is well and truly out of the bag. I wonder how he found out, especially about the portrait. You did not become so carried away in the throes of carnality you became careless, did you?'

'Of course I did not. Pieter has never asked me any questions nor said anything at all. I am no wiser than you. But I do know he intends to glean every advantage from the situation he has created. He has gone to Melanie now. To "console" her was the word he used.'

Ric's brows contracted in displeasure. 'You are slipping, Adeline. You promised to keep him occupied and away from Melanie.'

'Don't blame me for any of this.' Delie was rapidly losing patience with her brother, who appeared a great deal less perturbed than she was by the unfortunate exposure. 'If you had not procrastinated you would have

179

secured Melanie before Pieter arrived. What are you going to do now?'

'Talk to her. In the morning.'

'In the morning?' Delie almost screeched her repetition of Ric's words. 'Pieter is with Melanie now and you think to wait until morning?'

The coldness of Ric's expression would have quelled any person other than his sister. 'What else, dear girl, do you expect me to do? Rush up to Melanie's room and engage in a fight over her body? Or perhaps you think the two of us should engage in some manner of sexual contest to ascertain which of us can give her the greater pleasure.'

'That might not be such a bad idea,' Delie retorted.

'Not in a million years. Unlike you, sister Adeline, I prefer my sexual encounters to be private affairs between myself and one woman only. As for Pieter, I will be very surprised if he does not find Melanie's door locked. She will not thank him for what he did tonight.'

Anger and shock sustained Melanie all the way up the stairs and along the passageway to her room. When she shut the door behind her she leant against it, hands pressed back against the cool wood. That was when her control snapped, the tears spilling out in such a rush she ran across the room to fling herself sobbing on her bed.

Pieter heard the sounds of distress from the passageway. Like Ric, he half expected to find her door locked but was triumphant when it opened on the turn of the handle. Walking silently over to the bed, he sat on the edge and reached a gentle hand to stroke her head. 'I am sorry, dearest. I did not mean to upset you.'

'Go away.' Melanie, her voice muffled against the pillow, continued to sob.

'Only if you insist. I came to see if you were all right and you are not. I cannot leave you in this state. Let me stay with you until you are feeling better.'

His hand resumed its gentle caress, stroking over her

head and shoulders. This time Melanie did not pull away. Gradually her storm of weeping eased to a few trickling tears. She turned and sat up to gaze at Pieter with troubled eyes. 'How could he deceive me so wickedly, Pieter?'

With a murmur of sympathy, Pieter drew her into his arms and cradled her head on his shoulder. 'I do not know. Hush now,' he murmured when her tears started afresh. 'Do not upset yourself any more tonight. I will call your maid to help you get undressed and into bed.'

Melanie dumbly nodded her assent. When the maid arrived, Pieter waited discreetly outside the room, ready to go back in the moment she departed. 'It is perfectly all right,' he assured the girl who objected strongly to his move to re-enter Melanie's room. 'Your mistress has asked me to stay with her until she falls asleep.'

Moments later he was assuring Melanie he wanted only to give her comfort. He stretched out on the bed beside her and drew her into his arms. 'Doesn't that feel better?'

Melanie was forced to admit his embrace was soothing. 'Nothing else, Pieter. Promise? I could not. Not tonight.'

'Of course not, my dear. I will merely hold you.'

By degrees so gradual Melanie was barely aware of it happening, the hand which stroked her hair in gentle solace began to impart a more sensual caress. First her face and shoulder then down to curve softly over the nightgown-shielded swell of her breast.

Instantly Melanie's eyes flicked open. 'Pieter, I don't –'

'Hush.' He interrupted her and bent to press a soft silencing kiss against her mouth. His lips worked gently over hers, imparting sensuality without sexual evocation.

Pieter was careful not to rush her, every action tender and reassuring until she at last allowed him to raise her nightgown over her head. His lips then continued the seductive arousal his hands had begun. They trailed kisses over her eyelids, nibbled gently on her ear lobes and teased at the corners of her mouth before taking the whole again in a tender, sensual kiss.

He knew she was taking comfort from him, aroused, though not yet with passion. There was time for him to adore her breasts one by one, licking and kissing until the softest of moans indicated an active response. He suckled her nipples to tight peaks of desire, grazing each through his teeth to ensure her response flowed down to the most desirable part of her body. The kisses were trailed farther over her scented skin, lingering around her navel before feathering down to the triangle of red-gold curls.

Acting purely from instinct, Melanie opened her thighs to enable Pieter's kisses to move lower. Even then he delayed the final contact, kissing the inside of each of her thighs as he guided them to a wider angle. For a long time he teased her by touching his lips to her thighs and the outer edges of her labial swelling without venturing anywhere near the sensitive central crease. When he did, it was to trail his tongue so lightly she became tantalised by its evasiveness. Before long Melanie was lifting herself in urgency towards his mouth. To maintain her arousal he nibbled gently at the tender inner folds and gloated at her protest when he drew away.

'Soon, my dear. I want to be naked too.'

Melanie's eyes flew open and he saw a glimmer of doubt come into them. Very quickly he bent to press a kiss on her mouth, at the same time sliding a finger along her moist crease. Though the actions gave her reassurance, Pieter wasted no time in shedding his clothes.

Kneeling between Melanie's thighs he placed his hands under her buttocks to raise her hips. He remembered how much she enjoyed being lifted to his mouth. Again he took his time, playing at the folds with his

182

tongue, never touching the highly sensitive peak. Only when he felt her body quiver did he probe his tongue more deeply into her sweetness. He drew from her not only her taste but a yearning need for fulfillment. Then, when she was driven to beg, he swept his tongue across her tight little peak of desire. Melanie's body tensed immediately. Pieter employed the tip of his tongue in a rapid stabbing action until her tension fractured with a tremendous convulsion of her pelvis. His mouth closed over her entire vulva to suck at the nectar her body was creating for his pleasure.

The moment the last drop was drunk he rose to enter her, sliding easily to his depth. Melanie cried out once before he captured her lips in a kiss, working his mouth over hers so that she could taste her own essence. Her response was the one he anticipated, her internal muscles contracting around his shaft. Convinced he had won completely, Pieter rose and swooped, over and into her, in triumph. Emotionally drained, tired, aroused, aching for a reassurance of her worth, Melanie welcomed his possession.

Whenever Delie was in a temper she craved sex. Good hard sex with which to expend her angry tension. The events of that evening had put her in such an ill-tempered mood that she soon reduced her poor maid to a trembling state near to tears. When the brush Mary was drawing through Delie's hair pulled painfully against a knot, Delie snatched the brush from the maid's hand and ordered her from the room. 'Useless girl. You are no good for anything. Anything at all. I need a man and the only one I can think of is Carstairs. Tell him to come here.'

'Will I come back too, ma'am?'

'Didn't you hear me, girl?' Delie's glare was scathing.

'Yes ma'am.' Mary scuttled from the room seething with resentment. She did not like to be excluded from the wonderful sexual pleasures her mistress devised. All

183

afternoon Mary's mind had been busy imagining what it would be like to have sex with the beautiful blond-haired man. Her thoughts had been extremely erotic but there had been no way to ease her ache. Carstairs had been busy all afternoon. Now, tonight, she was to miss out again. That hardly seemed fair to Mary.

While she waited, Delie oiled her wooden phallus. She could have used it herself or asked Mary to give her the pleasure. The notion of making the supercilious butler her sexual servant held more appeal. Delie's mind formed pleasant images of how she would use him, of the things she would make him do to give her sexual satisfaction.

He came eagerly into her room, his trouser front in advance of the rest of his body. Delie laughed, scorning the material-covered erection. 'You may be given a chance to use that. You may not. There are other services I require of you. Get undressed.'

Carstairs naturally wasted no time in obeying. For all the pleasure he had enjoyed with this woman and Mary, he had been immensely chagrined at not being allowed to thrust his organ into the raven-haired wanton's rapacious sex hole. No matter what she said, he intended to satisfy his own lustful yearnings.

Delie lay back on the bed to watch the butler disrobe. All the while she stroked herself externally with the wooden phallus. Her eyes taunted. 'This is how hard I like a man's organ to be. You will pleasure me with this hardness but first you will pleasure me with your mouth.'

On that command she lifted her knees and held them with her hands to pull her naked sex lips wide. Carstairs knelt on the bed. Before Delie gleaned even the slightest inkling of his intention his hands were on top of hers pressing her knees back towards the mattress and his throbbing penis was driving straight into the place it had long ached to be.

Delie's shock was rapidly surmounted by excitement.

Never would she have suspected the butler capable of such mastery, his thin organ a great deal more stimulating than she had imagined it would feel. Held immobilised against the bed she was totally at his mercy. Carried away by his lustful victory he pumped into her with as much finesse as a rutting stag. Delie relished every thrust, her delight increasing tenfold when he added a curving motion which massaged every cell in the lining of her sheath.

'Am I hard enough for you?' he managed to ask between panted breaths.

'Not yet,' Delie goaded him, to be rewarded when he drew right back then slammed into her so hard she thought he would break through her womb. 'Harder. I need it harder.' She continued to goad, suggesting he was not giving her satisfaction even while the rapid build-up of her inner tension told her the imminent orgasm would be truly tremendous. It tore from her with such force she screamed her ecstasy, the warm flood driving the butler to greater effort until, with three hard thrusts which jolted right through Delie's body to her head, he triumphantly shot his ejaculate deep into the place which had caused him such torment.

'Now,' he declared, 'I am in control. I will do what you asked, only you will clean me with your mouth while I do.'

Delie found their positions rapidly reversed with Cartairs lying on his back on the bed. Kneeling astride his torso Delie took his organ into her mouth, licking and sucking at his command. He rewarded her by expert manipulation of the wooden phallus, alternating the thrusts he made with it by rubbing the end against either her clitoris or her anus. Soon he was rock hard in her mouth and she was jerking her hips back against his manipulation of the phallus until they were both of them again in climax.

* * *

In the passageway outside Delie's room Mary knelt, eye to the keyhole, watching everything with a lascivious envy which was equalled only by the intensity of her arousal. Her yearning to be a sexual participant had her unbuttoning her bodice in order to gain some gratification from massaging her own breasts. The self-caress exacerbated instead of easing her ache for sex and she fumbled beneath her skirts to plunge her fingers in her wet and ready sex place.

This was the sight which startled Ric when he eventually made his own way upstairs. He had no idea who Delie might be with but hoped it was the sexual antics of his sister and Pieter van Heuren which caused the maid's excitement. So absorbed was Mary in her auto-eroticism that Ric was almost next to her before she became aware of his presence.

Her first fearful start quickly changed to rapacious delight. Ric found his movements hampered by two surprisingly strong hands which gripped the waist of his trousers.

'What do you think you are doing?' Ric demanded, at the same time attempting to break her grip on his trousers. The woman appeared positively sex crazed and he was in no mood for games tonight.

'You've got to help me. I'll go mad if I don't have it.' She moved one of her hands to rub it over his groin.

To his intense annoyance Ric felt his manhood stir. He knocked the maid's hands away and stepped to go around her.

Mary moved faster, grabbing his ankle to send him pitching headlong to the floor. Only his reflex action in stretching out his arms prevented Ric from falling heavily. He barely rolled over before she was on top of him, tearing open his trousers then pushing her hot wet sex down over his semi-aroused organ. It did not remain softened for long, rising in response to her voracious gyrations. She hardly appeared aware of him as a person, merely the instrument of her satisfaction. Head held up, eyes closed, ecstasy imprinted in every pore of her face, she appeared concerned only with the necessity of creating her own orgasmic rapture.

For Ric, his physiological reaction was beyond the control of his mind. He could hardly believe what was happening. This woman was raping him in the middle of the passageway, yet the more she bounced and gyrated on his shaft the greater became his own arousal. Her own climax came fairly quickly, spilling in a copious flood to wet his shaft and stain his trousers. The woman's frantic movements gradually became more steady. Her hands massaged her breasts and she emitted a series of drawn-out groans of satisfaction.

Ric was certainly not satisfied. He pushed the maid off his pelvis and, scrambling to his feet, dragged her up and into his room. There he pushed her over the bed, plunged into her from behind and satisfactorily finished what she had started.

A chill air crept over her body, waking Melanie from her slumbers. She realised she was lying on her bed naked, without any covers. The recollection of why she was so brought her mind to full alertness. Rising from the bed, she tied a warm robe over her nakedness then went to the window to draw the curtains wide. Perched on the window seat, arms encircling her crooked knees, she gazed out over the night-clad landscape.

In her thoughts she reviewed everything that had happened since she first set eyes on her dark stranger, when she had not the slightest inkling he was the unknown Alaric Wilberforce she had spoken so scathingly of to her cousin Dita. The grandson who believed she had no right to any of Jeremiah's wealth. She realised in hindsight there were any number of things which should have made her suspicious. Not least of which were his hurtful scathing comments about her sexuality.

When he followed her to the knoll and their passion

became wild and abandoned she believed his feelings matched those she held towards him. How wrong she had been. Ric had deceived her with callous indifference to her feelings. For that she would never forgive him. In the morning she would send both Ric and Delie away. If she married anyone it would be Pieter who had shown her tonight how kind and compassionate he could be. Though perhaps she might be happier if she opted to become a merry widow with a string of ardent lovers.

Less than a half-hour after she woke, Melanie was again crying tears over Ric, accepting that she was too confused to know her own mind. How she wished her dear cousin was here. She so desperately needed someone understanding with whom she could talk. When the pearly glow of dawn was giving shape and form to the darkness outside her window, Melanie lit a lamp and sat down to write a long letter to Dita.

Chapter Eleven

*F*or Constable Robert Smith the one day a month he had to himself was the highlight of an otherwise unremarkable existence. His beat on the streets of suburban Sydney afforded him no more excitement than the mundane arrests of inebriates and users of foul language. In all his twenty years as a policeman he had never once made an arrest for a serious crime. That particular honour always seemed to fall to his colleagues. His meagre pay afforded him a cramped room in a boarding house and what little money was left quickly followed the galloping horses around the race track. Therefore he was always eager on his day off to ride up to Arlecdon to visit his aunt.

Although he was rarely given an opportunity to venture beyond the servants domain, he received a vicarious thrill from being able to enter that grand mansion and walk around the lovely grounds. If he was lucky his visit would be enhanced by the sight of the beautiful young widow. On one occasion he actually met her when he was walking in the garden. She had so charmed him with her pleasant friendly manner that he immediately wished he was both younger and better situated in life. From that day on he created for himself a delightful fantasy in which he was able to do her so great a service she became indebted to him for life.

The lovely lady had been away from home on one of his visits and his aunt, assuming her privilege as house-keeper, had taken him on a tour of the mansion. This was something she had never dared to do when old Mr Wilberforce was alive. Luxury and elegance of such a degree were beyond anything the poor policeman had imagined. Constable Smith's Utopia was evermore embodied in Arlecdon and its beautiful mistress.

On this fine sunny morning the only glimpse he was to receive of the woman of his dreams was a fleeting one when her carriage rolled past him on the road. Although he doffed his cap she did not, to his intense disappointment, even appear to notice him.

If a brass band had been performing at the side of the road Melanie would probably not have noticed. She was reliving in her mind the earlier scene with Ric.

In light of the various events of the previous evening, Melanie breakfasted in her room, not wanting to face any of her guests until she felt herself ready. Least of all Ric. When she did venture downstairs she located him in the library again, contemplating his father's portrait. Melanie made a mental note to order the painting returned to the attic. The likeness was too great for her to wish to have it in sight as a reminder of Ric's treachery. Nor did she waste breath in demands for any explanation. Chin tilted with all the pride she could muster, she told him to leave Arlecdon.

Ric regarded her steadily. 'Will you give me a chance to explain?'

'That is not necessary. You planned to contest Jeremiah's will, discovered you could not prove it invalid so sought to employ the only other means by which you could grab his fortune.'

'At first,' Ric agreed. 'I admit that was my plan. Until

190

yesterday. Will you believe me when I say I would marry you if you were penniless?'

A hard scornful little laugh denounced his declaration. 'I remember yesterday very well. All you wanted was your share of sex. Nor have I forgotten the other times you have called me the foulest of names. I understand them as well now. You think I used sex as some kind of weapon to force Jeremiah to change his will.'

The stony silence which greeted her challenge was confirmation enough. Pain and bitterness clawed in her gut. 'I might have forgiven you even that if you had not made it plain from the start you accepted my invitation to Arlecdon for the sole purpose of engaging me in a sexual liaison.'

'Wasn't that the very reason the invitation was offered?'

'Yes.'

'Then why do you deem my behaviour any different from any of the other men with whom you have enjoyed sex?'

'With everyone else, even with Simmonds, there was always honesty. An agreement of sex for mutual pleasure. You not only concealed your identity, you deceived me by pretending you cared enough to want me for your wife.'

'Was van Heuren's offer of marriage prompted by an attraction to you or your money?'

Melanie immediately flared to Pieter's defence. 'He is not tarred with the same brush as you. He is kind and compassionate and disturbed to have caused me distress by revealing what he thought I already knew.'

'I take it you welcomed him into your room last night.'

'Yes I did. And we did not have sex, we made love.'

Ric tensed, his hands clenching tightly before he willed them to relax. His voice held a forced calm. 'I would make love to you too if you would allow me.'

'I want nothing more to do with you. By the time I

191

return from town I expect both Delie and you to be gone. Neither of you is any longer welcome in my house.'

'Your house?' Ric shouted the words, his temper having finally got the better of his efforts at self-control. 'I have more right than you to be in this house. I was born here. Morally, if not legally, Arlecdon is mine. One day I will have it and everything in it. No, Melanie. I have no intention of walking away and leaving Arlecdon in your hands. Marriage would be a perfect solution.'

'For you, not for me.'

'Very well then. I will find some other means.'

Melanie had left him then, too angry, too close to tears to continue the argument. But she would have a great deal to say to Mr Bartlett when she arrived at his office. The solicitor was undoubtedly cognisant of Ric's deceit. That betrayal, by a man she had known and liked all her life, was almost as hurtful as Ric's behaviour. If both men had been honest with her from the start she would willingly have given Ric more than half of his grandfather's fortune. She wanted no one saying she had schemed to deprive Ric of his inheritance.

Voices, as Pieter had previously discovered, carried extremely well through the library window. On realising Melanie was about to confront Ric within that room, Pieter had hurried out of the house by a near door to take up his eavesdropping position. What he heard only satisfied him in part. He wanted Ric out of Arlecdon before Melanie could be tempted to relent and forgive. While he would not care if Melanie had a dozen lovers in the house giving her sex, he was cunning enough to realise her feelings for Ric had gone beyond lust. Unfortunately, Pieter could conceive of no means by which he might be rid of Ric before Melanie's hurt began to fade.

A few minutes after the carriage departed with Melanie, Pieter saw Ric stride out to the stables dressed to go riding. With those two out of the way it seemed an opportune time to pay Delie another visit. While the gentle loving episode with Melanie the previous night had served its purpose, he was not averse to engaging in some more of Delie's wickedly carnal varieties of sexual indulgence.

On his way back into the house Pieter was astonished to see a police constable come riding up the tree-lined drive. For one heart-stopping second he thought the dishonest activities of his past had caught up with him. Only when he saw Mrs Godwin greet the man with warmth did he realise the constable's visit was unofficial.

An idea germinated in Pieter's mind. Very thoughtful, he walked back into the house. The first person he met being the maid, Mary, the jigsaw puzzle of the whys and wherefores of executing his embryonic plan fell into place. He had absolutely no trouble in persuading the girl to accompany him to his room. Before they were even inside, the maid was breathing heavily, her eyes hot with lust. Pieter laughed inwardly. The maid's concupiscence would render her malleable to his will.

He told her she could undress then turned to gaze out of the window, more interested in the outside scene than her disrobing. The suggestion of indifference on his part would make her even more eager to please him. 'I saw a police constable with the housekeeper,' he said without turning around. 'Who is he?'

'Mrs Godwin's nephew. He visits her once a month.'

'How long does he stay at Arlecdon?'

'Usually for most of the day. He likes to pretend he will be master here one day.'

Pieter was surprised. He could not imagine the man holding any appeal for Melanie as a lover. 'How does he hope to achieve that status. Is your mistress attracted to the man?'

'Goodness no. He is besotted with her. He dreams of performing some great service for which she will be forever in his debt.'

'How interesting.' Pieter lapsed into silence.

193

'I am undressed now.'

'Are you?' Turning from the window Pieter gave the naked maid a cursory glance, walked over to the armchair and sat. Legs outstretched, hands behind his head, he gazed at the ceiling. 'I need your help, Mary.'

'I am good with my mouth.'

Pieter ignored the eagerness. From the corner of his eye he saw that she was beginning to fidget, uncertain of what she was expected to do. 'I plan to marry your mistress. Nothing must stand in my way. Especially not any other man. Earlier this morning Mrs Wilberforce asked Mr Liddell to leave the house. Unfortunately he has refused. You, Mary, are going to help me ensure he does leave.' He rapidly brought his bright blue gaze to focus on her face. 'Did you say you are good with your mouth? Don't you think you had better show me how good?'

Mary rushed to kneel beside the chair, fumbling in her haste to unfasten his trousers. Her eagerness was so great she was unable to prevent herself from exclaiming in disappointment on discovering his appendage in no way resembled the vibrant organ she had expected to unclothe.

'You did claim to be good.' Pieter reminded her.

'Can I pull your trousers down, sir?'

'If you think it necessary.' He did assist by raising his hips to enable her to slide his trousers and undergarment down to his ankles.

Mary went to work with a will, taking very few minutes to prove her claim of expertise. Allowing his enjoyment of the manner in which Mary licked and sucked the column she had raised to rigidity to take precedence over his plans, Pieter vowed to one time have sex with Mary and Delie together. He told the maid so simply to arouse her even more.

'That is enough for now, Mary.' Pieter pushed the maid's head away. 'Listen carefully while I explain what I want you to do.'

Pleading eyes gazed up at his face. 'Can you tell me later? Please. I need my pleasure too.'

'Do you?' The expression on Pieter's face suggested he had not considered such a possibility. 'Stand up then.'

When Mary stood he pushed a hand between her thighs, wriggled a finger into her cavity then began to work the digit up and down. 'Now, where was I? Oh, I know. This is what I want you to do for me.'

His instructions were quite specific, the action of his finger totally erotic. When Mary protested at what was asked of her, Pieter brought his thumb into play against her clitoris.

'Oooh,' shrieked Mary, forgetting all about objecting to the callous dishonesty of Pieter's demand. When she began to whimper with the imminence of her orgasm, Pieter took his hand away. 'No,' she cried, trying to grasp his hand to drag it back between her thighs. 'Keep doing it to me.'

'Will you do what I ask of you?'

'Yes, yes, anything.'

'Promise?'

'I promise.'

'Very well, Mary. Now since my organ is so hard you had better make good use of your work.'

Mary was astride his lap, sliding her wet sheath over him almost before he finished speaking. Placing his hands once more behind his head, Pieter took no part in the coital movements. From the frenzied manner in which the girl was bouncing up and down he held no doubt she would bring him to a climax. But Pieter wanted her to be only partly satisfied. While she continued to long for him to do all manner of things to her she would be far easier to control.

The initial setting-in-place of his scheme having been successful, the next stage of Pieter's strategy was to keep Delie occupied while Mary carried out his instructions. He was whistling a soft cheerful tune when he went to find the other woman. Sex was such a powerful bargaining tool, he found himself thanking the long-dead parents who had given him the physical wherewithal to wield that power.

It being not much after mid-morning, Pieter suspected Delie would not yet have emerged from her room. His assumption was correct though he did not expect, on opening her door, to be greeted with a furious, 'Where have you been?'

'Oh,' she continued, without apology, on seeing Pieter, 'I thought you were Mary. I have been ringing for that wretched woman for ages.'

'You must not blame your maid. The fault is mine for keeping her detained.'

'Really?' Delie was sarcastic. 'Did she enjoy herself?'

A smile quirked Pieter's lips, his eyes dancing with amused memory of Mary's ecstatic sexual gyrations. 'I believe so.'

'Good. Now go find the girl for me.' She broke off when Mary came hurrying into the room. 'About time too. I want you to prepare a bath for me.'

'Yes, miss.'

The maid hurried away and Delie turned back to Pieter. 'Tell me how you found out about Ric. He thought I had told you.'

Pieter's smile changed from one of amusement to one of victory. 'You did in a way. I was passing the library window in time to hear an extremely elucidating conversation between you and your brother. As I recall, you were the one who made mention of his grandfather and the expectations of an inheritance.'

'I did not think anyone would be eavesdropping.'

A shrug of Pieter's shoulders dismissed Delie's ire. 'Chance is a wonderful thing.'

'Were you deliberately trying to turn Melanie against Ric?'

'My need of a wealthy wife is greater than your brother's.'

196

'I doubt that very much. My father left us penniless with the Hall falling down about our ears.'

'Ah yes. Some mention was made of that matter. Never mind Delie, with your sexual talents you should have no trouble ensnaring a wealthy husband. In that way Melanie was far smarter than you. I might even consider sharing some of Melanie's fortune with you if you become my mistress.'

His total conceit amazed Delie. 'Don't you care about anybody other than yourself?'

'No more than you do. It is a pity you are not the one with the money, Delie. We would suit each other very well.'

'Do you think I want any more to do with you after your little game last night?'

'Of course you do. You live for sex and you know we were good together.'

'Excuse me, miss.' Mary came back into the room. 'Your bath is ready. Will you need me to assist you in bathing?'

'I will do that,' Pieter declared, his dismissing nod for Mary followed by a lecherous smile for Delie. 'You will need somebody to wash your back.'

Recalling her fantasy about having underwater sex, Delie agreed. Pieter was right about them being good together. She would be silly to deny herself sexual gratification out of a sense of loyalty to Ric. Her brother was capable of looking after himself and if he had any sense he would already be setting things right with Melanie.

Arlecdon being equipped with every modern convenience, there was a special bathroom with a tub in which one could lie full-length. Delie stretched out in the warm scented water and smiled up at Pieter. 'What are you waiting for? You said you were going to wash me.'

'I will, after I get undressed. I do not want to have water splashed all over my clothes.'

'Of course not,' agreed Delie. One knee crooked, arms

draped over the sides of the tub, she reclined her back against the sloped end. Her breasts were half in, half out of the water, her nipples barely breaking the surface.

Pieter washed those firm mounds first, soaping his hands well before swirling them over Delie's breasts, massaging and kneading while he washed. There was no need for him to work her nipples to hardness, the brown peaks having been in a rigid state from the moment she stepped into the bath. Leaving her breasts, Pieter washed each of her arms then asked her to lean forward so that he could wash her back. When his hands reached the base of her spine he worked a finger between the cheeks of her buttocks to rub against her anal opening.

Emitting a gasp of delight, Delie curved her body farther forward to take the pressure from her buttocks and allow the probing finger more room for movement. Nothing lax, Pieter pushed his finger into the narrow passage.

'Ooh yes.' Delie gave fervent approval. 'I want to have sex there.'

'Later. I am going to finish washing you first.' Removing his finger from her anus he moved along the bath and proceeded to wash Delie's legs. Starting at each foot he worked slowly up the leg to the inner thigh to finish with his fingers pressed into her vulva.

Delie's response was zesty. The hardness of her breathing indicated the growing urgency of her need for coition. Pieter did not wait to be asked to join her in the bath. Stepping in the opposite end of the bath, he sat facing Delie who raised herself to enable him to fully extend his legs beneath her buttocks. She carried her body forward until her feet were either side of his torso and her knees against his armpits. Resting her arms on the sides of the bath she lowered herself over Pieter's rigid organ.

Positioned as they were, there was no possibility of either one initiating coital action, intense though the pleasure was from being so joined. His own arms already resting on the edge of the bath, Pieter placed his hands over Delie's and began to slide his buttocks back and forth. The unique stimulation created by his shaft pressing first against the front then against the back of her canal had them both exclaiming their excitement.

Aware her orgasm was building rapidly and afraid from Pieter's grunts he was close to his own, Delie cried out for him to stop. As soon as he ceased the sliding action she lifted herself free to reposition her body for Pieter to enter her anal opening. With his hands holding her buttock cheeks wide, Pieter assisted her to slide herself down. Little cries and loud gasps came with every extra fraction of an inch he penetrated. Her torso of a necessity angled backward to be able to accommodate his shaft, Delie drew in her legs to stretch them up over Pieter's shoulders.

Once again Pieter initiated movement. Exhorting Delie to do her share, he kept only one hand on the edge of the bath to maintain stability. The thumb of the other was pressed into her vagina, the adjacent forefinger hooked over to rub against her clitoris.

Delie's orgasmic tension rebuilt very rapidly, her lusty cries of pleasure rising to a crescendo of ecstasy when her orgasm broke, the climax heightened by being able to feel the spasms of Pieter's ejaculation, so tight was he in her rear.

They remained in the bathroom for a great deal longer than was required to take a normal bath. While Pieter's main objective was to allow Mary sufficient time to carry out his instructions, he was not averse to indulging either his, or Delie's, sexual appetites for as long as they were able to sustain their lust. The discovery of a number of ways the bath could be utilised to assist in the achievement of unusual sexual entry positions kept their libidos energetic for a very long time.

* * *

After having told Mr Bartlett exactly what she thought of his part in aiding and abetting Ric's deception, Melanie was then forced to listen to the solicitor extolling the advantages of marriage between the young couple. All he succeeded in doing was to reinforce Melanie's conviction that Ric was interested solely in getting his hands on his grandfather's wealth. In no mood to face any of her guests, Melanie paid her parents a visit. A few hours of her mother's company, with the conversation being no more taxing on the emotions than the problem of what to wear to the Governor's ball, restored her to a more equable frame of mind. While Melanie was not disposed to forgive either Ric or Delie, she returned home feeling better able to insist on their departure from Arlecdon.

Within minutes of walking through the front door the composure she had found in her mother's company became severely taxed. Carstairs greeted her with an expression of utmost gravity on his face. 'Madam, there appears to have been a theft of several valuable items.'

Naturally, Melanie was startled. 'Will you be more specific please, Carstairs.'

'Yes, madam. You know Mr Wilberforce had a collection of rare figurines and another of miniatures. There are pieces missing from both collections.'

'Are you certain?'

'Quite certain. Mrs Godwin discovered the theft not more than ten minutes ago.'

'Send Mrs Godwin to me,' Melanie commanded. She walked rapidly to the main drawing-room, peeling off her gloves as she went. A glance at the cabinets which housed the valuable collections confirmed there were several pieces missing.

Mrs Godwin hurried into the room followed by her nephew. Melanie's eyebrows rose on sight of the constable. 'Ten minutes and you already have the police here?' she asked of Carstairs with a suspicion of something being not quite right.

'No, ma'am,' Mrs Godwin hastened to explain. 'Constable Smith is my nephew. He visits me every month on his day off.'

Constable Smith hurried forward, his florid complexion rendered even brighter by the excited notion he was about to fulfil his fantasy. 'I am pleased to be able to offer you my assistance in solving this theft, Mrs Wilberforce.'

'Proceed as you wish then,' said Melanie, even though she found his ingratiating manner highly distasteful.

The constable became all zealous efficiency. 'The house must be searched first. When all within have been cleared of involvement we can assume it was an intruder who stole the valuables.'

'Are you suggesting, Constable, one of my servants would steal from me?' Melanie voiced the query in her most severe tone.

'Everyone in the house is under suspicion, even your guests, madam.'

'That is preposterous.'

Constable Smith was not at all rattled by Melanie's indignant reaction. A woman could not be expected to think with the rationality of an experienced police officer. His big chance to do her a great favour had finally arrived and he was not about to leave any stone unturned in his endeavour to apprehend the thief. The beautiful widow would be grateful for his zeal when her valuables were returned. He also knew exactly how he would suggest she show her gratitude. 'I insist on the house being searched, madam. Perhaps, with the guests being fewer in number than the servants, we could start with their rooms first.'

'Before you begin I feel it would be courteous to apprise them of the situation. Do you know where any of them might be, Carstairs?'

'I believe Miss Liddell is resting in her room, ma'am. Mr Liddell went riding this morning and has not yet returned. Mr van Heuren's whereabouts I do not know.'

'I am right here,' declared Pieter, coming at that moment into the room. He cast a puzzled glance over the group. 'Has something happened, Melanie?'

'There has been a small theft, Pieter. Constable Smith wants to search everybody's room.'

'I have no objection.' Pieter was perfectly affable, the clarity of his blue gaze epitomising honesty. 'A process of elimination, I presume, Constable. How very wise.'

'Quite right, sir. Perhaps we could start with your room.'

Pieter cheerfully led the constable upstairs followed by Melanie who was followed in turn by the butler and housekeeper. A thorough search of Pieter's room revealing nothing incriminating, Constable Smith sought Melanie's advice on which room to search next.

'I do not think we should disturb Miss Liddell's rest.' In a few short days Melanie had learnt enough about Delie to be reluctant to burst in on her unannounced.

'Then the other gentleman's room?'

'This one here.' For some ridiculous reason there were butterflies in Melanie's stomach, her tension increasing with every second which passed. She told herself Ric would never stoop to an act so low yet when the valuables were found hidden in a bag beneath the bed her acceptance of his guilt was total.

Constable Smith was triumphant. 'These identify your thief, madam. All I need to do now is to arrest the man.'

Mrs Godwin was the only one who appeared reluctant to accept the evidence of Ric's guilt. She became quite flustered, torn between pride in her nephew and loyalty to the man she had crooned over when he was a babe. 'There must be some mistake. Why would Mr Richard steal his own things?'

Her thoughtless admission of knowledge of Ric's identity did not go unnoticed even if Melanie allowed it to pass without remark. 'Because they are not his, Mrs Godwin. They belong . . .' But she did not get any farther.

Ric stood in the doorway, body tense, a cold-eyed

gaze sweeping over the assembled company. 'What are not mine?'

'Aha!' Constable Smith bounded forward full of official zeal. 'I arrest you, sir, on the charge of stealing these valuables from Mrs Wilberforce.'

Ric stared at the items now laid upon the bed, then individually at the face of every person in the room before returning his attention to the self-satisfied policeman. 'That is absolute rot, Constable. Mrs Wilberforce knows I have no need to steal anything.'

'Exactly what I said,' declared Mrs Godwin, folding her arms across her bosom with the air of one who could only be right.

'Now Aunt, the evidence is right here.'

'We all saw where Constable Smith found the miniatures and figurines, Mrs Godwin.' Melanie spoke quietly to the housekeeper.

'Good God, Melanie. You do not believe I stole those things.' Ric was incredulous.

A painful lump needed to be cleared from Melanie's throat before she could reply. Nor could she look directly at Ric. 'I must believe the evidence of my own eyes. This morning you declared you would take everything you could by one means or another.'

'That's it then.' Constable Smith was full of confidence. 'I am taking you in. I suggest you come quietly, sir.'

'And if I refuse?'

'Then I must handcuff you, sir.' The action rapidly followed the words.

Melanie averted her eyes from the sight only to feel the intensity of Ric's gaze compelling her to lift her head. His eyes were as hard and bright as black diamonds, his lips compressed in a thin angry line. 'I will be back, Melanie. Then, by God, I will make you pay for this.'

'It won't help you to threaten Mrs Wilberforce, sir. Now I suggest you walk slowly downstairs and refrain from forming any notion of escape.'

* * *

203

Unable to bear seeing Ric led away in handcuffs, Melanie sought the sanctuary of her room. There, however, she succumbed to the temptation to look out of her window and watch the two ride down the drive, Ric's horse on a leading rein to prevent his escape. She had no idea Delie witnessed the same sight until the woman came bursting into Melanie's room, hair in disarray, face contorted in fury, shrieking, 'What the hell is going on?'

Chapter Twelve

Such was the ferocity of Delie's outburst that Melanie's instinctive recoil was not unnatural. The other woman appeared perfectly capable of inflicting physical injury.

'I'm sorry, Delie. Ric has been arrested for theft.'

'Are you mad?'

'No. Hurt, upset, yes. He was implicated not only by the discovery of the missing items in his room but by the vow he made only this morning to take everything from me by whatever means he could.'

'How convenient for you.' Delie's sarcasm would have done her brother justice.

'What do you mean?'

'Ric would not steal. He does not have a dishonest bone in his body.'

'I can not see that there is a great deal of difference between dishonesty and deceit.'

'Which, I imagine, is what this is all about. You were upset by the truth so you decided to have him arrested for theft. I had not thought you would be so vindictive.'

'I wasn't.' Melanie exclaimed, aghast at Delie's accusation. 'I might have wanted you both to leave but I would never stoop to laying false charges against Ric.'

'Who else would do such a thing?' Delie demanded, only to become suddenly still, her eyes narrowed in speculation. 'I wonder ...'

Melanie waited for an elucidation of Delie's thoughts.

'Pieter was determined to marry you.'

'Now you are being ridiculous. Pieter has never given me any reason not to trust him implicitly.'

The sweep of Delie's gaze was denigrating. 'Lord, what a gullible fool you are. Pieter has amused himself with me and with my maid. He was even planning to have the two of us together later today.'

'You are only saying that to make me think Ric innocent.'

'Ric is innocent. If you believe Pieter is then perhaps you might offer to take my place with Mary this afternoon. I have no intention of remaining in this house any longer than it will take me to pack my bags. The Grimshaws will be happy to take me in.'

'I bet they will.'

'At least they are honest about their enjoyment of sex, which is more than I can say for you. Ric will not forgive you for this day's work. Neither will I. Run for cover while you can, Melanie, because when Ric is released we will both be seeking revenge.'

The seed of doubt about Pieter's integrity which Delie had planted in Melanie's mind grew slowly but surely. Perhaps the first truth she acknowledged was a lack of concern about Pieter's sexual activities. She discovered she was indifferent to the idea of Pieter having sex with Delie, the maid, or anybody else. From that point she began to wonder just how interested Pieter was in her fortune. Had his exposure of Ric's identity really been accidental?

Now that she thought back in sequence, Melanie realised the denouncement had occurred after she had told Pieter she was going to marry Ric. The natural progession from sly mischief-making to deliberate

206

implication in theft was too horrid to contemplate. Yet it seemed to answer so many puzzling questions. Melanie decided to do a little investigating of her own.

Even under threat of dismissal the maid, Mary, would do no more than admit to having sex with Pieter. 'You can not hold that against me, ma'am,' she declared in a sullen voice. 'I did the same for Mr Liddell.'

The fury which surged through Melanie was so great she was forced to clench her hands to prevent herself from striking the girl. A mental image of Ric with the maid made her shake with anger though she was unable to tell whether her anger was with Ric or the maid, or even why she should be angered. Mary, being the only one present, received the full force of Melanie's displeasure.

'I will not have insolence from my servants. Your employment is terminated from this moment. I will tell Mrs Godwin to settle your wages and you can leave first thing in the morning.'

The maid's face paled. 'You can not put me off like that, ma'am, without notice or a reference.'

'I just did.' Melanie's anger had coalesced into a hard unforgiving core. 'Now be off with you and tell Mrs Godwin I wish to see her immediately.'

On the defensive and fearful her services, like those of the maid, were about to be dispensed with, Mrs Godwin reluctantly admitted knowledge of Ric's identity but willingly recounted her conversation with Mr van Heuren. Tempted to give her own opinion on the matter of who should have inherited Arlecdon she took one look at Melanie's haughty expression and clamped her mouth shut. While she constantly declared to the other servants her low opinion of the young mistress she held no desire to be evicted from the comfortable quarters which had been home to her for so many years.

Having been given a great deal upon which to think, Melanie dismissed the housekeeper and sat for a long time doing nothing other than reviewing her thoughts.

Her sense of justice was deeply troubled by an uneasy conviction that Ric might be innocent of the theft for which he had been arrested. Conversely, she found it difficult to believe Pieter would stoop to so low a deed to be rid of a man he could rightfully consider his rival.

There was, she decided, only one thing to do and the sooner it was done the better for her peace of mind. Melanie rang for her maid and asked to girl to bring Pieter to her sitting room.

A half-hour elapsed before he arrived, Pieter having been occupied with consoling a distraught Mary. The girl had come to him in tears and he felt the least he could do was to take her up to his room and reward her loyalty by having her naked on his bed and slamming his organ into her with a force which had her near to swooning in delight. With the promise to intervene on her behalf, he suggested she make herself comfortable in his bed to await his return.

Melanie, of course, knew nothing of these matters.

'Are you all right, my love?' he asked on entering the room. 'You have received two severe shocks in less than 24 hours. I shudder to think of you having to cope without me here to give you support.'

'I do not need your support, Pieter. Nor do I want you here.' For all Melanie spoke quietly, her voice was firm. 'I think, under the circumstances, I would feel happier if you were to leave Arlecdon too.'

'Come now, my dear, you do not mean that. You must be quite distraught.' Pieter had moved swiftly to take her hands in his and now attempted to draw her into his arms. 'Let me make love to you to help you forget your troubles.'

Melanie pulled her hands free. 'You tried that ploy last night.'

'With considerable success, you must admit. You enjoyed it. So did I. Melanie, my love, I still want to marry you.'

'I do not want to marry anyone, Pieter. Not Ric. Not you. I was far happier on my own.'

The tenderness of expression Pieter was employing to soften her defences did not alter except in the nature of the glint in his eyes. 'If I was to push you down and seduce you right now you would soon change your mind. Your body would tell you to.'

'That is only sex, Pieter. The same as it was in Cape Town.'

'Of course.' Pieter's attitude changed swiftly. 'Why did I not think of that before? I am not a gracious loser, my love. As my wife you would be protected from scandal, but I do wonder what people would think if they were to learn exactly what you were doing when your very wealthy husband was dying.'

'You wouldn't dare.' Melanie was aghast at the threat.

'I would. What a weapon that would give Ric in the matter of the contentious will.'

'Oh. Does that mean you do not care about my money?'

'Naturally I care. You do not think I want to marry you for sex alone, do you? I have that from you for free.'

'Get out!' Melanie was furious.

'Not until you promise to marry me. I need a rich wife I admit, but I also want a beautiful amorous wife. Which is why I have chosen you.'

'You can not force me to marry you.'

'I will use whatever means are necessary. With Ric out of the way I have you all to myself.'

'Did you hide those things in his room?'

'When would I have had the opportunity? I was with Delie all morning.'

'Before or after the maid?'

'Did you dismiss the girl because you are jealous, my dear? Quite unfair of you. I will never object to you taking other lovers. Actually, I have told Mary not to worry. I promised her she will always have a position in our household.'

'You astound me. You have the most incredible conceit of any man I know.'

'Thank you, my dear. I am pleased to hear your appreciation of my worth.'

Exasperated beyond the point of saying any more, Melanie moved to stride from the room. Except Pieter caught her in his arms to crush her body against his and grind his mouth down on her lips. Melanie struggled furiously but Pieter lifted his head only far enough to demand, 'Marry me.'

'Never.'

'Very well.' All pretence of loverlike tenderness abandoned, Pieter dragged her through the connecting door into her bedroom. There he pushed her down on the bed, ripped the cord from the curtains and bound her ankles and wrists. Her furious struggles did not impede his actions one iota. Finally he tied a gag across her mouth.

'Do not panic, my love. I am not going to hurt you. I simply do not want you to run away before I am ready to make you change your mind about marriage. By the morning you will have and I want to make certain a priest is available to perform the ceremony immediately.' He walked to the door and turned to look back at her. 'You know, you look quite irresistible trussed up like you are.' He came back to the bed and bent over her to roll her on to her back. Lifting her skirts he pressed her knees apart then slipped a hand through the opening of her pantaloons to insert two fingers into her defenceless sex.

'Ah, dear Melanie.' He was gloating, his fingers having slid easily against the moisture they encountered. 'You can always be counted on to be ready for sex.' He masturbated her rapidly, eyes gleaming down at hers.

For a long minute or two Melanie managed to stare back in defiance, to hold herself tensed against arousal. Her body refused to be controlled by her mind. With a moan which was more of self-anger than anything else she closed her eyes aginst the inevitable only to open them swiftly when Pieter took his hand away.

'Rest well, my dear. I will tell the servants you are indisposed and not to be disturbed.' Whistling softly, he walked from the room then locked the door behind him. The tears which trickled from the corners of Melanie's eyes were more from frustration and anger than fear of coming to any harm. Pieter had aroused her so thoroughly that the yearning throb in her vulva had her twisting on the bed in an attempt to precipitate her own release.

Eventually she dozed off, to open her eyes to almost complete darkness. For how long she lay alone she could not tell. Perhaps it was only minutes. It seemed more like hours. The sound of the key turning in the lock heralded Pieter's return. He lit the lamps then brought in a tray he had apparently left outside the door.

'There is only soup,' he apologised with complete insincerity. 'Being too indisposed to leave your room you could hardly be expected to consume a hearty meal. But you will need some nourishment to sustain your stamina. Mmm. I think I will feed you. I do not trust you. You look as if you would like to throw the soup in my face.'

He removed her gag and Melanie, wanting to tell him what she thought of him, was frustrated by the dryness in her throat. When Pieter held a glass of wine to her lips she drank thirstily.

'How long to you intend to keep me tied up?'

'Only until you have eaten all your soup. Then I am going to give you such a night of pleasure you will, by morning, be more than willing to marry me.'

While Melanie could have told him he was going entirely the wrong way about making her change her mind, she obediently ate all the soup then drank a second glass of wine. The languid warmth it generated flowed through her blood to her vulva to bring recollection of the unfulfilled orgasm. Whatever Pieter did to her she hoped she would soon be given sexual release.

'Now, my dear,' he said, after he had put the tray aside. 'We need to get you undressed. The lower half first, I think.'

The cords were removed from Melanie's ankles then Pieter began to strip away her skirts, petticoats and pantaloons without any concern for whether they became torn in the process. Helpless, with her wrists still bound behind her back, Melanie was surprised to discover the degree to which she was becoming aroused. Despite the suggestion of savagery in Pieter's actions she was not receiving any hurt. But when he slipped a finger into her crease she cried out in protest at the clenching of her bladder. 'I need to relieve myself.'

'Of course you do.' Pieter assisted her from the bed and walked with her to her adjoining private bathroom.

'You are not going to watch,' she exclaimed in horror.

'No, just make certain the outside door is locked. Call me when you are finished.'

'Why?'

'I will wash you. I want you perfectly clean for me to taste.'

The washing was, in itself, an act of sublime eroticism. The fact she was naked from the waist down, fully clothed on top and had her hands tied behind her back heightened her awareness of every intimate touch. Pieter took so long to cleanse each crease and fold that Melanie was trembling with need well before he declared her to be properly cleansed.

On their return to the bedroom he told her to lie on the bed where, to her intense surprise and even greater shock, he tied her ankles not together but one to each end corner post of the bedstead. With her thighs parted, her intimate places opened to view, the arousal she was already feeling became intensified.

Pieter stood at the end of the bed gazing at her feminine folds. 'Do you know, my dear, that I can actually see how wet and eager you are. Your lovely pink sex lips are glistening with your juices already.' The effect on Melanie of those words was to make her body produce more of the secretion which made her genitals glisten. His almost tactile gaze added a throb to her awareness. Feeling her vulva begin to twitch, Melanie gasped in disbelief. Surely Pieter could not induce an orgasm merely by gazing at her.

As the minutes ticked by with her internal tension increasing more and more she realised he could. He apparently chose not to, walking away from the bed to pour himself a glass of wine. Quite ridiculously, Melanie felt more naked now that she was no longer covered by his gaze. The tension which had built almost to its zenith became transmuted to a dull ache between her thighs.

After he had drunk a little of the wine Pieter returned to the bed to tip the remainder, drop by drop, on Melanie's abdomen. Her muscles contracted against each cool drop which hit her warm flesh, each contraction incorporating muscles which would rather be clenching around a hard male organ. With a hand behind her head he raised her to drink the last of the wine, then he bent over her to lick away all the wine he had spilt on her abdomen.

His tongue swirled back and forth, cleaning the cool red wine from her warm white skin. He circled around her navel and probed into the tiny hollow to clear the wine which had pooled there. Then he licked away the drops which led down to the triangle of red-gold curls, stopping tantalisingly close to her soft aching sex.

Melanie begged.

Pieter raised his head to gaze along her body at her fevered eyes, his own bright with sensual power. 'I do not think you are yet ready to be given release.'

Pulling her up to a sitting position, he untied her wrists to enable him to remove her upper garments. Her wrists, like her ankles, were then secured to the

213

bedposts so that she was spreadeagled on the bed, unable to move more than an inch or two.

Then began what Melanie considered a refined sexual torture. Not that Pieter caused her any pain – the touch of his hands and lips was far too light for that. Her torment came from the expertise with which he aroused and stimulated her body to such a degree of need she was reduced to begging for release. Each time she begged he would tell her she was not ready, cease his caresses until her fevered body cooled, then begin all over again.

She swore at him, called him the foulest of names, reviled him for everything under the sun. Pieter remained unmoved until, begging him yet again, her voice broke on a sob.

'Will you marry me?'

'No!'

'Then your need for release can not be as great as you would have me believe. Arousing you, however, has rendered the attention to my own sexual needs somewhat imperative.' He walked across to open the sitting room door. 'We are ready for you now, Mary.'

Shock, embarrassment and anger all surged through Melanie at once to be followed by the most repulsive thought of all. She cast a horrifed look at Pieter's smiling face. 'Don't you dare let her touch me.'

'I promised you pleasure, not to force you into an act I know you would find distasteful. I arranged for Mary to be available for my benefit only. I can hardly keep you in a state of mindless arousal if I am distracted by my own need for release.'

The maid apparently knew what she was expected to do. Kneeling in front of Pieter she eased down his trousers and undergarment. His magnificent erection sprang free, the sight of it making Melanie ache to have it thrust between her thighs. With his trousers removed, Mary then stood to take off his coat and shirt. All the time he was being undressed, Pieter gazed at Melanie and she at him. Melanie knew exactly the thoughts circulating in Pieter's head. She wondered if he had any inkling of the true nature of the ones going through her own mind. Despite the intense degree of her sexual arousal, one small part of her mind was able to logically assess her situation.

She forgot all about doing that when Mary knelt once more to take Pieter's rampant organ into her mouth. A shudder went through Melanie from head to foot. Rejecting the arousal the sight engendered, she closed her eyes and turned her head away. But she was unable to shut out the pleasure-driven sounds both man and woman were making nor prevent her body from responding to the sexual stimulus.

When she heard the maid cry loud approval she was compelled to open her eyes and look. Neither Pieter nor the maid was any longer taking notice of her. Mary was bent over with her hands resting on the arms of the chair. Pieter, his own arms curved around Mary's pelvis, was jerking furiously into her from behind.

Wetness pooled between Melanie's thighs. She licked suddenly dry lips, unable to tear her gaze away from the frenzied coupling. Pieter was intent on the taking of his pleasure with the maid, stirring her to the zenith of her own. Only when both had climaxed did he again look across at Melanie. She hastily turned her head away, not looking back when Pieter ordered the maid to thoroughly wash his genitals. The image in Melanie's mind was vivid enough. When that task was completed he sent Mary away.

Melanie did not open her eyes until she sensed Pieter had come to stand beside the bed. Their gazes connected, hers resentful, his disarmingly tender. 'How are you feeling, my love?' His hand slid between her thighs, his finger pressing against her tight swollen bud before slipping into her moistness. Melanie cried out once, her orgasm tearing through her body with such painful force that she was incapable of further sound. Yet she was left unsatisfied. That was not the way she had wanted to be given release.

And then the torment began all over again with Pieter caressing her body to fever pitch yet never allowing her the ultimate pleasure. Then he knelt astride her chest. Hands behind her head, fingers entwined in her hair, he lifted her to take his hardened organ into her mouth. Near to being sapped of her will, Melanie accepted the vibrant shaft, hoping if she pleasured him well he would reward her with the satisfaction for which her body now burnt. She was even prepared to take him orally to a climax.

Before he reached the point of no return he moved away then released the bonds which secured her to the bed. Lying down beside her he drew her into his arms. 'I do love you,' he said.

A sob tore out of Melanie, silenced by his lips pressing over hers. He kissed her deeply, holding their bodies close together until she was trembling uncontrollably in his arms. 'Marry me,' he urged.

'Yes,' Melanie whispered, 'yes, yes.' Anything to ease my torment, she cried silently in her mind.

Pieter rolled over in a fluid movement, taking his body into hers with one sweet thrust. Crying out with joy, Melanie arched to meet him. She was being carried away on a tide of sexual ecstasy. Nothing mattered except the fact Pieter was driving into her to fill her silken warmth with his strength and master her body with his possession.

Nor was that the only time. All the hours of the night were to be used for sex, few to be lost in sleep. Until the morning when both, exhausted by their lust, fell each into a deep dreamless sleep.

Melanie stirred before Pieter. Her vulva was swollen and sore, her body aching from the excess of sex. For a few moments she lay quietly, thinking. If the night had taught her anything it was that Pieter van Heuren was a man of whom to be wary. Though she had been sexually

216

stimulated and sated beyond her wildest dreams, Melanie had no intention of becoming Pieter's wife. While he had done nothing to cause her physical harm, she feared he might easily be driven to do so if she again refused to marry him.

He continued to sleep soundly beside her. Moving quietly, so as not to disturb him, Melanie left the bed and quickly gathered together several items of clothing. In her sitting room she dressed unaided then hurried downstairs to order her carriage. She spoke briefly with her maid, telling her to secretly pack a small trunk and send it to The Crown Prince, one of the hotels which she owned. Melanie was gone from the house for more than two hours before Pieter awoke.

Assured by her faithful maid that Melanie had only gone to visit her parents to tell them of her forthcoming marriage, Pieter roamed around the house, ordering the servants and imagining himself already master at Arlecdon.

Melanie spent a nervous day and restless night wondering if Pieter would come after her, if her maid really had managed to get the trunk away in secret. Her wealth could give her protection but what she really needed was someone understanding in whom to confide. Melanie needed her beloved cousin Dita. In the morning she boarded the island schooner for Paradise Island.

Chapter Thirteen

*E*mily and Jonathon Grimshaw had welcomed Delie with enthusiasm. Neither saw any reason to question her assertion that she enjoyed their company far more than Melanie's. They had what Emily termed a 'quiet night' when there were no visitors. The lack of company did not prevent the three of them from amusing themselves with all manner of sexual games, during which Delie shared the aids to stimulation she had obtained from Conrad J Irving. Responding with lusty enthusiasm to Delie's manipulation of the wooden phallus, Emily vowed to make the acquaintance of the importer of exotic goods. Such a man would be a great asset to their little group.

The next morning, Delie, troubled over Ric, set out for the city watch house. She was allowed only a brief visit with her brother whose bitterness would have frightened her if it had been directed at herself.

'What is our deceitful whoring widow doing now?' he demanded, after giving Delie the briefest of greetings.

'I have no idea, nor do I care. I left Arlecdon within an hour of your arrest.'

'Then why didn't you come here straight away? You might have saved me a most unpleasant night.'

'I needed to find somewhere to stay. The Grimshaws have given me a room and I must confess I find their hospitality far more to my liking. They made me welcome immediately.'

Ric scoffed. 'There is no need to elaborate, dear Adeline. Do you ever think of anything other than sex?'

'I think of you, dear brother, or I would not be here. If you are not nice to me I will go away again.' Delie wrinkled her nose in distaste. 'Lord, what a foul smelling place.'

'You noticed,' Ric observed dryly, his stomach having experienced considerable difficulty in coping with the odorous proximity of two drunken cell mates. 'When I am freed I intend to make certain that conniving red-headed bitch is going to pay for every minute of my imprisonment.'

'How long do you think you will be kept detained?'

'No longer than it takes you to fetch Mr Bartlett and bring him here.'

The expression on his face said a great deal more than his words. Delie pursed her lips. 'Then you are going to be avenged on Melanie.'

Ric's eyes narrowed. 'Do I detect a hint of disapproval?'

'There is something about this matter which does not ring true. Yesterday I was furious with Melanie – now I wonder about this framing of you for theft. I had really begun to like Melanie. It seems out of character for her to have done such a thing simply because you deceived her over your identity.'

'Van Heuren?'

'Undoubtedly. The question is whether or not she knows and, more importantly, whether he will persuade her to marry him. He told me himself he is after her fortune.'

'Which is why I must get out of here without delay. I have no intention of losing Arlecdon to van Heuren.'

'How do you propose to get it for yourself?'

'In exactly the same manner. Even if I have to kidnap her and drag her to a priest, I will marry that woman.'

'Then discard her, penniless.'

His coal-black eyes burning with maleficence, Ric's mouth thinned in a ruthless line. 'Not any more. She will be penniless certainly, but I will be better able to make her suffer by keeping her as my wife.'

A small shake of Delie's head acknowledged Ric's vengeful intention. 'There are times, brother of mine, when I do not like you very much.'

Ric's responding laugh was harsh and cynical. 'My dear Adeline, the feeling is mutual. That is why we are so loyal to each other. Now be a good girl and fetch Bartlett before this place drives me insane.'

When Delie arrived at the solicitor's office it was to discover the door locked, with a notice pinned upon it advising any callers that Mr Bartlett was going to be absent from the city for a period of two weeks. Delie's heart sank. Knowing exactly how Ric was going to react, she wished she was not the one who had to convey to him the unfortunate information. On her return to the watch house, however, she was told the prisoner was allowed only one visitor a day and advised to return the next morning.

No amount of flattery or sexual cajolery on her part could even persuade the constable on duty to deliver a note to Ric. The man was not averse to taking a kiss, squeezing Delie's breasts nor lewdly suggesting she meet him when he came off duty. But he would not be swayed into taking a message to the lady's brother. Tempted to knee the odious constable in the groin, Delie restrained herself lest the man refuse her permission to visit on the morrow. A visit she anticipated with dread. She shuddered to consider the anger with which she would be greeted. Ric would undoubtedly believe she had deserted him to pursue her own pleasures. And on that subject she offered a fervent hope Emily had something entertaining organised which would take her thoughts away from anticipation of her brother's ire.

By the time Delie returned to the Grimshaws' it was to discover that Mary had arrived, in accordance with the arrangements Delie had made with the girl before she left Arlecdon. Mary was eager to recount the things Pieter had done to Melanie. 'Ooh, miss, it made me all wet and excited seeing the way she was tied to the bed and not a stitch of clothing on her body.'

'Would you like to be restrained in bonds, Mary, and forced to submit to whatever was done to you?'

'I think I would, miss.'

'Then I will talk to Emily to see what we can arrange.'

While being agreeable to pandering to the maid's fantasies, Emily insisted she must also be shaved and suggested that task be performed immediately. Emily did not touch Mary sexually as she had done with Delie. She concentrated solely on whisking away the dark pubic hairs. Only when the task was finished did she rise to begin removing her clothing. Delie did the same.

Emily exchanged a conspiratorial smile with Delie before turning her smile on Mary. 'If I am to allow you, tonight, to take your pleasure in the manner you desire you must prove yourself worthy. You must be able to satisfy both Delie and me without giving either of us greater pleasure than the other.'

The ingenuity of Mary's method for achieving that result assured her of a permanent position in Emily's household. After she had toyed simultaneously with the responsive genitals of both women until they were moist with desire, Mary asked them to lie on the floor. There she helped each into a position on her back with knees pulled back towards shoulders, hands holding feet and vulva lifted and exposed. They were positioned as mirror reflections of each other, Mary assisting them to move closer until their buttocks were touching.

She then knelt beside them. With the two naked vulvas

so closely aligned Mary was able to sweep her tongue back and forth from one to the other. While she employed her tongue to give pleasure to one of the women she maintained the stimulus to the other with her fingers. Then she would change about. Sometimes she fingered both while her tongue moving rapidly from vulva to vulva.

With perfect understanding she judged the rapidity of their breathing, keeping them both to an equal degree of arousal. When she sensed they were close to maximum arousal, she rubbed the tight nubs of both women with her thumbs and darted her tongue at each tingling crease to take them both to simultaneous climaxes.

Thrilled by Mary's expertise, Emily was only too willing to then take the maid to her own climax. In all, the remainder of the afternoon passed in a manner pleasurable to all three women.

The mirrors on the ceiling fascinated Mary. They threw back their reflection of her lying on her back on the padded dais, her legs outstretched, secured to the corners and her wrists bound together then secured by a length of rope to a point behind her head.

Emily and Delie had fastened her bonds then left her, without telling her when they would return or giving any indication of what was going to happen next. To pass the time, Mary studied the reflections of her nakedness from the multitude of angles depicted in the mirrors. The effect was to arouse her to a degree where she wished she could free a hand to satisfy the terrible ache between her thighs.

She was wondering if she was going to be left in bondage for the entire night when two men entered the room. They were so alike in appearance that Mary immediately realised they were twins. Both smiled at her without speaking and began to undress. The combination of anticipation and uncertainty made Mary extremely moist between her opened thighs. Because

222

they had not spoken, she was hesitant to ask them what they intended to do to her.

They came to stand beside the dais. One brother tossed a coin and both looked at the side which faced up. The one who had tossed the coin smiled at the other, giving a nod of his head. His brother then climbed on to the dais to thrust his erection into Mary's wet and ready place.

'I'm Edgar,' he said and gave a dozen strokes which thrilled Mary to the core before he moved away and his brother took his place.

'I'm Crispin.' He thrust a dozen times then it was Edgar again.

The excitement generated by being tied down, unable to do other than accept the thrusts of their organs, was heightened for Mary by the agreement they appeared to have for each brother to pump into her exactly twelve times before relinquishing his place to his twin. Having already enjoyed a number of orgasms that afternoon, Mary was still highly sensitised to stimulus. By the fourth change over she was bucking with her orgasm, only to feel like she had been wrenched apart when Crispin pulled out half-way through her climax. Edgar rapidly thrust his organ into the void to carry her through the rest of her sexual cataclysm.

Neither twin had yet climaxed. Mary was wondering who was going to be first when Delie and Emily, who had entered the room unnoticed by Mary, came over to the men and orally performed that service on one twin each.

While that was happening a big dark-skinned man, with the largest male organ Mary had ever seen, approached the dais where he proceeded to release her ankles from their bonds. He rolled her over, pushed her knees forward, pulled up her hips and slowly but surely pushed his great organ all the way to its fullest depth. Mary felt herself filled to such a hurtful degree she cried out, half in pleasure, half in protest.

'You are supposed to be enjoying this,' the man said, his voice sounding disapproving of her protest. His hand delivered a stinging slap to her buttocks. Pain seared right through to Mary's aching canal, making it contract around the bulk which filled it. Again and again the large hand delivered the stinging slaps until she could no longer tell which sensation was pain and which was pleasure, the tension from both exploding in another dramatic orgasm.

Rufus ceased slapping her then, gripping her hips instead to pump back and forth with so devastating an assault on her sexually cognisant nerve endings that her orgasm had no end. On and on it went in waves of stupendous sensation which rose and receded with each of his thrusts. His sexual stamina was quite phenomenal. Mary lay limp and exhausted long before he was anywhere near reaching the pinnacle of his own satisfaction. When he did he gave one monstrous thrust, held himself deeply embedded and pressed a finger against Mary's already swollen clitoris. The intensity of sensation was too much for her to bear. She screamed out loud, her senses swimming in a half-swoon.

They were not yet finished with her. She was turned on her back for her ankles to be restrained in their former position. A man the others called Jonathon was led over to the dais, shuffling because his ankles were bound together. He was assisted to kneel between her legs from which position he rapidly inserted his rampant organ into Mary's now very well-stretched and lubricated canal.

Coming into her so soon after the big dark-skinned Rufus, Mary received only mild pleasure from the movement of Jonathon's shaft sliding into place. She wondered at the bonds on his ankles until his arms were pulled wide, his weight resting fully on her body while his wrists were secured to the top corners of the dais.

A gasp, combined of disbelief and incredible arousal issued from Mary's lips. They were virtually bound together. Jonathon would not now be able to fully withdraw his manhood from where it nestled in her silken warmth. He moved the upper part of his body, abrasing her nipples against his chest. Mary felt the nerve endings in her vulva begin to pulse and attempted to lift her own hips to gain greater pleasure from the organ that remained motionless inside her.

Then the unbelievable happened. Rufus took up a position alongside the dais, a short multi-thonged whip in his hand. He raised his arm then brought it down to flail the leather across Jonathon's buttocks. Jonathon screamed, the instinctive recoil from the lash driving his shaft harder and deeper into Mary. Eact stroke of the whip seemed not only to make him thrust harder but also to make his organ grow bigger and stronger. Mary soon realised Jonathon relished both the pain and the state of bondage. She began to feel every blow in an erotic extension of sensation through her own body. When she saw the whip begin to descend she tensed, ready to arch up to meet Jonathon's downward thrust. The entire situation was so wonderfully, sexually bizarre that she was soon in climax again.

Later she was surprised to discover that although Jonathon's buttocks were covered in angry red welts the skin had not been broken. After he had orgasmed he was lifted away from her and carried to a pile of cushions where he lay face down while Emily rubbed a soothing lotion on to his buttocks.

Mary's bonds were cut and she was allowed to sit up. That was when she discovered Delie was very much occupied with both of the twins. There was only Rufus left alone. He came to kneel behind her, reaching his hands over her shoulders to massage her breasts. The caress being more soothing than stimulating, Mary leant back against his broad chest and closed her eyes. Soon, she knew, he would take her again. When he did she would be ready to do whatever he wanted. Having, during the course of this unbelievably wonderful night, experienced so many new and exciting sexual sensations, she wondered how she had ever been excited by Carstair's unimaginative thrusts.

Almost at the same time the sails of the schooner were swelling with the breeze that would carry her out of Sydney Harbour and Melanie to Paradise Island, Delie was waiting in the small room at the watch house where she was again allowed a brief visit with Ric. Before he had a chance to vent his fury upon her she succinctly explained the situation. Her brother's reaction was one of despairing disbelief.

'Why, of all weeks, did Bartlett have to decide to go away now? I was counting on him to have me released. When it did not happen yesterday I was certain I would be freed today.'

'Is there no one else we can call?'

'Melanie.' Ric's voice rose a degree. 'Delie, you must go to see Melanie. Ask her to withdraw the charges against me. Beg her if necessary.' He stopped speaking to stare at Delie. 'Now what is the matter. Why are you looking like that?'

'We parted company in a less than amicable manner. I doubt Melanie will agree even to speak to me, much less listen to a plea on your behalf.'

'You must try. Actually, now that I think about it, my plans will be better served this way. If Melanie comes personally to withdraw the charges, rather than Bartlett arranging my release, I can beg her forgiveness for deceiving her and persuade her of the sincerity of my reasons for proposing marriage.'

Delie's pursed lips and the slight shake of her head indicated her opinion of her brother's scheming. 'In that case I will do what you ask. But do not blame me if I have no success.'

The schooner was well out on the high seas before Pieter was able to verify where Melanie had fled. When she had not returned the previous evening, he bullied her maid into divulging the address of Melanie's parent's home. Demanding a horse be saddled for him he set out for the Griffiths', only to discover they were not at home. He did manage to elicit the information that Melanie had visited her mother the previous day but had not been to the house since.

It was at that point Pieter realised Melanie had run away. With no idea where she might have gone, he returned to Arlecdon to reassess the situation. There he was forced to contend with an antagonistic housekeeper who saw no reason why he should remain in the house with the mistress absent. Mrs Godwin's bluster was no match for Pieter's determination. Muttering in doom-filled tones about the master turning in his grave if he could see such goings-on, she retired in a huff to her own quarters.

The meal Pieter was served had evidently been put together in a hurry and the wine which accompanied it was most definitely not one of the better vintages. By the end of the meal he was in none too good a mood. He had misjudged Melanie. Or perhaps he had overesti-mated the degree of sexual control he had over her. Now she had given him the slip. His bad mood was farther exacerbated by not having either Delie or Mary available to provide physical diversion. If he had known where Delie was, he would have gone to see her, but of her whereabouts he was as ignorant as he was of Melanie's.

Pieter therefore decided he might as well fill in the remainder of the evening searching for anything which might give him some clue as to where Melanie might have gone. He was not yet about to relinquish his plans to marry a fortune. When he found Melanie, and he was determined he would, he would go about the matter of persuading her to become his wife in a far different manner.

Starting his search in Melanie's private sitting room, he had some success almost immediately. When he lifted the top of her escritoire, he found the letter she had written to her cousin. The contents were, in themselves, extremely elucidating. If Melanie was unsure of her own feelings, Pieter had no trouble defining exactly with whom her heart was engaged. If he did not want to lose both Melanie and her fortune he knew he must act quickly; before Ric Liddell was released to become a renewed threat to his scheming.

The next morning Pieter rode in to the town where he encountered little difficulty in locating the shipping agent who had booked Melanie's passage to Paradise Island. The man, being a romantic at heart, commiserated with Pieter. 'You have only missed your lady by a matter of hours.'

Which fact sorely taxed Pieter's urbanity. 'How soon will the next ship be leaving for the islands?'

'*The Lady Jane* sails a week today. I can book you a berth if you wish.'

'Is there none going sooner?'

'Well, there is a cargo ship due to leave the day after tomorrow. They can carry one or two passengers but the cabins are not so comfortable and the trip takes longer.'

'I will put up with the discomfort.'

His passage booked, Pieter returned to Arlecdon to wait out the two days in comfort.

He had not been back at the house more than half an hour when Delie, with Mary accompanying her to lend moral support, arrived at the door.

'Tell Mrs Wilberforce I wish to speak with her, Carstairs.' Delie swept into the hall with Mary following confidently in her wake.

The butler stared at the maid who was now dressed in the manner of a well-paid companion. Her fashionable attire was not what intrigued him the most. There was an air about her, an aura of confident sexuality which she had not possessed before. He felt his manhood rise in lust, only to be chagrined by the small amused smile

228

she gave in recognition of his arousal. The effect of that smile was to make him long to rip her clothes from her there and then and drive himself into her body.

'Are you going to inform your mistress I am here?' Delie queried in her most autocratic manner.

Though unable to do anything about his bulging manhood Carstairs schooled his features into their professional blandness of expression. 'Mrs Wilberforce is not at home, miss.'

'When will she return?'

'I do not know, miss. She has gone away.'

'Gone where?' The imperiousness of Delie's manner crumbled from the shock of the unexpected.

'That I do not know, miss.'

Delie's foot tapped angrily on the floor. Now what was she going to do? Her silent question was answered by the arrival of Pieter who immediately dismissed the butler then led the two women into the small drawing-room.

'One would think you are master here,' was Delie's sarcastic comment of the manner in which he took charge.

'I soon will be.'

'Really? Then why has Melanie gone away? If she is intending to marry you, I would not have expected her to want to be parted from your company.' A brief flare of anger in Pieter's eyes confirmed her suspicion over Melanie's absence. Part of her tension eased. While it might prove damned inconvenient for Ric, he could at least rest assured he was not in immediate danger of losing Melanie, plus all that marriage to her included, to Pieter van Heuren. 'Do you know where Melanie is?'

'How could I? She told me she was going to her parents' house to inform them of our impending marriage. All I know is that she did not go there. Nor has she returned.'

Delie laughed at him. 'So you were not quite as clever

as you thought. One can assume Melanie did not take too kindly to being tied down.'

A lascivious gleam came into Pieter's eyes. 'Actually she enjoyed it very much. You enjoyed it too, didn't you Mary?'

Once again Delie laughed. 'More than you will ever know.' The women exchanged conspiratorial glances before Delie again questioned Pieter. 'Are you quite certain you do not know where Melanie might have gone?'

'I have not the faintest idea. I have reconciled myself to waiting for her to return.'

'You intend to wait in comfort, of course.'

'Why not? This house is far preferable to any hotel. There is only one thing missing. I have no lovely ladies with whom to while away a few pleasurable hours. We never did have the little get-together we planned. Shall we make up for lost opportunities now?'

Delie pursed her lips in consideration of the suggestion, for once weighing her loyalty to her brother against her own sexual urges. Deciding that to give in to the latter was not going to harm Ric she looked across at Mary. 'Shall we?'

'I am willing.' Mary grossly understated her eagerness.

'I rather think I am too.'

While Pieter might have thought to control their activities, he had not counted on Delie's dominating streak nor Mary's new-found confidence in her enjoyment of sex. In an unspoken agreement between the women, Delie locked the drawing-room door while Mary drew the curtains across the window. They then proceeded to undress each other, taking a great deal of time over the removal of each garment, adding a good degree of erotic touching and fondling.

Assuming they were doing everything for his entertainment, Pieter settled himself on the sofa to watch. His erection grew even harder when he saw that Mary's quim was now shaven like Delie's. Recognising in the maid the sexual aura the butler had noted immediately, Pieter wished he knew where the two women indulged their sexual appetites and with whom.

When they were both naked, Delie sat on the sofa beside him. Swinging one leg over his lap to press against his cloth-covered erection, she exhorted him to lick her breasts while Mary gave attention to the other place which responded so well to oral stimulation.

Initially excited into complying, Pieter soon realised this was not the scenario he had envisaged. He had planned to have both women doing all manner of wonderful things to him. Abruptly pushing Delie's leg away, he stood to remove his own clothing. He then knelt on the sofa across Delie's lap to urge her to take his aching organ into her mouth.

While Delie pleasured him with her lips, Mary rose to stand behind him. She rubbed herself against his back, making certain he felt the hardness of her nipples scraping on his skin. When the eroticism of her actions began to affect her also, she pressed closer to bring her pubic bone into contact with Pieter's buttocks.

Moaning out loud, she swirled and rubbed herself against his back in an excess of sexual abandon. Pieter became more aware of Mary's arousing herself on his body than he was of Delie's lips sliding over his shaft. Eventually, Mary's libidinous moans became too great for him to ignore. Breaking their grouping apart, he pushed Mary down beside Delie, knelt, spread her thighs and delved with his tongue to carry her through to the summit of her arousal.

For a while Delie was content to masturbate herself, the two women taking it in turns to flick an erotic tongue against the other's breasts. When Delie realised Mary was becoming too absorbed in her own sexual euphoria, she moved from the sofa to a position behind Pieter. Her finger being well lubricated with her own secretions, she

231

toyed only briefly with Pieter's anus before probing her finger into the opening.

His gasp was muffled in Mary's vulva, the sensations imparted by Delie's finger making him even more ardent in his pleasuring of Mary. Delie used her free hand to rub her own pleasure spot, eager to orgasm in conjunction with the other woman.

Not one of them was aware the door connecting with the main drawing-room had been opened a fraction. Nor did they realise Carstairs, his erection not having softened from the time the two women entered the house, had watched everything from the unfastening of the first bodice button. This time he was not going to spill his seed uselessly in the air.

Trousers unbuttoned, stiff throbbing organ projecting forward like a battering ram, Carstairs hurried silently over to the trio, came down on his knees behind Delie and thrust triumphantly into her canal before any of them realised he was there. Her gasp of astonished delight penetrated the sexual singlemindedness of the other two. The realisation of what was happening carried each one rapidly closer to the pinnacle of climactic joy.

For Mary and Delie, both vaginally stimulated, the rush towards that peak became greatly accelerated. Carstairs relished the delight of pumping into Delie's wonderful moist passage. Pieter's only stimulation came from Delie's finger wriggling in his anus. In desperation he reached down to enclose his throbbing organ in the circle of his hand. Four climaxes came like a series of exploding fireworks and Pieter silently vowed the two women, before they left, would be made to compensate him for making his first orgasm happen in so humiliating a manner.

Ric's reaction to hearing of Melanie's disappearance on Delie's afternoon visit was one of mixed feelings. After railing against remaining locked up, he brightened with the realisation he would be brought before the magistrate

232

on the morrow. 'I suppose I will survive another night in this hell hole. I can take my mind off the squalor by planning all the things I will do to Melanie when I am free.'

'You need to find her first.'

'Does van Heuren know where she has gone?'

'He pretends he doesn't, though I feel certain he does.'

'Will he wait for her to return, do you think, or will he go after her?'

'Melanie ran away. Why, I cannot begin to guess. But I feel certain Pieter will not sit around hoping she will come back.'

'In that case, my dear Adeline, you had better keep a close watch on his movements.'

Having more exciting plans for the night than keeping just one man entertained, Delie sent Mary back to Arlecdon. The girl was perfectly willing. Delie knew Mary would undoubtedly satisfy both Pieter and the butler then persuade them to jointly attend to her own sexual pleasure.

The next day Ric was brought before the magistrate. Constable Smith, puffed up with his own importance presented the case. His cockiness was deflated with the release of the prisoner due to there being no witnesses to the alleged crime.

Overjoyed at the verdict, Delie performed the unprecedented act of embracing and kissing her brother, which he acknowledged with a wry smile. 'My dear Adeline, I had no idea you cared so much.'

'I shouldn't, seeing how you persist in calling me by that ridiculous name.'

Ric's laugh was more a manifestation of his relief at the dropping of the fabricated charges. 'Our dear mother's taste in names did leave something to be desired. Now I hope, dear sister, you have brought my things. I can not wait to find a hotel where I can shave, bathe and change into clean clothes.'

'Yes, you do smell a little.' She wrinkled her nose at him and they were both laughing when they walked down the steps of the courthouse.

It was Delie, turning to speak to her brother, who saw the familiar carriage coming down the street. 'Ric, look. That is Melanie's carriage.'

'With van Heuren in it and luggage on the back. I am willing to bet my freedom he is going after Melanie. Wait for me at The Prince of Wales, Delie. I am going to follow him.'

Bounding down the last few steps, he dashed along the street in the wake of the carriage, sometimes forced to run to keep it in sight. Before long he realised it was heading for the wharf but was surprised to see Pieter board a cargo vessel. With an assumed air of nonchalance, Ric engaged one of the wharf workers in casual conversation. He quickly learnt the cargo ship was about to depart on a regular run to the islands and normally did not carry passengers.

From that point it was easy for Ric to discover to which island Melanie had gone. The only annoyance came from the necessity of having to wait two days until the next schooner sailed.

'*The Lady Jane* is a lot faster, sir. She will probably reach Paradise Island only a day or so after the cargo ship.'

Which piece of information made Ric feel a great deal better. He would only be a day after Pieter in reaching Melanie. There was not, he reasoned, a great deal of harm the other man could do in 24 hours.

Chapter Fourteen

*B*eyond the shade of the trees, the sun beat with glaring brilliance. The colours of the tropical flowers, the sand, the sea, were all of a brightness which hurt the eyes. Taking a sip of her iced lemonade, Melanie fanned her face with a rattan fan. 'I fully understand why you and Aunt Eleanor favour these loose shifts. If I was wearing one of my fashionable gowns I am quite certain I would expire from the heat. I do not know how you endure it month after month.'

The cousins were sitting on the cool shaded verandah of Dita's new house. Though it was now late afternoon, the heat was still enervating. At least to Melanie. Both Dita and her mother appeared to thrive in the tropical climate. When Melanie made that observation soon after her arrival, Dita had given a sultry laugh. 'The tropics are made for love and sex. Matt thinks it quite wonderful that I wear so little.'

'Where is Matt?' Melanie had immediately asked. 'Is he working on the plantation?'

'He has gone off to visit some of the other islands.' Her smile held secret memories. 'He will ever be an adventurer, Melanie. I could never tie him to my side, nor would I wish to. He loves the life here and gets on extremely well with both my parents. But he could not resist the urge to go exploring. I know he will make up for his absence when he returns.'

Melanie was selfishly pleased to have her cousin all to herself. When Dita recovered from her surprise and pleasure to question her, Melanie indicated her visit was the result of an impulsive decision. For all she desperately wanted someone in whom to confide she had no idea, now that she was with Dita, how to broach the subject of her troubles. There were too many confusing issues to know with which one to start.

Therefore the cousins spent the first 24 hours in laughing reminiscences of their childhood. They talked of other unimportant matters until finally Dita turned to Melanie and asked, 'What is wrong Melanie? You have lost a great deal of your sparkle and not once, in all the time you have been here, have you called me "dear coz" or "sweet coz". That is so unusual as to cause me the greatest alarm.'

The sigh Melanie gave was one of such unhappiness that Dita became even more concerned. She clasped her cousin's hands. 'Tell me, dear.'

'Do you remember I told you that Jeremiah had a grandson?'

'Alaric Wilberforce. You presented a most unflattering description of the man even though you had never met.'

'Well we did meet, and he is nothing like I imagined he would be. He is tall, dark, extremely good-looking –'

'And you have fallen in love with him!' Dita finished her statement on an air of triumph.

'It would be better if I had not.'

'Doesn't he return your love?'

'I do not have the slightest notion of his feelings; he changes towards me from one moment to the next. However, that is only a part of my worries. Things are a great deal more complicated than a case of unrequited love.'

'Then you must tell me everything. Isn't that the real reason you came to Paradise Island?'

Now, after several days on the island, Melanie's spirits were greatly restored, though she was not yet ready to face the problems which would be awaiting her in Sydney. She knew Ric was unlikely ever to forgive her for allowing him to be arrested then doing nothing to secure his release. For that she despised herself. If the officious Constable Smith had not been at Arlecdon, Ric would never have been arrested. Melanie would have chosen some other means of resolving the matter of the alleged theft.

This was something which continued to trouble her thoughts. While she was no longer convinced of Ric's guilt, she was also less able to believe Pieter would have acted in so underhand a manner. Melanie constantly wondered if either man would be eager to marry her if she was penniless. She wished there was some way she could make that test. Would the relationship between Ric and herself have developed differently if they had met under other circumstances? That was something she would never know. He had taken her body, taken everything she had given willingly, with only one end in mind. Pieter had at least desired her before she became a wealthy widow.

'Oh, look,' said Dita, breaking into Melanie's thoughts. 'The cargo ship is coming into the bay. I do hope there is tea on board. I have very little left. Do you feel like coming down to the wharf, Melanie?'

'Do you mind if I don't?'

'Of course not. You do whatever you want. I will go across to Mother's. She will undoubtedly be eager to see what goods have arrived.'

For a while Melanie remained on the verandah watching the distant bustle of the vessel being tied up. She saw the figures of Dita and Eleanor walk out along the jetty.

Then, on impulse, she left the house herself to take her favourite walk along a path which wound through tropical gardens then lush natural forest to end at a cliff overlooking a tiny cove. Several times she had come alone to this place to sit and to think.

On reaching the top of the cliff, Melanie took her customary seat at the base of a shady tree. Looking down at the beach below she saw two of the islanders, a man and a woman, run naked across the sand to plunge into the waves. Melanie admired the skill with which they swam, watching them for a while before turning her gaze out over the turquoise water.

When she looked back at the cove she saw the couple were standing in a close embrace with the foaming waves frothing around their ankles. The man's hands slid over the woman's buttocks to pull her hips closer to his, which thrust against her in a carnally suggestive action.

With a laugh the woman pushed him away and turned to run along the beach, laughing back over her shoulder. He sprinted after her to catch her within a few paces, his arms going around her waist and his erection sliding between her thighs. Melanie could not tell whether he penetrated her or not for she soon broke free to spin around to face him and take a few steps backward. She then began to caress her firm coffee-coloured breasts, rolling each dark nipple between thumb and forefinger. Her tongue circled provocatively over her lips. All the while she continued to take steady steps away from the man.

The man matched her steps pace for pace, lips parted in a white-toothed grin, his hand making lewd movements over his rampant manhood. Laughing back at him, the woman stopped. While continuing to roll her nipples, she thrust her pelvis towards him in a sexual mimicry of his action. When he lunged for her, she slipped past him to run in the opposite direction. Again he caught her, this time in a tackle which pitched both of them forward on to the sand. He recovered quickly to kneel back on his heels. Grasping the woman's legs, he dragged her back to lift her sex to his mouth.

Melanie experienced a surge of moisture in her own sex place. With it came a regret for the days when she had enjoyed sex with the same uncomplicated abandon as the couple on the beach. Witnessing the woman's joyful appreciation of her orgasm was too much for Melanie's hedonistic body. Adjusting her position, she probed a finger into her own moistness, acutely aware of how many days had passed since she last enjoyed sex. And that had been with Pieter.

The man now lowered the woman so that she was able to slide over his organ. Her facial expression portrayed the delight she experienced with every inch she encased with her sheath. Pressing her fingers deep inside her warm opening Melanie imagined herself to be that woman. Seated on the man's lap, her knees on either side of his, the woman rotated herself around the pole her sex encompassed. The man reached around her hips to stimulate her clitoris with both hands. Melanie used her other hand to rub her own. With the woman obviously being aroused to a second climax, the burning in Melanie's vulva increased. She wished there was a man, any man, to give her the same degree of pleasure.

Down on the beach the woman now knelt on all fours with the man pumping energetically into her from behind. Their ecstatic cries rose to the cliff top. Listening to them, responding to their carnal message, Melanie masturbated herself to a very unsatisfactory climax.

Though she realised she should return to the house, she remained where she was, indulging herself with memories of various wonderful lovers she had known. She thought of the night she had taken two young lovers together, then shocked Dita with her confession. That was in the days before Dita met Matt and learnt to enjoy the pleasures of the flesh. Melanie did not think about Matt. To do so seemed disloyal to Dita. She thought about Simmonds and wondered if he had bought his farm. She thought about Ric and she thought about Pieter.

His voice spoke nearby, repeating the words with which he had greeted her at Arlecdon. 'Melanie, my love, are you surprised?'

Shock better described her reaction. For a moment she refused to believe her eyes. How could Pieter be here, smiling down at her with the worldly sexual charm which had attracted her when first they met? Recalling what she had just been doing, and thinking, she started to scramble to her feet. 'How did you find me?'

'You know the saying about there being a way if one has sufficient will.' He reached out a hand to assist her to her feet. Immediately his arms went around her to crush her body to his. His erection pressed into the softness of her abdomen and she looked up at him with a question in her eyes. His smile was lecherous. 'I had not thought you would be one to enjoy voyeurism, my dear. Has watching them aroused you to the degree they have aroused me?'

Melanie glanced down at the beach to discover the couple, who had swum again after their vigorous coupling had come out of the water. The man lay on his back with the woman riding joyously up and down on his shaft. A telltale tremor ran through Melanie.

Pieter gave a triumphant laugh, crushing her body even closer. 'I have missed your beautiful body. Have you missed me too? Is that why you tremble?'

Finding it extremely difficult to concentrate on anything other than the shape of Pieter's arousal and the ache between her thighs, Melanie pushed her hands against his shoulders to force a little distance between their bodies. 'I ran away from you, Pieter.'

'You are not running now.'

'I cannot. You are holding me too tightly.'

Pieter released her and took a step back. 'You are free.'

When Melanie did not move, Pieter gave another soft

240

triumphant laugh. He unfastened his trousers, stepping out of them to allow Melanie to feast her hungry eyes on his godly organ while he stripped off his shirt.

Melanie remained unmoving. Pieter stepped up to her to lift her loose-fitting garment over her head. His breath sucked in when he discovered she was naked underneath the bright print material. 'Now that is a mode of dress of which I approve.'

Placing his hands under her armpits, he lifted her, positioned the head of his organ at her moist opening then allowed her to slide down until they were perfectly united. Melanie coiled her legs around Pieter's waist, her arms around his back, her head resting on his shoulders. He felt so good inside her, so right, she began to wonder why she had ever run away.

For several moments they remained motionless, simply revelling in the sensual pleasure of being conjoined. Then Pieter's hands gripped her buttocks more firmly and he began to pump her up and down, his actions increasing in urgency until Melanie's arms, legs and internal muscles gripped him more tightly with the joy of her orgasm and he was jerking rapidly to his own.

Naturally Pieter was triumphant. The first flush of sexual urgency satisfied, they lay on their discarded clothing to more leisurely enjoy the pleasures they could give each other. Pieter interspersed his caresses with apologies for his behaviour at Arlecdon and his kisses with pleas for her forgiveness. Their pinnacles of sexual gratification having been reached a second time, he stroked leisurely inside her, his weight supported on his arms. His bright blue eyes smiled lovingly down at her. 'Tell me you will still marry me, my love.'

'Do you love me?' Melanie asked, pushing him away. 'Would you marry me if I was poor?'

'I will be honest with you my sweet. If you had asked me that question before, I would have said no. When you ran away I realised how much you mean to me.'

His voice trembled with sincerity, its cadence so

emotive that Melanie was almost convinced. But not entirely. She needed more time to think.

That evening they dined with Dita's parents, the older couple being completely charmed by Pieter's manners and his obvious adoration of Melanie. Even Dita, assessing him with Melanie's interests at heart, was favourably impressed. Before they retired for the night, she sat on the foot of Melanie's bed, in a reversal of Melanie's youthful habit of bouncing into her room with tales of her latest lover.

'Your Pieter is a very charming man and exceedingly good-looking. I know now why you succumbed to him in Cape Town. If I was not so much in love with Matt, I might be tempted myself. I find it difficult to believe he would stoop to the underhand activities you attributed to him.'

'Do you think I was lying?'

'Of course not. However, he does appear to be very devoted to you. Perhaps he acted purely out of jealousy. The important thing is for you to analyse how you feel about his arrival today.'

'I was surprised.'

'And?'

'All right. We had sex almost straight away. I have no control over my body, Dita. I never have. Show me a presentable man and I am aching to lie beneath him and have him thrust his organ between my thighs.'

'Then Pieter does not mean more to you than any other lover.'

'I honestly do not know. He told me he would marry me even if I was poor.'

'Which you are not.'

'Nor will I be as wealthy for very much longer. I will not part with Arlecdon but I intend to give everything else to Ric. In the morning I am going to write to Mr Bartlett to instruct him to make the appropriate legal arrangements. The letter can then go back on the schooner. When he has the necessary documents ready for my signature I will return to Sydney. You do not mind if I stay here for a while?'

'You are welcome for as long as you like. There is just one more question I would like you to answer. Why are you going to give everything to Ric?'

'Because it should have been his. I want to prove I am not a gold-digging hussy, that I did not coerce Jeremiah into changing his will.'

'Why is that important?'

Melanie gave her cousin a glance which held affectionate reproach. 'You said only one question.'

'Two. You did come to me to help you sort out your feelings.'

'I know, and you have.'

'Then please answer my question.'

'My feelings towards Ric have not changed. It hurts to have him think badly of me.'

'Then I have just one piece of advice for you. Melanie, my dear, do not even contemplate marrying anyone else if you love Ric. I speak from experience. I have travelled that road and know the heartache it can bring.'

While Melanie knew her cousin's advice to be sound, Pieter's determination to convince her of the sincerity of his feelings was difficult to withstand. He asked her to show him around the island, taking advantage of one secluded place to demonstrate his desire and prove how much she enjoyed their sexual union.

They came eventually to the place on the cliff. Far in the distance they could see the sails of the schooner. 'We can be on her when she sails this afternoon,' Pieter declared. 'I spoke with the missionary this morning. He will marry us immediately.

He was standing behind Melanie, encircling her body with his arms, one hand moving over her breasts, the other pressing down between her thighs. Despite the arousal she was experiencing, Melanie shook her head. 'I have not said yes.'

'Do you need more convincing?' The hand between her thighs pressed farther, one finger pushing into her moistness without concern for the barrier of material between.

The tingle in Melanie's vulva immediately increased. 'It is only sex, Pieter, not love. You were amusing yourself with both Delie and Mary while you were trying to convince me we should marry. You would have wasted no time having sex with Dita if she had been willing.'

'Are you jealous?'

'No. I do not care with whom you have sex.'

'Nor would I prevent you from having other lovers. You see, we would have a very amiable marriage.'

'I am giving everything to Ric.'

'What?' Pieter released her immediately. Melanie turned to face him.

'Thank you, Pieter. Your reaction has made up my mind. Now that I know you do care about the money, I will never marry you.'

'Never is a long time, my love. I followed you to Australia, then to this island. If you think I am going to go quietly away, you are very much mistaken.'

'You cannot force me to marry you.'

'I tied you down once, Melanie. That time you experienced only pleasure but you learnt the lengths to which I am prepared to go. Next time there will be considerably more pain. I might even be tempted to mark your beautiful face and body. No other man would want you then.'

Melanie took a step back, fearful incredulity on her face. 'You are mad!'

'Ruthless would be more accurate. I will get what I want by whatever means are necessary. The decision is yours. How much do you value your beauty?'

There was no doubt in Melanie's mind that Pieter

would carry out his threat. A shudder of horror ran through her with the image of what he might do to her if she continued to refuse marriage. How safe would she be even as his wife? 'How do I know you would not harm me after we were married?'

'I give you my solemn promise. I threaten you only to get what I want. If you attempt to thwart me, I will have no compunction carrying out those threats. I did what was necessary to get rid of Ric. When I have control of your fortune you will have nothing more to fear.'

Dita's warning echoed through Melanie's mind. But what could she do? She was not brave enough to call Pieter's bluff. The thought of her face and body being scarred filled her with horror. So much so that when she agreed to marry Pieter and he pulled her down to the ground to take her in triumphant possession, she was unable to respond.

In a deeply troubled frame of mind, Dita helped Melanie dress for her wedding. She suspected there was a great deal more to the suddenness of the decision than Melanie had disclosed. Charming though she had found Pieter to be, Dita was convinced he was not the right man for her dear cousin to marry. She wished Matt was there to advise and support her. But Matt was off adventuring and Melanie had withdrawn into an uncommunicative silence. That in itself gave Dita cause for alarm. So concerned was she about the entire affair she gave no note to the arrival of *The Lady Jane*. Only when the cousins set out to walk to the church did she see the schooner tied up at the jetty and realise it must have been berthed for some time.

Pieter was waiting for them outside the tiny palm-thatched church. He grasped Melanie's hands, drawing her to him to place an affectionate kiss on her lips. When she did not respond, he placed a finger under her chin to tilt her face up, forcing her to raise her eyes to his. The tenderness of his expression even fooled Dita, who felt some of her unease dissipate.

'There is no need to be nervous, my love.' Pieter spoke gently to Melanie. 'I gave you my promise. You will be the most cherised wife in the world.'

'But not your wife, van Heuren.'

The harsh declaration startled them in different ways. Melanie's heart surged with a joy which lit her face. Observing it, Dita offered a silent prayer of thanks for Ric's timely arrival, his identity concluded immediately.

Pieter's handsome face paled before suffusing with angry colour. Recovering himself, he placed a possessive arm around Melanie's shoulders. 'Melanie wants to marry me. Don't you, my love?'

'Do you?' Ric stared hard at her, his black eyes piercing through to her soul. He saw the emerald eyes were dull and clouded, the plea in them recognisable even though she answered in the affirmative.

Giving Ric a mocking salutation, Pieter turned to hurry Melanie into the church. Ric moved faster. He caught hold of the other man's arm to pull him around and throw him to the ground. Pieter recovered quickly to come back at Ric, only to be sent staggering with a hard-fisted blow. Melanie's screams for them to stop went unheeded. The two men circled each other warily, each seeking an opportunity to land a telling punch.

'I have waited too long for this,' said Ric. He sprang forward suddenly to deliver a right upper-cut which set Pieter on his backside. Surprised more than stunned, Pieter kicked out a foot to trip Ric and send him tumbling also. From that point there were no holds barred, each man intent on inflicting the greatest possible damage on his opponent.

A few islanders had stopped to watch when the fight first started. Soon they were joined by others, the crowd swelling to form a ring around the battling men. Encircled in Dita's arm, Melanie was near to being distraught when Pieter appeared to be getting the better of Ric.

Fearful of what Pieter might do, Melanie blurted out the threats he had made to coerce her into marriage. Utterly horrified by the disclosure, Dita vowed to protect her cousin no matter what the outcome of the fight. She looked across the circle to where Delie, tense and white faced, urged her brother to retaliate.

Ric ducked under Pieter's next punch, his evasive action upsetting Pieter's balance and giving Ric the opportunity to regain the advantage. Thirty minutes later the fight was over. Bloodied, dishevelled and near exhaustion, Pieter lay face down, unable to summon the strength to get up. Also bearing the physical evidence of the ferocity of the fight, Ric walked over to toe Pieter in the ribs and roll him on to his back.

'I could kill you, van Heuren. I am sorely tempted except I value my life more. When the schooner leaves, you had better be on it and if you know what is good for you, you will take the first boat back to Cape Town.' He turned away from the beaten man to walk over to where Melanie stood in the protective circle of her cousin's arm. 'We need to talk.'

'My house is up there,' said Dita.

'Good.' Grabbing Melanie's hand, Ric strode in the direction of the house. His anger and tension seeming to increase with every wordless pace Melanie stumbled silently in his wake.

Dragging himself painfully to his feet, Pieter found himself face to face with Delie. Her expression was mocking. 'You do look a sorry sight.'

In an attempt to regain his composure, Pieter dusted off his jacket, smoothed his hair with his hands and managed a passable semblance of his customary charming smile. 'You wouldn't care to come to Cape Town with me, would you, Delie?'

Delie shook her head. 'I was happy enough to take my pleasure with you before but not any more. I do not even feel sorry for you. You use everybody for your own

247

purposes. Oh, yes.' She gave a scornful half-smile at the questioning rise of his eyebrows. 'Mary told me what you had done. You are a fool, Pieter. You should have left Melanie to Ric and concentrated on me. After all, Ric has promised to share his fortune with me.'

'It is not too late, Delie. We were good together.'

'My, but you do have the most phenomenal conceit. You do not need me, Pieter. I am quite certain you will find some way of feathering your nest. There must be some willing heiress somewhere who would count herself fortunate to be the object of your selfish attentions.' She turned away from him and walked across to introduce herself to Dita. Cautiously sizing each other up, theirs was not an immediate affinity of friendship. However, Dita knew her obligations of hospitality to all visitors to Paradise Island.

'I think we should leave Melanie and Ric alone. Would you like to come over to my parents' house for some refreshments?'

As they walked through the scattered groups of islanders, Delie noted the nubile young women and the virile physiques of the men. The warm bold eyes of some returned her stares, one man making a surreptitious suggestive action with his hand. Moisture pooled between Delie's thighs, her eyes relaying a silent message to the man. Whatever Ric decided he was going to do, Delie hoped she might be able to spend more than a few days on the island.

Only when they reached the verandah of Dita's house did Ric halt. His eyes questioned Melanie. Without a word she led the way to her room. There she tipped water from the ewer into a bowl, wetting a flannel and wringing it out. 'Let me clean your cuts.'

'I am all right.'

'I insist. You do not want them to become infected.'

Ric submitted, wincing when she touched the worst grazes. When she declared herself finished, he grabbed

248

her wrist, his eyes boring into hers. 'Were you really going to marry van Heuren?'

Melanie lowered her gaze. 'Yes.'

'Why? Did I misunderstand that plea you sent with your eyes?'

'No. Pieter had threatened to hurt me if I refused. He said nobody would want me if my face was marred.'

'My God! I should have killed the bastard.'

'I am glad you did not.' She turned away from him to rinse out the flannel.

Ric came up behind her to take her shoulders and fold her into his arms. He cradled her head against his shoulder. 'I shudder to think I almost arrived too late to prevent the marriage. The thought of you being harmed fills me with horror.'

'He would not have hurt me after we were married. All he wanted was my money. The same as you.'

'How can you compare us? I would never harm a hair of your head. Even if you have driven me to fury at times.'

'Perhaps you would not hurt me physically, though you cannot deny your aim was to take everything away from me.'

'Can I convince you that is no longer true?' There was tenderness in his voice. He held her away to gaze down at her with a sincerity which made her heart ache. Her trust had been abused too many times for her to believe him. She broke from his embrace to take out the letter she had written to Mr Bartlett.

'I would like you to read this.'

When Ric saw to whom the letter was addressed, he gave her a questioning stare. With a slight shake of her head, Melanie walked out on to the verandah. Hands on the railing, body tensed, heart thumping, she awaited his reaction. He seemed to take forever to read the letter. Then she heard his footsteps and felt him come to stand beside her. When she did not look at him he took her shoulders to turn her about.

'Why are you doing this, Melanie?'

'I never intended to rob you, Ric. I did not even know of your existence until Mr Bartlett informed me of your intention of contesting the legality of Jeremiah's will. Naturally, I resented that when you were some unknown person in England. If you had told me from the start you were Jeremiah's grandson I would have given you everything then.'

'Not Arlecdon.'

'I must have something for myself.'

'Would you share Arlecdon with me? As my wife?'

'There is no need for you to marry me now.'

'But I want to. More than ever.' He saw a look of sadness come into her eyes. 'What is the matter. Do you no longer love me?'

'I do, I do. Oh, Ric. How can I promise to be a faithful wife? Even after I loved you I was more than willing to fall into Pieter's arms.'

'Pieter will no longer be around.'

'What about Simmonds? There will always be men like Pieter and Simmonds to tempt me. I fear I am too weak and my flesh too willing for me to be able to resist temptation.'

'Is that the only reason you hesitate?'

'Yes.'

'Then there is a perfectly simple solution. I will have to keep your body so well satisfied you will have neither the inclination nor the energy to contemplate sex with anyone else.

'Oh?' Melanie lifted wide green eyes to gaze up at Ric with a good degree of her old sparkle. 'Do you think you will be able to?'

'Most certainly. Shall I prove it to you right now?'

'Please do,' said Melanie.

BLACK LACE NEW BOOKS

Published in November

THE STRANGER
Portia Da Costa

When a confused and mysterious young man stumbles into the life of the recently widowed Claudia, he becomes the catalyst that reignites her sleeping sensuality. But is the wistful and angelic Paul really as innocent as he looks or is he an accomplished trickster with a dark and depraved agenda? As an erotic obsession flowers between Paul and Claudia, his true identity no longer seems to matter.

ISBN 0 352 33211 5

ELENA'S DESTINY
Lisette Allen

The gentle convent-bred Elena, awakened to the joys of forbidden passion by the masterful knight Aimery le Sabrenn, has been forcibly separated from him by war. Although he still captivates Elena with his powerful masculinity, Aimery is no longer hers. She must fight a desperate battle for his affections with two formidable opponents: a wanton young heiress and his scheming former mistress, Isobel. Dangerous games of love and lust are played out amidst the increasing tension of a merciless siege.

ISBN 0 352 33218 2

Published in December

LAKE OF LOST LOVE
Mercedes Kelly

Princess Angeline lives on a paradise island in the South Seas. She has a life of sensual fulfilment which she shares with her hedonistic friends. When her husband's gorgeous young manservant, Adam, is kidnapped and taken to nearby Monkey Island, Angeline sets about planning his rescue. Adam is being held captive by the Powerful One – a woman of superhuman desires – who is using him as her sex slave. Can Angeline confront this fearful female and return Adam to the Île de Paradis?

ISBN 0 352 33220 4

CONTEST OF WILLS
Louisa Francis

Sydney, Australia – the late 1870s. Vivacious young Melanie marries a man old enough to be her grandfather. On a trip to England, their journey is cut short by his sudden death. Melanie inherits his entire fortune unaware that her late husband has a grandson in England who is planning to contest the will. The louche and hedonistic Ric Lidell and his promiscuous half-sister travel to Sydney in a bid to get their hands on the money. Concealing his true identity from Melanie, Ric uses his satanic good looks to try and charm her. But other suitors have designs on the highly-sexed young widow. Who will win Melanie's heart and their way to her fortune?

ISBN 0 352 33223 9

SUGAR AND SPICE
A Black Lace short story anthology
£6.99

This is the long-awaited first collection of original Black Lace short stories. The book contains 20 unique and arousing tales guaranteed to excite. With contributions from female authors from Europe, Australia and America, this compendium provides a variety of settings and themes. Explicitly sexual and highly entertaining, *Sugar and Spice* is a kaleidoscope of female fantasy. Only the most erotic stories get into Black Lace anthologies.

ISBN 0 352 33227 1

To be published in January

UNHALLOWED RITES
Martine Marquand

Allegra Vitali is bored with life in her guardian's Venetian palazzo until the day sexual curiosity draws her to look at the depraved illustrations he keeps in his private chamber. She tries to deny her new passion for flesh by submitting to the life of a nun. The strange order of the Convent of Santa Agnetha provides new tests and new temptations, encouraging her to perform ritual acts with men and women who inhabit the strange, cloistered world.

ISBN 0 352 33222 0

BY ANY MEANS
Cheryl Mildenhall

Francesca, Veronique and Taran are partners in Falconer Associates, a London-based advertising agency. The three women are good friends and they're not averse to taking their pleasure with certain male employees. When they put in a bid to win a design account for Fast Track sportswear they are pitched against the notorious Oscar Rage who will stop at nothing to get what he wants. Despite Francesca's efforts to resist Oscar's arrogant charm, she finds him impossible to ignore.

ISBN 0 352 3221 1

BLACK LACE BACKLIST

All books are priced £4.99 unless another price is given.

––––––– ✂ ––––––––––––––––––

Please send me the books I have ticked above.

Name ....

Address ....

....

....

.... Post Code ....

Send to: **Cash Sales, Black Lace Books, 332 Ladbroke Grove, London W10 5AH.**

Please enclose a cheque or postal order, made payable to **Virgin Publishing Ltd**, to the value of the books you have ordered plus postage and packing costs as follows:

UK and BFPO – £1.00 for the first book, 50p for each subsequent book.

Overseas (including Republic of Ireland) – £2.00 for the first book, £1.00 each subsequent book.

If you would prefer to pay by VISA or ACCESS/MASTERCARD, please write your card number and expiry date here:

....

Please allow up to 28 days for delivery.

Signature ....

––––––– ✂ ––––––––––––––––––

WE NEED YOUR HELP . . .
to plan the future of women's erotic fiction –

– and no stamp required!

Yours are the only opinions that matter.

Black Lace is the first series of books devoted to erotic fiction by women for women.

We intend to keep providing the best-written, sexiest books you can buy. And we'd appreciate your help and valued opinion of the books so far. Tell us what you want to read.

THE BLACK LACE QUESTIONNAIRE

SECTION ONE: ABOUT YOU

1.1 Sex (*we presume you are female, but so as not to discriminate*)
Are you?

Male ☐
Female ☐

1.2 Age

under 21 ☐ 21–30 ☐
31–40 ☐ 41–50 ☐
51–60 ☐ over 60 ☐

1.3 At what age did you leave full-time education?

still in education ☐ 16 or younger ☐
17–19 ☐ 20 or older ☐

1.4 Occupation _____

1.5 Annual household income

    under £10,000 ☐   £10–£20,000 ☐

    £20–£30,000 ☐   £30–£40,000 ☐

    over £40,000 ☐

1.6 We are perfectly happy for you to remain anonymous; but if you would like to receive information on other publications available, please insert your name and address

_____

_____

_____

_____

SECTION TWO: ABOUT BUYING BLACK LACE BOOKS

2.1 How did you acquire this copy of *Contest of Wills*?

    I bought it myself ☐   My partner bought it ☐

    I borrowed/found it ☐

2.2 How did you find out about Black Lace books?

    I saw them in a shop ☐

    I saw them advertised in a magazine ☐

    I saw the London Underground posters ☐

    I read about them in _____

    Other _____

2.3 Please tick the following statements you agree with:

    I would be less embarrassed about buying Black Lace books if the cover pictures were less explicit ☐

    I think that in general the pictures on Black Lace books are about right ☐

    I think Black Lace cover pictures should be as explicit as possible ☐

2.4 Would you read a Black Lace book in a public place – on a train for instance?

    Yes ☐   No ☐

SECTION THREE: ABOUT THIS BLACK LACE BOOK

3.1   Do you think the sex content in this book is:
      Too much   ☐   About right   ☐
      Not enough   ☐

3.2   Do you think the writing style in this book is:
      Too unreal/escapist ☐   About right   ☐
      Too down to earth   ☐

3.3   Do you think the story in this book is:
      Too complicated   ☐   About right   ☐
      Too boring/simple   ☐

3.4   Do you think the cover of this book is:
      Too explicit   ☐   About right   ☐
      Not explicit enough ☐

Here's a space for any other comments:

SECTION FOUR: ABOUT OTHER BLACK LACE BOOKS

4.1   How many Black Lace books have you read?   ☐

4.2   If more than one, which one did you prefer?

4.3   Why?

SECTION FIVE: ABOUT YOUR IDEAL EROTIC NOVEL

We want to publish the books you want to read – so this is your chance to tell us exactly what your ideal erotic novel would be like.

5.1 Using a scale of 1 to 5 (1 = no interest at all, 5 = your ideal), please rate the following possible settings for an erotic novel:

    Medieval/barbarian/sword 'n' sorcery ☐
    Renaissance/Elizabethan/Restoration ☐
    Victorian/Edwardian ☐
    1920s & 1930s – the Jazz Age ☐
    Present day ☐
    Future/Science Fiction ☐

5.2 Using the same scale of 1 to 5, please rate the following themes you may find in an erotic novel:

    Submissive male/dominant female ☐
    Submissive female/dominant male ☐
    Lesbianism ☐
    Bondage/fetishism ☐
    Romantic love ☐
    Experimental sex e.g. anal/watersports/sex toys ☐
    Gay male sex ☐
    Group sex ☐

Using the same scale of 1 to 5, please rate the following styles in which an erotic novel could be written:

    Realistic, down to earth, set in real life ☐
    Escapist fantasy, but just about believable ☐
    Completely unreal, impressionistic, dreamlike ☐

5.3 Would you prefer your ideal erotic novel to be written from the viewpoint of the main male characters or the main female characters?

    Male ☐   Female ☐
    Both ☐

5.4 What would your ideal Black Lace heroine be like? Tick as many as you like:

Dominant	☐	Glamorous	☐
Extroverted	☐	Contemporary	☐
Independent	☐	Bisexual	☐
Adventurous	☐	Naïve	☐
Intellectual	☐	Introverted	☐
Professional	☐	Kinky	☐
Submissive	☐	Anything else?	☐
Ordinary	☐	_____	

5.5 What would your ideal male lead character be like? Again, tick as many as you like:

Rugged	☐		
Athletic	☐	Caring	☐
Sophisticated	☐	Cruel	☐
Retiring	☐	Debonair	☐
Outdoor-type	☐	Naïve	☐
Executive-type	☐	Intellectual	☐
Ordinary	☐	Professional	☐
Kinky	☐	Romantic	☐
Hunky	☐		
Sexually dominant	☐	Anything else?	☐
Sexually submissive	☐	_____	

5.6 Is there one particular setting or subject matter that your ideal erotic novel would contain?

_____

SECTION SIX: LAST WORDS

6.1 What do you like best about Black Lace books?

_____

6.2 What do you most dislike about Black Lace books?

_____

6.3 In what way, if any, would you like to change Black Lace covers?

_____

6.4   Here's a space for any other comments:

_____
_____
_____
_____

Thank you for completing this questionnaire. Now tear it out of the book – carefully! – put it in an envelope and send it to:

Black Lace
FREEPOST
London
W10 5BR

No stamp is required if you are resident in the U.K.